Dark Coven

Shifter Squad: Book 3

J.C. DIEM

Titles by J.C. Diem:

Mortis Series
Death Beckons
Death Embraces
Death Deceives
Death Devours
Death Betrays
Death Banishes
Death Returns
Death Conquers
Death Reigns
Shifter Squad Series
Seven Psychics
Zombie King
Dark Coven
Rogue Wolf
Corpse Thieves
Snake Charmer
Vampire Matriarch
Web Master
Hell Spawn
Hellscourge Series
Road To Hell
To Hell And Back
Hell Bound
Hell Bent
Hell To Pay
Hell Freezes Over
Hell Raiser
Hell Hath No Fury
All Hell Breaks Loose
Fate's Warriors Trilogy
God of Mischief
God Of Mayhem
God Of Malice

Loki's Exile Series
Exiled
Outcast
Forsaken
Destined
Hunter Elite Series
Hunting The Past
Hunting The Truth
Hunting A Master
Hunting For Death
Hunting A Thief
Hunting A Necromancer
Hunting A Relic
Hunting The Dark
Hunting A Dragon
Half Fae Hunter Series
Dark Moon Rising
Deadly Seduction
Dungeon Trials
Dragon Pledge
Unseelie Queen
Nox Saga
Hexed On Halloween
Tricks And Treats
All Hallows' Apocalypse
Trickster's Treachery
Blissful Demise
Oblivion's Kiss
Fatal Glamor
Lethal Charms
Devil Uncaged
Hellion Unleashed
Battle For Nox

Titles by J.C. Diem:

Shifter Squad Next Gen Series
Ink Cursed
Invisible Chains
Risky Bargains
Alpha Rivalry
Rex's Thrall
Spectral Justice
Prince's Bride
Mystical Schemes
Twins' Bond
Old Gods

Chapter One

Shaky and trembling, I was only dimly aware of a sharp rock pressing painfully into my knee. I was still in shock from discovering that my mother wasn't quite as dead as I'd always believed her to be. My arms were wrapped tightly across my chest. I was trying to hold myself together both physically and mentally.

Before I could come to terms with the bombshell that had just been dropped on me, I heard footsteps rapidly drawing closer. I looked up when Reece skidded to a stop at my side. Some of my confusion cleared away when he put his hand on my shoulder. "Are you all right?"

The concern in his tone almost brought tears to my eyes. My answer was a mute nod. As always, direct contact with him strengthened our bond. Armed with a handgun, he searched the area for danger. The peril was already gone, but I wouldn't truly be safe until the sun came up. That was still hours away and I wasn't sure I'd be able to resist the lure that had drawn me from my bed if I tried to go back to sleep.

Kala and Flynn arrived seconds later. "What's wrong?" Kala asked. Both she and Flynn were also armed and were ready to kill anything that threatened us. Her short hair was a tawny gold color and stuck out in all directions. It was annoying that she could be so pretty even when she'd just woken up.

"I'm not sure," Reece replied. While he couldn't see any adversaries, he knew that something dangerous had been here mere seconds ago. I clamped down on my thoughts before he could glean the truth from my mind. I wasn't ready to tell them that my mother was alive yet. Of course, 'alive' was a subjective term when it came to the undead.

Huffing and puffing from his lengthy run, Mark finally reached us. Like the rest of the squad, he was dressed in nightclothes. Thankfully, he wore a t-shirt and drawstring pants rather than just boxer shorts like Reece and Flynn. Kala wore a singlet and sleeping shorts similar to mine. I kept my gaze away from Reece. One look at his mostly naked body would drive my desire to the surface and he'd know exactly what was on my mind.

"Are you all right, Lexi?" Mark asked. He waited for me to nod before launching into his next question. "What happened?"

I wasn't fond of lying, but I wasn't about to admit the truth either. It was still too raw and painful to divulge to anyone. "I'm not sure. I think I was sleepwalking again." That wasn't a complete lie. While I'd been asleep, my mom had lured me outside with her evil siren song. She had a hold over my mind that was impossible to refuse.

He looked at me sharply and everyone's head swiveled to me. "What do you mean 'again'?" Kala asked. "Since when do you sleepwalk?"

Some of my anxiety returned when Reece broke our contact and dropped his hand to his side. "I woke up in the woods in the middle of the night a couple of times after I was bitten," I explained as I stood.

As surreptitiously as possible, I tugged my singlet forward to cover the bite mark on my right shoulder. No longer old and faded, it was fresh and new again. If they saw the scar, I'd have no choice but to explain how the changes had occurred.

Mark nodded at my explanation. "I've heard of this happening to the newly infected. Sleepwalking is a common occurrence just after they've been bitten. Their instincts force them to run beneath the moon even before they've completely turned."

Flynn looked doubtful about the theory. "Why is she sleepwalking now? She's already had two full changes. Shouldn't it have worn off by now?"

Mark sent me a troubled glance. "Alexis seems to differ from most shifters. There's no telling what differences she'll have from the rest of you." Usually, he was a calming influence. Right now, he wasn't helping my anxiety much.

"Are you talking about how her spirit is supposedly being torn between two opposing forces?" Kala asked. She unconsciously moved closer to me, offering me comfort and protection without realizing it.

A voodoo priestess had laid the knowledge that my spirit was under siege on me a few days ago. I'd had no idea what she'd been talking about. Privately, I thought she was a little crazy. I had to revise that notion now. Maybe she wasn't as mentally unstable as I'd believed.

Our boss nodded. "Whatever is happening to Lexi seems to be heightened by our close proximity to New Orleans." The team moved in to surround me as we headed back to the base. "It might be too dangerous to stay here until morning," he decided, to my intense relief. "Get dressed and meet me in the garage in ten minutes. We're leaving now."

No one argued with his decision, despite it being the middle of the night. We filed back into the base through the door that led to the kitchen. It was cool inside the two story concrete building. If I'd still been human, goose bumps would've erupted on my arms and legs. As a werewolf, my body ran hotter than normal. The cold didn't bother me as much as it used to.

I was conscious of Reece's eyes on me as I climbed up the spiral staircase to the second floor. My clothes were fine for wearing to bed, but they were far too skimpy to wear in front of others. Kala showed no signs of self-consciousness at all. She was as confident as she was pretty. Apparently, I was the only one who was unhappy about wearing so little.

Safe and sound back in my bedroom, I was glad to have a few moments of privacy. Leaning against the door, my body shook in delayed reaction. Only now did I realize how close I'd come to being turned into an even worse monster than I already was.

Working for the Track and Kill Squad was as dangerous as it was unpredictable. Our latest mission had taken us to New Orleans. We'd been tasked with hunting down a bokor before he could raise an army of zombies.

I'd quickly discovered that the bokor's minions weren't the only things haunting the city. My mother had begun stalking me shortly after we'd arrived. She'd felt a faint link between us and curiosity had driven her to seek me out. Katrina had recognized me instantly, which came as no surprise. I was almost a carbon copy of her, if far less beautiful.

She'd watched me for a few nights before finally making her move. At least some of the lore about vampires was real. Katrina hadn't had a reflection when she'd ambushed me in a restaurant restroom.

I'd heard someone behind me, but had only seen my reflection when I'd glanced into the mirror. When I'd turned around, she'd been standing only inches away.

Feeding from me when I'd been a baby had given her the power to control me. She'd put me beneath her spell, then had bitten me directly over the scar that she'd left so long ago. It had healed and it looked much newer now, rather than faded with time.

Using her undead mojo, she'd erased the memories of our next confrontations after feeding from me again. I'd grown weak and dizzy from blood loss without realizing what was wrong with me.

When she'd tried to bite me again only a few minutes ago, Reece had sensed that I was in danger. He'd lent me the strength to resist her spell without realizing what he was doing.

I'd been able to resist my mother's third attempt to take over my mind and had finally remembered every encounter that we'd had. I was now aware of the full truth. She hadn't been murdered by anything as mundane as a human. She'd been turned by a vampire. One of her first acts as the undead had been to feed from her own child.

Katrina had weakened my bond with Reece each time she'd fed from me. According to the voodoo priestess, I'd come close to going over to the dark side, so to speak. Renewing the bond was the only thing that could have saved me. That meant Reece had had to sleep with me again. Physically, it wasn't exactly a hardship for either of us. Mentally, it was torture for us both.

This time, she hadn't been able to wipe my memories and I remembered every word that she'd uttered. She'd told me that she wanted us to be a family again. Her plan was to change me into a vampire like her. If that happened, I'd be lost to the darkness forever.

Katrina wasn't going to give up on trying to turn me and I couldn't guarantee I'd be able to resist her next time. Mark was right, we had to get out of here. I lurched into motion and dressed in jeans, a white t-shirt and thick soled boots. I slipped on my holster and covered it with my red leather jacket. The jacket hid the fact that I was armed and had the added bonus of being very stylish.

I'd already packed my suitcase before going to bed. I was glad I didn't have to waste any time frantically packing now. The black backpack that held my custom made sniper rifle and spare ammo was still sitting in the closet. I slipped it over my shoulder, then carried my suitcase into the hall. Once upon a time, both bags would have been heavy for me. I could now carry them without any effort at all.

Being a shape shifter had many benefits, including increased strength, sight, smell and hearing. The downside was that I turned into a murderous beast for three nights out of every month. Strangely, Reece and I no longer turned into mindless monsters. Thanks to our link, we were able to retain some awareness while we were in our half-wolf forms. I wasn't sure if that would still be the case if we were separated before we changed.

The others reached the garage just ahead of me. Flynn took my suitcase and crammed it into the back of the sleek black SUV along with the rest of our luggage. I slid into the middle of the seat between Flynn and Kala with my backpack on my lap. Reece took off as soon as the garage door opened.

After twenty minutes on the road, we sped past a narrow dirt track that led deeper into a marshy swamp. It also led to the body of a cop serial killer. Reece and I were the only ones who knew about Officer Mallory's death. The cop had intended for me to be his latest victim, but he was the one who had ended up feeding the alligators. My only regret was that I hadn't been the one to strangle him to death. Reece had beaten me to it.

Pushing thoughts of attempted rape and murder aside, I wasn't in the mood to rehash them again. I just wanted to get away from this place and to go back home. It was still a surprise to realize that I didn't really have a home now. My old life as a normal teenager was gone. I was now an agent of the Paranormal Investigation Agency.

Our team was officially called the TAK Squad, but we had our own private name for the team. We were the Shifter Squad and we were the only supernatural creatures who worked for the PIA.

Our job was to hunt down anything that threatened human lives and to make sure the bad guys disappeared forever. So far, the job was turning out to be far more eventful than I'd anticipated.

Chapter Two

Passing through New Orleans, we drove for another half an hour before reaching a private airfield. We tended to avoid domestic airports. It was difficult to explain why we were carrying a small arsenal. The PIA had a jet on standby whenever we needed it so we could avoid any delays and awkwardness.

Mark checked his watch as the SUV coasted to a stop near the tiny runway. "The jet should be here in about four hours."

Kala groaned in disappointment. There were no televisions or magazines handy to keep her occupied. We'd only just arrived and she was already bored. I was exhausted and all I wanted to do was rest. Staying in the SUV, I curled up on the seat and attempted to nap. My attempt failed miserably. I was too keyed up to be able to fall sleep.

Three hours later, my stomach was rumbling constantly. I gave up on trying to sleep and joined the others. Mine wasn't the only stomach complaining that we should have been eating breakfast by now. A chorus of rumbles was coming from everyone but Mark.

"Did anyone bring any food?" Flynn asked.

Mark's expression was regretful. Not because he felt bad about his lapse in planning, but because he'd have to listen to us complain for the next few hours. "We left in too much of a hurry for me to even think of it."

"Great," Kala grumbled. "I hope there's going to be food on the jet." There hadn't been the last couple of times. I didn't have my hopes up that this trip would be any different.

We heard the jet long before it appeared. Dawn was just breaking and the runway was still dark. We didn't have any way to light the path for the pilot. He circled the area until it was safe to land and eventually coasted to a stop nearby.

We didn't waste any time stuffing our luggage into the small cargo hold. The sooner we were in the air, the sooner we'd be able to eat.

Reece was the first on board. "There's no food," he said over his shoulder after a quick look around. He received three groans of disappointment at that news.

"It's going to take us three hours to reach Colorado," Flynn reminded us unnecessarily.

"If we don't make it," Kala said to Mark in a tragic

tone as she climbed the stairs, "make sure you bury me as far away from Reece and Lexi as possible. I don't want to spend eternity lying in a grave next to a pair of mangy mongrels."

Our boss sent her a sardonic look as he entered the plane. I snorted out a laugh, while secretly wondering if we really would starve more quickly than humans.

Flynn was the last on board. He pulled the stairs up as the pilot emerged to assist him. They secured the door then the pilot had a quick word to Mark. Over fifty, the captain was trim and fit. He looked ex-military to me. I could spot a soldier easily just by their bearing. "What is your intended destination, Agent Steel?" he asked.

"We're heading back to our base in Colorado," Mark replied.

"Copy that. I'll take off as soon as you're all buckled in." He watched to make sure we strapped ourselves in before disappearing back into the cockpit.

Kala usually sat next to me when we flew. This time, we each took a row to ourselves. As soon as we'd taken off and levelled out, we all tried to nap. My stomach rumbled almost constantly during the flight.

I managed to doze, but I couldn't quite fall into a deep sleep. That was fine with me. Dark dreams were circling and I wasn't looking forward to succumbing to true slumber. I sat up when the jet finally began to descend. I'd seen the countryside near Denver often enough not to bother opening the shutter on the window.

After landing, we quickly retrieved our luggage. The pilot remained on board and saluted Mark through the cockpit window when he waved to indicate that we were done. He was ready to take off again as soon as we were clear of the runway.

This airstrip was just as small as the one we'd left behind in New Orleans. A hangar was the only building on the grounds. Kala walked over to it and opened the door. Taking a look inside, she shook her head. "Nothing. Not even a vending machine," she said grumpily. "I'd kill for a burger."

I wouldn't have been surprised if she meant that literally. I was so hungry that shooting a cat and roasting it over a fire was beginning to sound like a good idea. Since Kala turned into a feline when she shifted, I wisely kept that thought to myself.

We headed to the SUV parked near the runway. It didn't look as if it had been sitting out in the weather while we'd been gone. Mark had a network of contacts that he could call on to perform various jobs whenever he needed them. Retrieving and delivering our vehicles was just one of the tasks he delegated to them.

Mark looked thoughtful as he climbed into the front passenger seat. I had a feeling he was debating about whether we should detour to Denver for a belated breakfast. My fingers were crossed that this was the case, but I was doomed to disappointment.

"Head straight to our base," he instructed Reece.

My empty stomach cramped in protest and I wasn't the only one to glare at him. Even Flynn was ravenous and his appetite wasn't as voracious as ours. Being a wereconstrictor, he didn't need to eat quite as often as other shifters.

"If I don't get food soon, I'm going to start chewing on the seat," Kala complained.

"I'll fight you for it," I muttered.

She turned an assessing gaze on me. "I could take you."

Flynn leaned forward and grinned cheekily. "Not if she turns alpha again and commands you to let her eat the seat."

Red flared in her cheeks as the SUV went into motion. "That only happened once and only because she caught me off guard."

Reece glanced into the rearview mirror and met my eyes. His were crinkled slightly at the corners as he suppressed a laugh. Being an alpha gave us dominance over others of our kind. While we were wolves, Kala was a cougar and Flynn was a constrictor. We weren't even the same species. Despite our differences, I'd managed to force Kala to obey me anyway.

Maybe that had been possible because we'd formed a small, if highly unusual pack. As far as I knew, Reece hadn't tried to bend the other two agents to his will. He didn't really need to, since they tended to follow his commands anyway. I wasn't sure if it was because he was an alpha, or because he was our team leader.

"No one is going to eat the seats," Mark said and turned his frown on us. "We'll be home in a couple of hours. Surely you can hold on for that long."

He obviously had no idea just how ravenous we all were. I was still new to being a werewolf and I wasn't used to feeling hungry all the time. It felt as if my stomach was trying to gnaw its way through my backbone.

Kala subsided into a sulk and the rest of us had little to say. Traffic was light and Reece zoomed past the other motorists. He drove with his usual disregard for the speed limit and we made it to the base in record time.

I was relieved when the thirty foot high fence that was topped with razor wire finally appeared. We drove through the electrified gate and for the first time in days, I felt safe again. I wished I could put the threat of my mother out of my mind and forget about her, but that wasn't possible. Sooner or later, I'd have to confess to the squad that she was alive and that she had a dreadful plan for me.

We sped up the winding driveway that was flanked on both sides by fragrant pine trees. When the base came into view, Mark used a remote device to open the garage door. Kala barely waited for Reece to park the SUV before she was climbing out. We took turns grabbing our luggage from the back.

Flynn was the first to reach the door. He placed his

palm on the scanner and green light flared as it read his prints. When the door clicked open, he stepped into the long corridor. It stretched out to the right with intermittent doorways on each side. There was only one door on the left. The base near New Orleans was identical to this one. I had a feeling that all of our compounds scattered throughout the country were exactly the same. The only thing that was different was the furniture.

Flynn opened the door that led to the main area. Dumping his bags on the floor in the living room, he headed past the dining room and entered the kitchen. Breakfast was long past and it was now lunch time. I didn't care what sort of food would shortly be on offer, I just hoped there would be lots of it.

I carried my bags upstairs to my room, but I was too hungry to bother unpacking. A new addition to the room caught my eye. Someone had retrieved my gun safe from Texas and had delivered it to my room. It had been placed in the corner near my bed.

A quick check of the closet and dresser showed that the rest of my clothing had also been delivered. While it was creepy that some unknown person had been touching my underwear, at least I now had somewhere secure to keep my weapons.

Chapter Three

After a quick bathroom break, I headed downstairs. The others had already started eating when I joined them at the dining table. Kala had piled several sandwiches on a plate. She hunkered over the bounty protectively, darting threatening glances at anyone who even glanced at her food. If I tried to filch anything from her plate, she'd probably stab me with a fork.

I piled my own plate high and started working my way through the feast. Mark shook his head at the sight of his four agents wolfing down our food. "Anyone would think I only fed you once a week," he complained.

"It feels like a week since I last ate," Kala said around a mouthful of food.

I laughed, then choked on a piece of bread that

lodged in my throat. Flynn helpfully pounded me on the back until I swallowed it down. "Thanks," I croaked.

He tipped me a wink. "Anytime." I hoped it wouldn't be necessary anytime soon. I was pretty sure he'd almost broken one of my ribs while helping me. Thankfully, I healed much faster than normal now and the pain was already beginning to fade.

"I noticed my gun safe and clothes have arrived," I said to Mark. I'd mentioned in passing that I'd like to retrieve them at some stage. I hadn't expected it to be handled in our absence.

"I organized it with your father," he said. "He allowed one of my contacts to pack your belongings and have them sent here."

Pain at the mention of my dad squeezed my insides and I fought to keep my expression neutral. "Thanks," I said lightly. "I appreciate it."

I was still smarting from learning that he'd lied to me. It didn't help that he and Mark were making decisions about me behind my back. It was petty and stupid to feel this way. I'd gotten what I wanted, but I wasn't happy about not being kept in the loop. It just proved that they both still thought of me as a kid.

After the sandwiches had been demolished, the team dispersed. Reece and Flynn headed to the boxing ring at the far end of the room to spar. Kala flopped onto the couch and turned on the TV. I headed to the kitchen to make coffee.

Food had been my first priority, but coffee was a

close second. Our fairy godmother, or maybe one of Mark's contacts, had stocked the cupboards and fridge in our absence. He would have arranged for the delivery well in advance of our return. He was sometimes almost scarily efficient.

Taking three mugs down from the cupboard above the sink, he studied me. "How are you feeling?" he asked as I poured water into the coffee machine. One thing the whole squad had in common was our addiction to caffeine.

I glanced at him to see him frowning a little in concern. I had the feeling he hadn't bought my excuse that I'd been sleepwalking. "I'm a little tired, but I'm okay."

"You'd tell me if there was something wrong?" he probed.

I'd only known him for a couple of months, but I trusted him almost as much as I trusted my father. Now that I was aware of the fabrications that I'd been told, I might even trust Mark more than my dad now. "Of course," I said with as much conviction as I could muster.

My problems were too personal to divulge to anyone. How could I possibly admit to the team what had really happened to me in New Orleans? It was my dirty little secret. Well, mine and my father's. He obviously already knew exactly what had happened to his late wife.

Kala angled her head to listen in on our conversation. She was a firm believer that there shouldn't be any secrets in the Shifter Squad. I didn't bother to ask her if she wanted coffee, her answer was always yes.

Mark spooned one sugar into each mug, then poured cream in next. He was fastidious about his coffee and believed it tasted better if he added the cream first. It didn't taste any different to me, but I wasn't going to argue about something so trivial.

I waited for the machine to finish brewing, then poured in the coffee and stirred the mixture so rapidly that the spoon was a blur of motion. Taking one of the mugs, Mark nodded his thanks and headed upstairs to the communications room. He spent most of his time up there, reading, researching our missions and keeping in touch with his colleagues.

Still feeling weary, I took a seat on the couch near Kala. She waited for me to place her mug on the coffee table in front of her before she leaned in close to speak to me. "I don't know what's really going on with you, but I highly doubt you were sleepwalking."

Caught out, I didn't want to compound my fib, so I shrugged. "I'm not in danger now that we're no longer in New Orleans."

"What was the danger?" she persisted. "I promise I won't tell the others." It went against her code, but she was concerned enough about my welfare to make the offer to keep a secret for me.

On the brink of spilling my guts, I hesitated, then chickened out. She was the first friend I'd had in years and I didn't want her to look at me like I was a freak.

"I really don't want to talk about it," I said plaintively.

"Okay," she said immediately, startling me with her quick capitulation. "Just remember that you can talk to me anytime about anything."

Her glance slid towards the gym where the two men were sparring. "Anything except how to get into Reece's pants," I said before she could.

"You already figured that one out for yourself," she smirked. She schooled her face into a serious expression and lowered her voice. "So, is he good in bed?" My face instantly flamed red and she snorted out a laugh. "I'll take that as a yes."

Normally, I'd have retreated to my room before she could embarrass me further. This time, I raised my eyebrow and waited for her mirth to fade. "If you must know, he's absolutely fantastic in bed. Not that I have anything to compare the experience with," I added.

Kala's grin was slightly wistful. "I've heard that sex with an alpha is mind blowing." Thankfully, we were talking too quietly for the guys to be able to overhear us. This conversation was already embarrassing enough without them knowing what we were discussing. "I can only imagine how good it would be between two alphas."

"It's awesome," I confirmed. "I only wish…" I trailed off, uncomfortable with sharing my innermost feelings.

Kala's expression turned almost pitying. "You wish the bond hadn't been forced on you both." It was a statement rather than a question.

"Yeah," I said with a sigh. If he'd been given the choice, Reece would never have chosen me to be his mate. It was only the intervention of a psychic known as Lust that had ended up with us sleeping together in the first place. She didn't know that he was a shifter and she didn't force him to bite me. That had just been an unhappy byproduct of our first sexual encounter.

The same telepath had gotten her mental claws into me. She'd forced me to seek out the man who desired me the least and I thought Reece was at the top of that list. That was the night of the first full moon after he'd bitten me and my wolfish instincts had taken over. I'd bitten him during our second bout of sex. That had cemented the bond between us, forcing us into permanent mental bondage.

"Fate is a funny thing," Kala said. "There's no telling where it'll take us and who it will bring into our lives."

I nodded in agreement, then let the conversation die. There was nothing I could do about it now. We were stuck together, for better or worse, just like a human marriage. I almost smiled at that. Reece had proposed to me when he'd realized that we were bonded. It was hard to say if he or I had been more horrified when he'd made the offer.

My father had stepped in to quell that idea, thankfully. He'd only been able to spend a few days with me before he'd returned to his overseas assignment. I had no idea where he was or what he was doing now. We usually spoke once a week, if he could find the time.

Now that I knew just how much he'd kept from me, I wasn't sure I even wanted to talk to him until I could process his lies. What could I possibly say to him? I know you've been lying to me for my entire life and that my mom is a creature of the night?

It hurt that he'd kept this a secret when I was a kid, but I was an adult now. He should have trusted me with the truth.

At least I had a new family now, of a sort. Being shifters, we four were drawn together even though we were very different. I was frankly amazed that Kala and I got along so well. She and Reece tended to bicker at times. Flynn had once told me that they fought like cats and dogs. I could appreciate the humor of his statement now.

Chapter Four

Being a member of the Shifter Squad wasn't all hunting monsters and trying not to die. We had some downtime, too. Between jobs, we had the chance to relax a bit more. When I wasn't training with the others, I spent my time lounging around watching TV or reading through my collection of ebooks.

Not all of my reading was purely for pleasure. I also dedicated part of each day to researching the PIA archives. A wealth of information was stored on the database. Cases had been documented dating back to four hundred years ago, well before the agency had been officially formed.

The archives could be sorted chronologically or by topic, which made it easier to search through them. Mark had provided me with my own laptop, which meant I didn't have to use the main computer. It gave me privacy to dig up the information I needed. It was a relief to be able to read through the files without someone looking over my shoulder.

I didn't have access to all of the files. Mark had informed me that there were ten levels of security. He was level eight and the rest of the team was at level five. Being new, I was a lowly level one. Some of the files were marked as being restricted and I didn't try to pry into them. My computer skills were rudimentary at best. I'd never be a master hacker.

Trying not to raise any red flags that might bring my research to Mark's notice, I'd downloaded a bunch of files on a wide range of topics to my laptop. I didn't want the boss to know that I was specifically researching vampires. If he knew what I was searching for, he might ask me what my interest was. That was a conversation I hoped to avoid for now.

Over the next two weeks, I learned as much as I could about the type of creature that my mother had become. No one truly knew where supernatural creatures had originated from. It seemed that we'd always been around and there was always someone trying to kill us.

I didn't blame the humans for hunting us down. If I wasn't penned up each time I shifted, I'd snack on them just as readily as I would any other animal. Unless I was with Reece when I transformed, of course. Then I had a better chance of remembering that people were taboo.

Most of my research was performed late at night

when I was supposed to be sleeping. I learned that vampires could be killed by sunlight, holy objects, holy water and any kind of weapon through the heart. Beheading them also killed them, but getting close enough to chop a vamp's head off was risky. They were fast, vicious and cunning.

To encounter a vampire and live to tell about it was rare. I felt a chill when I realized just how easily my mother could have killed me. In a way, I was lucky that she'd wanted to turn me. If she succeeded, she'd become my master and she'd have absolute power over me. Given a choice, I'd rather die than become her slave. I'd already had a taste of being beneath her control and I'd hated every second of it.

My sleep had been restless ever since we'd left New Orleans. I was cranky and out of sorts. It didn't help that I had to spend eight hours each day being pummeled by my fellow agents.

Speaking of which, I was currently getting my butt kicked once again. Flynn circled me, looking for an opening. He was trained in several different martial arts styles and had the annoying habit of changing his tactics each time we sparred. I'd only had a few weeks of training in hand to hand combat and I still wasn't very good. Some people had a natural aptitude for this kind of thing. Unfortunately, I wasn't one of them.

"Keep your guard up," Kala warned me. Instead of helping, it was a distraction and I made the mistake of glancing at her. Reece was on the far side of the room, lifting a ridiculous amount of weights. He was watching our match with interest.

Seeing that my focus had shifted away from him, Flynn seized the opportunity and sent a sidekick at my stomach. Catching his movement just in time, I managed to deflect the blow. The moment his foot touched the ground, he immediately performed a spinning roundhouse kick.

I was unprepared for the move and his heel caught me on the chin. I went down with my ears ringing. While I didn't pass out completely, I did lose a couple of seconds. When my head cleared, Reece was standing over me protectively. A low, threatening snarl was coming from him. Flynn was wary, but not quite alarmed.

Kala was standing between the two men. "Calm down, Garrett," she said. "Lexi is fine. See?" She pointed at me and all three of them turned to watch me struggle into an upright position.

With a sidelong look at Reece, Flynn stepped around him and knelt beside me. "Are you okay?"

"Sure," I replied brightly. "I love getting kicked in the face. I wish I could do this every day."

"You do," Kala pointed out with a snicker.

Flynn helped me to my feet and moved aside to let Reece examine me. Avoiding his eyes, I busied myself brushing imaginary dirt off my clothes. He took my chin in his hand and lifted my gaze to his. Our eyes met and I was instantly lost.

This was exactly what I'd been trying to avoid.

Being close to Reece always affected me and this time was no different. It was bad enough that he knew what his touch did to me. The others didn't need to witness how pathetic I was. A wave of heat swept through me when his glance shifted to my mouth. A memory of us kissing floated to the surface of his mind and I swayed towards him in invitation.

"Earth to Reece and Alexis." Kala's amused voice broke into the fog that had momentarily clouded my mind.

"What?" Reece asked and took a step back, wisely distancing himself from me. We'd been dangerously close to dropping the shields that we'd erected to keep our thoughts private.

After two weeks of very little contact, I was craving his touch, even if it was just a brush of his hand on mine. I thought it was just me, but I had a sense that he felt the same need. We knew so little about the bond that we didn't really know what to expect from it.

"Mark's phone just rang," Kala said. "It sounds like we have a new mission."

"Thank God," I muttered. Our lives would undoubtedly be in danger again, but at least I'd have a break from being humiliated in the boxing ring for a while.

Upstairs in the coms room, Mark's chair rolled back from the computer table. We couldn't hear the person on the other end of the line, but his response had us all moving. "We'll be there as soon as we can," he said and hung up. "Pack a bag," he called down to us, not realizing that we were already on our way up to him. "We're heading for West Virginia."

"What's happened there?" Kala asked as she bounded to the top of the stairs.

"My superior wasn't very specific," Mark replied. "He's received a report of strange occurrences and he wants us to investigate them."

"That's pretty vague," Reece complained. As an alpha, his instinct was to lead. I wasn't sure how he managed to cope with Mark as his boss. Mark compensated by allowing Reece to take charge in other ways, such as always being behind the wheel and sometimes leading our missions.

"I'd noticed," Mark agreed in a wry tone. "I'm sure we'll discover exactly what is going on when we arrive in Bradbury."

Unsure how long this mission would take, I packed my suitcase with enough clothes for a couple of weeks, then headed to the garage. Mark had already called the pilot to arrange for him to take us to West Virginia. During the drive to the airfield, he called someone else to make sure we'd have transportation upon our arrival. His network of contacts must be spread out all over the country. The organization obviously had deep pockets. They were deep enough to ensure that we always had a jet on standby to ferry us to wherever we needed to go.

I'd lived in Virginia for a few months a couple of years ago. I knew roughly what to expect when it came to the towns, countryside and weather. My father was a soldier and we'd moved frequently, sometimes several times a year. A crack sniper, he'd taught me everything he knew about weapons. It was thanks to his tutelage that I'd ended up in the TAK squad in the first place. Mark had needed a sharp shooter and my dad had been on an assignment overseas. He'd sought my father's permission to borrow me for a short time. Due to a quirk of fate, I was now a permanent member of the team.

My dream had always been to follow in my father's footsteps and to join the army. That lifelong plan had been shattered on the night of my eighteenth birthday when I'd been bitten by Reece. If any of the men and women I'd once hoped to serve with ever found out what I'd become, they'd shoot me. Then they'd probably burn my corpse for good measure.

Chapter Five

Mark had planned well this time and food was waiting for us on the jet. He didn't want to listen to us whining about being hungry during the lengthy flight to West Virginia.

Bored and restless after listening to her music after an hour or so, Kala left her seat and plonked down next to me. I lowered my ereader to my lap when she gestured at my face. "How's your chin?"

I touched my chin and found it to be intact. "It's still there," I replied and she grinned. The pain hadn't lasted long and I'd almost forgotten that I'd come close to being knocked out.

"You're lucky Bailey didn't break anything. He must have pulled his kick."

"I'm glad he did," I said with a shudder, privately amused at her habit of sometimes calling her fellow agents by their surnames. It was something I'd managed to break myself from, although I backslid sometimes.

"Who wants a snack?" Flynn asked, oblivious that we were talking about him. The plastic bag he was searching was rustling too loudly for him to be able to hear us.

Kala and I put our hands up and he tossed us both a chocolate bar. I might not be able to fight very well, but at least I could catch. Kala tore into the wrapper with her teeth and stuffed half of the bar into her mouth.

"So, how are things between you and the eye candy?" she asked with her mouth full. Her eyebrows went up and down suggestively. "I haven't heard you sneaking into each other's rooms at night."

Wrinkling my nose at the brown stain on her normally white teeth, I sat up high enough in my seat to see Mark and Reece conversing at the front of the jet. Flynn was still rummaging around in the bag, searching for food. Kala had spoken quietly enough that none of the guys had heard her. She was making an effort to keep our conversation private.

"Everything is fine," I lied. In reality, we were doing our best to pretend that we weren't mated. We might share a bond, but that didn't mean we had to spend every minute together.

Snorting in derision, she chewed and swallowed before speaking. "I don't get why you two don't just admit that you're attracted to each other. It's so obvious to the rest of us."

"If he's so attracted to me then why did he tell me that I wasn't his type and that there could never be anything between us?" His rejection still stung even now.

Her brows rose in surprise. "When did he say that?

"After we returned to our base when you three tore Greed apart." That was a sight I wasn't about to forget in a hurry.

Her mouth quirked up in a brief smile of remembrance. Mark had been called away for a couple of days and had left Reece in charge. We'd tracked down one of the Seven Deadly Sinners and she'd come close to flash frying me with her psychic power. The others had taken exception to that and had ripped her arms and head off. "We got a bit carried away that time," she said, then returned to our topic. "Obviously, Garrett lied. He's had the hots for you from the moment you pulled your gun on him."

That was another episode I wasn't going to forget. He'd tried to intimidate me and I'd pulled my Beretta to show him that I wasn't as defenseless as I looked. "How could you possibly know that?"

"Because I grew up with him. I've never seen him act so weird around a girl before."

"Kala's right," Flynn said as he took the seat across the aisle from us.

Alarmed that he'd overheard us, I checked to see if Mark and Reece were still occupied. They were and I sank back down into my seat in relief. "What are you talking about?"

"He's never acted this way before," Flynn leaned over and whispered. "He was ready to rip my head off when I knocked you on your butt."

"It's the bond," I said and waved away his erroneous idea that Reece cared about me. "It makes him territorial."

"There's more to it than that," Kala argued. She hesitated, then said what had obviously been weighing on her mind. "I think he bonded you on purpose."

Flynn's brows rose in surprise. "I had the same thought."

I'd heard his theory before, but this was the first time Kala had voiced it. "He's regretting it now," I said with a hint of bitterness. "I'm the last person he wants to be chained to."

Kala shook her head in instant denial. "You're wrong, Lexi. I'm pretty sure you're the only person he'd have chosen."

Flynn nodded in agreement and I scowled at them both. "I can sense what he's feeling, remember?" I said quietly. "Even if he was attracted to me and lied about it, it doesn't change the fact that neither of us wants to be mated for the rest of our lives."

"Don't you?" Flynn asked far more shrewdly than was normal for someone of his age. He was only twenty, barely two years older than me.

"You two are bonded, it's permanent and there's nothing you can do about it," Kala said. "If I were you, I'd make the most of it." Her lecherous wink told me how she'd go about doing that and my face turned red.

Flynn was more perceptive than our blonde companion and his expression was sympathetic. "Look at it from their point of view," he told her softly. "They're stuck together for life and they'll never have the chance to find their true mates now."

Kala turned an assessing gaze on me. Whatever she saw on my face killed her amusement. "I've seen the way Reece looks at you. He feels more than just physical attraction."

I knew exactly what he felt, but I wasn't about to enlighten the pair. Reece hadn't protected me from Flynn because he cared about me. He'd done it because he felt a sense of ownership over me. He'd claimed me body and soul and I was his until death.

"Are you going to eat that?" Kala asked, pointing at the half eaten chocolate bar in my hand. My appetite had fled and I shook my head and handed it to her.

I returned to reading as Kala and Flynn tried to guess what kind of monsters we'd be facing this time. The words blurred before my eyes and I couldn't concentrate. No matter how hard I tried to suppress the bond, I could always feel Reece in my head, just as he could feel me. Our ties were mystical and they were far more binding than any mere marriage could ever be.

A few hours later, the pilot advised that we were about to land. We dutifully buckled ourselves in. Once again, we'd utilized a private airfield. The usual black SUV was waiting for us when we disembarked from the jet. Reece slid behind the wheel as the rest of us stowed our baggage in the back.

"Where to?" he asked when Mark claimed the passenger seat up front.

"We won't be able to stay at our base this time. It's too far away from Bradbury and we'll need to be closer to the action," Mark advised. "It isn't ideal, but I've booked us into a Bed and Breakfast nearby. It will have to serve as our base of operations." He used the inbuilt GPS to key in the address and we motored away from the airfield. The jet was already speeding down the runway. It would return to wherever it rested when we didn't need it.

We drove for several hours and it was late by the time we arrived at the bed and breakfast. The house was a large three story structure. A gigantic picture window overlooked the expansive, well-tended front lawn. The house might have been Victorian in design. I knew little about architecture and I wasn't interested enough to learn more. From the outside it was charming, with fresh white paint and light blue trimming. A discreet sign near the steps named the building as 'Dawson's Retreat'.

Mark knocked on the door and waited for a few seconds. Flynn shook his head to indicate that no one was approaching. Mark tried the handle. The door was unlocked and we filed inside. Well preserved antique furniture graced the long hallway. A rug ran the length of the corridor. In shades of red, gold and royal blue, it was worn and faded. Black and white photos of long dead people hung at regular intervals on the walls. Faded wallpaper with a rose print added a touch of pink to the decor.

We passed a huge dining room on the left. A dozen small square tables with four chairs each were spaced neatly around the room. A door to the right led to a cozy parlor. I glanced inside to see an antique coffee table, overstuffed armchairs and a couple of chaise lounges. The chairs were a few shades darker than the beige carpet. I could imagine sitting beside the fire in winter, snug and secure against the cold and reading a good book.

If we hadn't been here on a mission, it might have been a nice place to spend the weekend with a loved one. My traitorous gaze slid over to Reece before I could stop it. It was a silly, sentimental thought and I hoped he hadn't picked up on it.

Chapter Six

A reception area waited at the far end of the hall. A staircase to the left of the desk led up to the second floor. An elderly man sat behind the desk, dressed in a worn gray cardigan and black trousers. Stooped, wrinkled and white haired, he looked old enough to have been around when the house had first been built. He snorted awake when Mark cleared his throat loudly.

Aged, faded blue eyes stared at us warily. They cleared when he realized we were customers. "You must be Mr. Steel and party," he said and laboriously climbed to his feet. We were going incognito, hence why Mark hadn't used his usual title.

"I apologize for arriving so late," Mark replied courteously.

The old man waved the apology away. "These

things can't be helped. My name is Edward." He gave us a courtly bow. "Your rooms are ready. I just need you to sign in."

As Mark was signing the register, movement above caught my eye. I looked up to see a small boy staring down at me. It was way past his bedtime, but he didn't look tired. Strangely, he wasn't wearing pajamas. Instead, he wore a dark brown suit, a white button up shirt and suspenders. He also wore cheap black shoes that didn't look at all comfortable. The whole outfit looked extremely old fashioned and made him seem like a really short adult.

Kids could be weird about what they wore. They'd insist on dressing in their favorite outfits every day for a month straight and throw a tantrum if their parents protested. I had no idea where he would have found an outfit like this, though. It wasn't the kind of clothing that someone would have stored in their attic. Maybe it had come from a fancy dress store.

His tiny hands clutched the railings. His skin was startlingly pale and his expression was far too solemn. I waved and after a moment he lifted a hand in return. It must have been a trick of the light, but for a second there it almost seemed like I could see right through him.

"Who are you waving at?" Kala asked me curiously.

I turned to see her staring upwards. "I was waving at the kid…" My voice trailed off when I realized that the little boy was gone. "That's weird. He was there a second ago."

"You probably saw one of our ghosts," Edward said. His tone was casual, as if seeing ghosts was a natural everyday occurrence.

"This house is haunted?" Mark asked and paused in the act of handing the pen to Reece.

"Oh, yes," the old man replied. "There are five ghosts that we're aware of." His smile was sunny, but it did nothing to warm me. I'd never seen a ghost before. The only reason I could be seeing them now was because I was a shifter. A glance at my friends told me that none of them had seen the child. Maybe being a werewolf wasn't the cause then.

With great reluctance, I acknowledged the possibility that my torn spirit was to blame. I didn't just have werewolf DNA in my system. I'd also been infected to some extent with vampirism. So far, I hadn't seen any visible evidence that I was turning into a bloodsucker. My skin had always been pale, but I wasn't as white as the kid. My teeth only turned into fangs when I became a werewolf. Most telling of all, I didn't have a craving for blood. Not yet anyway.

"My daughter, Margaret, will be serving breakfast between seven and eight in the morning," Edward said as I signed my name in the book. "Dial one on the phone if you need anything and she will answer your call." I put the pen down and he gestured to the stairs as he shuffled out from behind the desk in a pair of ratty gray slippers. "I'll show you to your rooms."

Edward didn't offer to help us with our luggage. I

didn't blame him for the lapse in courtesy. He had to be at least in his eighties. I'd have felt pretty low asking him to lug my bags up the stairs.

Another ghost appeared when we reached the second floor. Thin and insubstantial, I could almost see through her. She'd been in her early twenties when she'd died and had been delicately lovely. She wore a corset beneath her dove gray dress that made her waist seem impossibly tiny.

Floating several inches off the floor, she was staring bleakly at an old sepia toned photo that had been taken when the nearby town had been new. Half a dozen stern faced men and women looked back at the camera. A backdrop of what looked like a general store was behind them. The three women wore black dresses with scratchy looking lace on the collars. Their hair was pulled back into a severe bun. The men wore black suits and white shirts. None were smiling.

All six looked very similar. It was obvious that they were related, but it was hard to tell which one was the oldest and which was the youngest. They looked roughly the same age. It seemed highly unlikely that they could be sextuplets. They were rare in this day and age let alone back then. Medical care had most likely come in the form of an untrained midwife. I was sure that the survival rate of babies had to have been much lower back then.

The ghost shifted her attention to us and she watched wistfully as we filed past her. Her gaze sharpened when she realized that I could see her. Holding out a hand beseechingly, her mouth moved, but she made no sound. I shook my head to indicate that I couldn't hear her. She clutched her hands together in despair, then disappeared.

Flynn had watched our silent exchange with interest. Unaware that she was gone, he drew in a breath to try to pick up her scent. As a wereconstrictor, he tended to taste the air rather than smell it. I couldn't pick up any scents that didn't belong to us or the other humans staying in the house. For all I knew, the ghosts were just figments of my overactive imagination. Yet Edward had seemed pretty certain that they were real. I obviously wasn't the only one who was able to see them.

We stopped at the first door in the long hallway and Edward handed a key to Mark. "This is your room, Mr. Steel. Unfortunately, I'll have to split your party up. We currently have a full house and two of you will need to stay up on the third floor."

"Alexis and I will take the rooms on the third floor," Reece said firmly.

I opened my mouth to argue, but Mark surreptitiously shook his head. "Agreed," he said, putting an end to my argument before I could voice it.

He didn't know everything that had transpired between Reece and me in New Orleans, but he probably suspected that we'd consummated our bond again. I grimaced inwardly at the predicament that we were in. My mother had come close to breaking the bond between us and sex had been the only thing that could strengthen it. In the event that our link came under threat again, it made sense for us to stay close together.

Kala's lips quivered with mirth, but a warning look from our boss quelled her laughter. She had the most playful personality in our team. She often had a hard time remaining serious.

Kala took the next vacant room down the hall and Flynn took the third. Then just Edward, Reece and I were left. We trudged slowly up the creaking stairs to the third and final floor. The hallway was much shorter and there were only four rooms up here. Reece was given the second last room down the end of the hallway and I was delegated to the last room.

"Have a pleasant night, what's left of it," Edward said with a smile and shuffled back towards the stairs.

The house was antiquated enough to still use actual keys rather than plastic keycards. I stepped inside my room, locked the door and shook my head at the feeble security. Someone with a bobby pin could probably break in easily enough.

It was late and all I wanted to do was crawl into bed and sleep, but I took the time to unpack and to take a quick shower first. Reece had the same idea. I could sense him on the other side of the wall as I soaped my body. A flash of heat went through me when I caught a glimpse of his thoughts. He was recalling pinning me down and bringing me to the edge with his hands and mouth. Did he know that I could see what he was thinking and did he have any idea what it was doing to me?

Shaking my head to dispel the image, I turned the water off. Drawing back the curtain, I let out a silent gasp of fright when I saw that I wasn't alone. A man stood a few feet away. His expression was eerily calm. Before I could let out a scream, I saw that he was floating. Realizing he was a ghost, some of my alarm faded.

The spectral intruder was a clean-cut, handsome man in his early twenties. He courteously turned his back as I snatched up the towel and pulled it around me. He was even more shadowy than the other two had been. His skin and clothes looked faded, like an old photograph that was losing its color. He wore an outfit similar to the small boy, but in black rather than brown. His hair was short and neat and was an indiscriminate shade of brown.

"Can't a girl have a shower in peace?" I hissed quietly at his back. "What do you want?"

Turning to face me again, he mouthed something. I tried to read his lips, but I couldn't work out what he was saying. "I can't understand you," I whispered quietly enough that I hoped Reece couldn't hear me. It was bad enough that I could see spirits. Now I was talking to them as well.

Frustrated, the ghost moved over to the mirror. There was enough steam in the room to fog the glass. I watched in astonishment as he drew his finger down the mirror and left a mark. It took all of his concentration to leave me a short message. Exhausted, he gave me a meaningful look before he faded.

I read the message again, feeling chilled despite my warm shower. It read; *ware the coven.* I wasn't an expert, but I was pretty sure a coven usually meant witches. Somehow, it didn't surprise me that witches existed. There was very little that could shock me now that I knew that monsters were real and that I had become one of them.

Chapter Seven

Falling asleep wasn't easy when I was trying to keep one eye open to watch for ghosts. Eventually, I slept and woke to a knock at the door a few hours later.

"Rise and shine!" Kala called far too cheerfully. "Mark wants us to meet downstairs for breakfast in ten minutes." I heard Reece groan through the wall. It was his only acknowledgement that he was awake and that he'd heard her message.

"We'll be right there," I called back. We'd raised our voices for the benefit of the humans who were still in their rooms on our floor. We had to blend in and that meant being as ordinary as possible.

Ten minutes wasn't long enough for me to recover from only a few short hours of restless slumber. I splashed cold water on my face, which helped a little. My long black hair was a tangled mess and I brushed it into a semblance of neatness.

I studied my reflection and noted how wan I looked. My eyes were dark brown, but now tended to lighten a few shades just before the full moon came around. That was only one week away now. If we were lucky, we could wrap up this latest mission before then.

I didn't even want to think about the consequences of being stuck in a small town when we turned next. Without the thirty foot high, electrified fence to keep us under control, people would surely die.

Dressing in fresh jeans and a black t-shirt, I took the stairs down to the second floor. I paused at the photo that the female ghost had been staring at last night. There was something eerie about the six siblings and I examined their faces closely. It took me a moment to spot what was troubling me. I couldn't pinpoint how old any of them were. Their clothes and expressions made them seem like they were in their forties or older, but their faces were unlined. They might have been a lot younger than they seemed.

Voices drew me downstairs and into the dining room. Most of the guests had already eaten and had left. Mark, Kala and Flynn had dragged two of the tables together so we could sit in a group. I took a seat next to Kala as Reece ambled in behind me. He sat beside Flynn, opposite from me. Mark sat at the head of the table. At a quick glance, he could have passed for our dad. Only Flynn's mocha colored skin shattered that illusion.

A woman in her fifties entered, pushing a trolley ahead of her. It held a variety of food including toast, fruit, cereal and less healthy alternatives such as bacon and scrambled eggs. "Good morning, I'm Margaret. I hope you had a pleasant night." Her smile was friendly and welcoming. Her figure was plump and her choice of dress was floral and bordering on dowdy.

"We did, thank you," Mark said on behalf of us all and not entirely accurately.

Margaret began offloading the food onto the table. Kala beat me to the pot of coffee and smirked at my sour look. Taking pity on me, she poured me a cup first. I must have looked even crankier than I felt.

"I understand that you can see the deceased," Margaret said to me. I nearly dropped my cup in surprise. "May I ask how many of our ghosts you've seen so far?"

"Three," I replied. The other two hadn't shown themselves yet. I kind of hoped they'd remain hidden. This new phenomenon was disturbing. It was one I wished I hadn't been burdened with at all.

She showed only mild surprise as she placed the last dish on the table. "You must have a strong gift. Does it run in your family?"

"I'm not sure," I said, but I sincerely doubted it. "As far as I know, my Dad can't see spirits. I lost my mother when I was very young and I know little about her."

Instant empathy flowed from her and she patted

me on the shoulder. "I'm so sorry to hear that, dear. Your mother must have passed this gift down to you."

I pressed my lips together to contain a highly inappropriate and cynical laugh. She'd passed it to me by biting me and draining my blood. Thanks to her unholy appetite, my soul was now in a struggle between remaining a wolf and becoming a vampire. It was a gift that I could have done without.

"Thank you for a wonderful breakfast," Mark said to distract her from her line of questioning. He knew I didn't want to talk about my mother. It was a topic that I didn't want to discuss with my friends let alone with a stranger.

"Will I be seeing you for lunch and dinner?" she asked.

"I'm not sure, yet. We might be otherwise engaged," he said. "I am certain that we'll see you at breakfast tomorrow, though." Even making that commitment was a stretch. There was no way to tell what would happen during our missions. We weren't even sure what we were dealing with yet. All we had to go on was the advice of a ghost. The rest of the team wasn't even aware of that development yet.

Too polite to question us about what business we had in the area, she left. I waited until she was out of earshot before I spoke. When I did, I kept my voice quiet. "One of the ghosts gave me a message last night."

Their surprise was almost comical. "What was the

message?" Mark asked.

"What ghost?" Kala asked at the same time.

"He was young, only a few years older than you," I said to Kala. "He tried to talk to me, but I couldn't hear him. He wrote a message on the mirror with his finger."

Flynn paused with his spoonful of cereal halfway to his mouth. "What did it say?" he asked.

"It said 'ware the coven'."

"Does that mean what I think it means?" he asked our boss.

"It's archaic, but he probably meant 'beware of the coven'," Mark replied. "That has to mean we're dealing with witches." He didn't seem very happy about that prospect.

"Have you dealt with them before?" I asked. I'd read only a fraction of the PIA archives and hadn't come across any files relating to witches yet. I'd brought along my laptop just in case I had a chance to do some more reading. I couldn't remember downloading any cases about witches onto it.

"Yes, unfortunately. They're generally a nuisance, but every now and then they can be truly dangerous."

"Dangerous how?" Kala asked. She bit into a piece of toast that was heavily coated in strawberry jelly. It made my teeth ache just looking at it. That much jelly would be far too sweet for my liking. I stuck to cereal and filled a bowl to the brim.

"They can cast some very nasty hexes on their victims," Mark explained. "You don't want to know the details." She took him at his word and didn't pry. She, Reece and Flynn had only been members of the TAK Squad for the past five years. I wasn't sure who Mark had worked with before then.

"Could they be the reason why we're here?" Reece queried. Mark's boss hadn't been very forthcoming about why he'd sent us here.

"Possibly. I did some digging and discovered that Bradbury has a reputation for random, unexplained disappearances. This has been occurring ever since the town was first established," Mark explained. "The missing are a mixture of both men and women. They are always young and attractive. The same number of disappearances occurs every year."

Remembering the ageless faces in the photo, I had a sneaking suspicion of who might be behind the disappearances. "I'm guessing that six people go missing each year, right? Three male and three female."

Mark looked at me with his brows raised. "How did you guess?"

It was nice to be able to surprise him for once. "I saw a female ghost staring at one of the photos last night. I think the people in it might belong to the coven." It didn't seem possible, since the photo had been taken so long ago, but that was the hunch I had.

"Which photo was she looking at?" he asked as he stood.

"It's the first one on the second floor."

He motioned for the rest of us to continue eating

breakfast. "Wait here. I'll be right back."

I concentrated on eating my cereal and the others did the same. As promised, Mark returned quickly. He'd taken a photo of the old picture with his tablet. He handed it around so the others could see. I'd already had a good enough look at the coven and handed the device to Kala after a cursory look.

"Wow, they look like they'd be a lot of fun at a party," she observed with a straight face.

Mark took the tablet back and ran a search on the group using a facial recognition program. His tablet was far more sophisticated than usual. It came equipped with all sorts of extra apps. This particular program was apparently designed to search the local newspapers for photos.

It took only a few seconds before news articles began to appear. "They're very prominent in Bradbury," he said after reading the article. "They are on every town committee and are heavily into charity work."

"Great," Flynn said with a grimace as he leaned over to look at the photo. "They're hiding behind do-gooder reputations while in reality they must be stealing the life forces of the townsfolk in order to stay young."

Mark handed the tablet to Flynn. He studied the article, then handed it to Reece. He read it quickly, then reached across the table to give it to me. With new clothes and in a far more modern setting, the coven no longer looked like they were in their forties.

Their expressions were still stern and unsmiling, but they appeared to be only in their late twenties now.

"Do witches usually steal people's lives to keep themselves young?" I asked Mark as I handed the device to Kala.

"This is the first case I've heard of," he replied and took the tablet from her when she was done. He slid it back into an inner pocket of his jacket. As always, he wore a dark suit. This one was charcoal gray. He'd teamed it up with a light blue button up shirt and a dark blue tie. Even if he'd been wearing casual clothes like the rest of us, he'd still look like a federal agent. "Most witches are benign," he explained. "Many believe that causing harm to others will bring harm back upon them threefold."

"It sounds like you're talking about wiccans," Reece said. He'd devoured his cereal and had pushed his empty bowl away. He was now working his way through six slices of toast.

Mark inclined his head. "Some are. Others think of themselves as white witches. They abhor the evil arts and classify dark witches as their enemies."

"I guess that means we're facing a dark coven," I said. "What can we expect from them?"

He paused to search through the files that were stored in his memory. "Witches and warlocks can have a variety of abilities. They're similar to the Seven Deadly Sinners in that respect." He was referring to the telepaths that we'd hunted down when I'd first joined the team. "Their abilities range from being able to befuddle minds, to casting spells and curses. This coven must be very powerful to have hidden in plain sight for so long."

"How have they managed to pull that off?" Flynn asked. "Surely the townsfolk must have noticed that the witches aren't aging."

"There are spells they can cast to mask their true appearance," Mark replied. "The townsfolk see only what the coven wants them to see. If I were to dig into the past, we'd find that they've changed their names many times over during the past couple of centuries."

"How old are they pretending to be at the moment?" Kala asked.

"In their fifties."

"I wonder what we're going to see when we meet them?"

"Since we are already aware of who and what they are, hopefully their glamour won't affect us."

"We can't just march up to them and gun them down," Reece pointed out. "We don't have any proof that they're behind the disappearances yet."

Our job was to track and kill anything that harmed humanity. We had to be especially careful when our quarry were human. Proof was required before we could detain or eliminate our targets.

Mark drummed his fingers on the table as he thought through our dilemma. "It would be a bad idea to enter the town as a group," he decided. "Five strangers showing up all at once will be noticed. We'll have to split up and investigate the coven without their knowledge."

Reece flicked a glance in my direction and Mark held up his hand in appeasement. "Lexi will remain with me, of course."

I'd only turned eighteen a few weeks ago and was considered to be the baby of the team. To be honest, pairing me up with someone was probably a good idea. I had a distressing tendency to run into trouble whenever I was alone.

Chapter Eight

Bradbury was only a ten minute drive away from the bed and breakfast. Dense trees grew on both sides of the road, creating a shady corridor. The woods that enclosed Dawson's Retreat on three sides extended right up to the edge of town. We passed several roads that led deeper into the woods to destinations unknown.

I grew nervous when I saw the sign welcoming us to town. I'd seen plenty of movies about witches and few of them had been nice. We already knew the coven was dangerous, thanks to the ghost's message. We had no way of knowing just what they were capable of yet. We would learn more as we performed surveillance on the town. Watching them without their knowledge was going to be tricky. We were strangers and we'd stand out no matter how hard we tried to blend in.

The instant that we crossed the town line, Mark jolted as if he'd been hit with a small surge of electricity. "Where are we?" he asked in confusion.

"We just entered Bradbury," Reece replied with a sideways glance at him.

Mark looked out through the windscreen and studied the houses and trees that lined the road. "This doesn't look like Colorado. Which State are we in?"

"West Virginia." Reece was frowning now and his concern was growing.

"What are we doing here?" Mark's bewilderment might almost have been funny if it hadn't been so frightening. Unsure about what was going on, I exchanged worried looks with Kala and Flynn. They looked as clueless as I felt.

"We're hunting a coven of witches," Kala said. "Don't you remember anything about our mission?"

Mark put a hand to his forehead, as if thinking hurt him. "I don't know. There's something…" His brow furrowed, then he groaned in pain and doubled over. Blood burst from his nose, quickly painting his clothes red.

Reece stomped on the brake and we screeched to a halt, drawing the curious stare of a young woman walking her little white terrier. I instinctively knew that staying in town would be the worst thing we could do. "We need to get him out of Bradbury," I said. The witches had cast a spell that had wiped his memory. Did they know we were coming and had they laid a trap in advance? If so, why hadn't the spell worked on the rest of us?

In full agreement, Reece swung the SUV around. We zoomed back across the town line far quicker than we'd entered. I turned to look through the rear window, half expecting to see six figures chasing after us on broomsticks. The only thing I saw was the young woman staring after us in astonishment. Her small dog barked shrilly in excitement.

Mark's groan of pain cut off as soon as we left town. He stared around in confusion, as if he couldn't remember where he was again. Blood caked the lower half of his face. The red stood out starkly against his shirt, but could barely be seen against his dark jacket. The smell clogged my nose, drowning out every other scent. "What happened?" he asked in a daze.

"The coven must have set up wards around the perimeter of town," Flynn said as Reece pulled over on the side of the road. There was barely room for another car to pass by without sideswiping us. The town was fairly secluded and ours was the only vehicle we'd seen so far. It was unlikely that anyone would be driving past in the next few minutes. "Do you remember our mission now?"

Wincing at a final stab of pain in his head, Mark nodded. "Six witches and warlocks are killing young, attractive people. They're stealing their life forces to prolong their own lives."

"It looks like you'll have to sit this one out," Reece said. "The wards didn't affect the rest of us."

"So it would seem," Mark said as he removed a handkerchief from his pocket and attempted to mop the blood from his face. "Their spells must only be targeting humans."

"Yay for us," Kala said with a factious grin. "They're not going to know what hit them when we show up and tear their faces off."

"There will be no face tearing," Mark said sternly. "Not until we have verification that the coven is responsible for the disappearances. We only have speculation at the moment."

Flynn asked a pertinent question. "Why hasn't anyone investigated the missing people before if it's been going on for so long?"

"They're very good at covering their tracks," Mark replied. "They don't just take people from Bradbury. They trawl the surrounding towns as well. They've only come to our attention now because they chose the wrong victim. One of the missing women is my superior's niece. She was on vacation from work and planned to pass through West Virginia on the way to visit her parents. She disappeared a week ago. After my research turned up so many missing people from this area, I determined that Bradbury is the most likely point where she vanished."

"How many people have gone missing in the area so far this year?" Reece asked.

Mark didn't need to consult his tablet. He'd stored the knowledge in his brain. "Three who match the profile."

"They'll already be dead by now," Kala said with what would have seemed like clinical detachment to anyone else. I knew it was just her innate animal practicality because I felt the same way. It was sad that so many people had lost their lives, but crying about it wouldn't bring them back. Finding proof that the witches were responsible and stopping the coven from performing any more sacrifices was our focus.

"What sort of time frame are we looking at between each disappearance?" Flynn asked.

"They always begin in November at the rate of one per week," Mark replied. I'd lost track of time and realized that we were in the final week of November now. "Another person will go missing sometime this week."

"Since you're out of commission, Lexi will have to team up with me," Reece said.

I bristled at his commanding tone. "I think we'll call less attention to ourselves if Kala and I pair up," I countered.

We had a short staring match before Reece grudgingly gave in. "Suit yourself."

"Yep, she's going to be an alpha all right," Kala grinned. She lifted her hands in surrender when I cut a glance at her. "You don't need to bend me to your will, oh Great and Powerful Overlord. I'll be a good little minion," she said in false panic that made Flynn snicker.

"I'm not going to become anyone's overlord," I said crankily. "Besides, you'd be a terrible minion."

She couldn't decide whether to be amused or offended by that comment.

"I'd be an awesome minion," Flynn decided. "Constrictors aren't as flighty as wolves and cougars." He winked to indicate he was kidding.

Kala immediately bristled. "I'm not flighty! I could be a good puppet if I wanted to."

"Sure you could," Reece teased. "You could become Lexi's pet kitty."

Before she could object again, Mark cut in. "I'll head back to base and do some more digging into the coven. Report in every fifteen minutes, unless something happens," he instructed.

We climbed out and I checked that the gun that I'd hidden in a pocket of my cargo pants wasn't showing. My pants hung more heavily on the right side, but it wasn't obvious that I was packing.

Normally, we'd keep in contact via small earpieces. Since we were moving around in broad daylight, there was a chance that they might be spotted. We'd all been issued with PIA cell phones. In the unlikely event that we ran into trouble, our teammates were only a phone call away.

We split into two groups as Mark slid across into the driver's seat. We waited for him to drive away before we recommenced our journey. Reece and Flynn entered the woods to circle around to enter Bradbury from the east. The bond ensured that I could always feel Reece, but I had to concentrate to pick up on his thoughts and emotions the further apart we moved.

My shoulders tensed in anticipation as Kala and I crossed back over the town line. I felt nothing, but that didn't mean we hadn't been noticed. For all I knew, we'd just triggered a magical alarm warning the coven that we were coming for them.

I glanced at Kala to see she was still sulking about being ganged up on. "I'm sorry I said you'd be a terrible minion," I said contritely.

"You all think I'm just a ditzy blonde who can't follow a simple order without being reminded constantly," she said with bitterness that took me aback.

"No one thinks that, Kala." I was shocked that she'd reached that conclusion. "What would make you say that?"

Silent for a few moments, she blew out a sigh. "Because it's true."

"What are you talking about?" I was genuinely flabbergasted.

"I have the attention span of a turnip," she confessed. "I get bored easily and lose track of what I'm supposed to be doing sometimes." She sent me a wry look. "Why do you think Mark gets us to check in with him every fifteen minutes?"

"Because he cares about us and he's concerned about our welfare?"

"It's partly that, but he knows what I'm like."

"Is your lack of concentration due to your cougar nature?"

She nodded and tucked a stray lock of hair behind her ear. "When I have a target in sight, I can stay focused until I've taken them down. That part is easy for me because I enjoy the chase. The rest of what we do tends to bore me to tears."

"Then it's just as well we work as a team. I won't let you lose focus and you can teach me how to be more effective when we're hunting down our targets."

She grinned and bumped my shoulder with hers affectionately. "I'm really glad you're on the team. It was kind of lonely being the only girl living with three guys."

"I'm glad, too." I said and meant it. This wasn't the career path I would have chosen, but at least I wasn't stuck in an office filing all day. That was my personal idea of hell.

"Why do I get the feeling that something happened between you and Garrett in New Orleans that you don't want the rest of us to know about?" she asked. She already knew that we'd had to strengthen our bond by having sex again. Only one other thing had occurred that no one else knew about. It mystified me how she knew we were hiding something. I felt ashamed when I realized I *had* thought of her as being a bit flighty.

"Do you remember Officer Mallory?" He and his partner had been plain clothes detectives. They'd followed us around a couple of times when we'd been investigating the zombie raisings. They'd suspected that we knew more than we'd been letting on.

Kala nodded. "He was the young blond cop with the pale, creepy eyes. I had the feeling there was something off about him."

"You're not wrong. It turns out he was a serial rapist and murderer."

She almost tripped in surprise, but her reflexes were good enough to save herself from falling. "How did you figure that out?"

"He cornered me when Reece was checking one of the cemeteries. He told me what he'd done to some other girls and he said I was going to be his next victim."

Kala shook her head in amazement at his stupidity. "Did you kill him, or did Garrett do the deed?" She knew both of us well enough to guess that we hadn't allowed him to live. Neither would she if she'd been in our situation.

"Reece beat me to it," I admitted. "He choked him to death, which was far quieter than the plan I'd had of blasting his head apart." I scowled that I'd been denied the kill.

Kala chuckled in amusement. "You really are one of us now. It's hard to believe how easily you've assimilated into becoming a shifter."

"What do you mean?" I knew very little about our kind. What I'd learned had come from reading through the archives and from firsthand experience.

"I went through hell when I first turned," she said as we walked past a house with a six foot high fence. A menacing growl came from the other side. I was pretty sure it was directed at Kala. "I was only fifteen and I didn't have anyone with me when I went through the process."

"Neither did I," I reminded her. "I didn't even know what I was until Mark told me."

"That makes it even weirder how well you've taken to it," she replied. "At least I knew I was going to turn long before it happened. I went through all kinds of mental torment for months afterwards. It was only when the guys turned a year later and we could all share the experience that I was finally able to come to terms with it."

Once again, I'd proven to be stranger than the rest of my kind. My hand rose to my right shoulder and rubbed the fresh scar. Maybe being bitten by a vampire when I was so young was to blame for my apparent ease at becoming a shifter. My body had already been compromised when I was a baby. There was a good chance that had helped to prepare me to become a monster.

"What did you do with Mallory's body?" she asked, breaking me from my maudlin thoughts. We were walking along the main street, heading towards the center of town. Few pedestrians walked the streets. They flicked nervous glances at us before hurrying on about their business. Strangers seemed to be fairly rare. Their town was off the beaten path and it wasn't easy to stumble across by accident.

"We dumped him in the swamp." We shared a smile at the poetic justice. "He was already being snacked on by alligators before we left."

"Serves him right," Kala decided. "You should tell Mark about it. He'll make sure the police are aware of what the cop had been doing in his spare time. I'm sure the girls' families would want to know what happened to them."

"You're right," I realized. It worried me that I hadn't automatically thought of the suffering that their families were going through. How much of myself had I lost when I'd become a shifter? Would I one day lose my compassion altogether? None of the others had so far, but we all knew that I was different from them. Who knew what I would eventually turn into, or if I'd be able to retain any of my humanity at all?

Chapter Nine

It was mid-morning on a weekday and the town was fairly quiet. There was nothing unusual about Bradbury that I could see. The nearby businesses included a hair salon, a gas station, several clothing boutiques, a used book store and a convenience store.

Kala pointed to a café on the next corner and we crossed the street to take a closer look. The sign above the door read 'Kate's Kafé'.

"I hate it when they use atrocious spelling like that," I complained. It was probably supposed to be eye catching, but it just grated on my nerves.

"You mean that's not how you spell café?" Kala asked, pretending to be the dumb blonde she thought she was. A bell jingled overhead as she pushed the door open.

Two customers sat at one of the small round tables.

In their late seventies, the two old women glared at us suspiciously as we walked past them on our way to the counter. If this was the welcoming committee, then I could see why the town had so few visitors.

The woman behind the counter turned around and I saw one of the faces from the old photo at Dawson's Retreat. I struggled to hide my alarm that we were standing so close to one of the witches we were here to investigate.

"Hi there. I'm Kate. Are you new to town?" she asked in a falsely bright tone. Her dark brown hair was pulled up into a neat ponytail. It was far less severe than the bun she'd worn in the old photo. Her mouth was smiling, but her cold green eyes assessed us both carefully.

"We're just passing through," Kala replied. She hid her reaction far better than I did.

"What can I get you?" the witch asked. She wore a demure skirt with a flower print and a virginal white blouse. If I hadn't known what she was, I'd have had a difficult time believing she was evil. I knew she'd cast a spell that made her look like she was in her fifties, but she looked like she was in her late twenties to me.

"I'll have a vanilla milkshake," Kala ordered.

"And you?" she asked me.

"I'll have a chocolate one, thanks," I replied with what I hoped was a friendly smile. I was beginning to realize there was far more to being an agent than simply blowing holes in the bad guys. I'd have to become an accomplished actress to prevent tipping off our targets that we were hunting them.

"Take a seat anywhere and I'll bring them right over," she said.

I followed Kala to a table near the window. We could easily overhear the two little old ladies talking on the far side of the room as we took our seats.

"Did you hear that a tourist went missing a few days ago?" one of them said. "Apparently, she stopped in Kate's Kafé for a meal. She went missing shortly after she left town." I'd be willing to bet that she hadn't left town at all. The coven had kidnapped her and used her for their nefarious means. One of the witches would have hidden her car where it wouldn't easily be found.

"What a terrible shame," the other woman replied. "Someone should do something about all the crime in this country."

Neither mentioned the other people who'd gone missing over the years. They didn't show much actual concern about the tourist's disappearance. I cocked an eyebrow at Kala. She had a theory ready for me. "The coven has probably laid a hex over the entire town. Their spells could be preventing anyone from questioning the disappearances too closely."

"Witches have that much power?" I asked skeptically.

"These ones seem to," she shrugged. Our conversation broke off when Kate appeared. I was reluctant to drink anything that one of the coven members had prepared. Feeling the same way, Kala furtively smelled her drink and took a cautious sip as the witch walked away.

"Do you remember our mission?" I asked her when the witch was safely behind the counter again. It was the only way I could think to check that Kala hadn't been fed a mind wiping potion.

"We're here to conquer and destroy," she replied woodenly, then smirked at my alarm. "Just kidding. We're on the prowl for the coven."

"Speak of the devil," I murmured when another familiar person strode past the window. One of the warlocks pushed the door open and entered the café. He nodded amiably at the two old women, then strode over to the counter. The elderly pair tittered coyly behind their hands. They were admiring the handsome man who they thought was only twenty or so years younger than they were. They clearly had no idea that he and his circle held the entire town captive by their black magic.

Kala took her cell phone out and sent a text message to Mark, checking in as ordered. She continued to play with her phone while listening in on the quiet conversation between the two coven members. I watched their reflections in the window as they spoke in hushed tones.

"One of the wards was tripped about twenty minutes ago," the warlock said in a low voice. His hair was the same shade of dark brown as his sister's. It hung at chin length and fell forward to half-hide his face. I caught a glimpse of his glittering green eyes and suppressed a shiver of dread. I could practically feel power emanating from the pair.

"Have they been reset yet?" Kate asked. She didn't look particularly concerned. This obviously wasn't the first time they'd been threatened. The fact that they still remained undiscovered meant that they were well practiced at facing their foes. So far, they'd always emerged as the victors.

"I just took care of it myself," he confirmed. "I checked the roads in and out of town and I didn't find any bodies this time. I don't know how they managed to escape before dying from an aneurism."

"Do you think these two are involved?" she asked and sent a suspicious glance towards our table.

He looked over his shoulder at us and was silent long enough for my shoulders to tense up again. "I doubt it," he said finally. "I'm not picking up anything suspicious from either of them." To me, they looked similar enough to be twins. They had the same eyes, nose and pointed chins.

I didn't allow my shoulders to slump in relief when he looked away. Instead, I took a sip of my milkshake. Kala rapidly sent a message, presumably to the others to warn them that the coven was aware of the breech in their defenses. We'd have to be extremely careful to remain under the radar now. It might be best if Reece and Flynn remained out of sight altogether. She received a message a few seconds later and turned her phone around so I could read it.

Reece had responded to her warning with confirmation that he and Flynn would keep a low profile. Mark had been right when he'd warned us that five strangers would be noticed. Only two of us had been spotted so far and we'd already drawn too much attention to ourselves.

"What's their story?" the warlock said and nodded towards us.

"The blonde said they're just passing through."

"Watch them to make sure they leave. I'm going to run a sweep of town and see if any other strangers are lurking around."

I stiffened and Kala darted a warning look at me not to blow our cover. She sent another message to the guys and received a reply a few seconds later. "They're going to bring the SUV to the café," she whispered almost beneath their breath. Only someone with supernatural hearing could have made out what she was saying. "Reece will park it around the corner, then head back to the B&B on foot."

"How long will that take?" I asked.

"At least half an hour."

While we could run very fast when we wanted to, the guys would have to remain out of sight while they retrieved the SUV. That would slow them down, which meant we needed to stall for time. "I'm hungry," I whined loudly enough for the witch to be able to hear me. "Can we have breakfast before we leave?" My tone was annoyingly wheedling.

Pretending to be irritated by my request, Kala

frowned and tore her eyes away from her phone. "You just ate an hour ago."

It was true and I smiled winsomely. "I'm a growing girl and I'm hungry again," I shrugged.

Rolling her eyes, Kala heaved a sigh and reached for the menu. "Mom and Dad are going to be pissed if we're late," she complained. It wasn't much of a stretch to pretend to be sisters. We lived together and were almost a pack, or pride in her case. We didn't look anything alike, but not all siblings looked like carbon copies of each other.

"They won't mind if we're half an hour behind schedule," I wheedled and slurped down more of the milkshake.

"Fine. You can take the blame if they ground us. What do you want?"

I took my time to peruse the menu and settled on bacon and eggs. It would take at least fifteen minutes to cook and I'd stretch out the meal for as long as I could. Heaving herself to her feet, Kala retreated to the counter to put in our order. She made it a double order so it would take Kate longer to prepare it.

My stomach should have rebelled against eating two breakfasts in such a short space of time. My metabolism had been boosted since becoming a shifter and I ate the entire meal, if more slowly than usual. Kala dawdled through hers as well. She was playing the role of a bored older sister well. Keeping most of her attention on her cell phone, she was doing her best to ignore me. In light of what she'd told me about her attention span earlier, maybe it wasn't an act at all.

Trying to blend in, I took my own cell phone out and started playing a game. My reflexes were much better now and the game posed little challenge. I pretended to be absorbed while keeping one eye on the target. Kate watched us covertly while cleaning the counter.

An elderly man entered and shuffled over to the counter to order coffee. He took a seat halfway between us and the two little old ladies. A newspaper was folded under his arm. He opened it and began to read. I could easily read the print as he turned the page. The top story was about the missing tourist. The local sheriff had no leads, which wasn't much of a surprise. The coven wouldn't have left any clues that would implicate them.

Pushing her plate away at last, Kala left some money on the table and motioned for me to follow her. "It's time for us to hit the road." Four sets of eyes watched us with varying degrees of suspicion as we stepped outside.

The SUV was waiting around the corner right where Reece said it would be. We climbed inside and drove back across the town line. Again, I watched for a tail and didn't spot one.

Kala pulled over to pick Reece up when he stepped out from the trees just past the town line. It was strange to have him sitting in the backseat rather than being behind the wheel. He sat on the edge of the seat, which put him almost close enough to touch.

I kept my eyes on the road ahead rather than on the rearview mirror. The air conditioning was cold enough to make a normal human shiver, but I could still feel the warmth of his skin radiating towards me. I couldn't afford to be distracted right now. Dwelling on how warm he made me feel would be a very bad idea.

Chapter Ten

Kala parked in the small lot behind the B&B. We filed in through the backdoor that led us past the kitchen. Margaret emerged and blinked at us in surprise. She hadn't expected us to return so soon. "Can I get you kids anything?" she asked.

"A pot of coffee would be great," Kala said with a smile. "We'll take it in the parlor, if you don't mind." We didn't need to search the building to know where Mark and Flynn were. We heard them talking even before we'd entered the building.

"Of course, dear," Margaret beamed. "Does this mean you'll be having lunch here after all?"

"Yes," Reece said. "We've had a change of plans." He didn't elaborate further and continued on down the hall. We trooped inside the parlor with Reece in the lead and me bringing up the rear.

Mark had washed up and had changed into a fresh suit. Still pale from his sudden copious blood loss, he was alert enough. "How are you feeling?" I asked as I took a seat on the chaise lounge across from him. Kala sat beside me and Reece took the armchair that was positioned between our two lounges.

His smile was wan. "I'm fine. It takes more than a nosebleed to keep me down." It had been the worst nosebleed I'd ever seen. He'd probably lost a pint of blood before we'd left town. I didn't even want to think what would have happened if we'd been any slower.

"He's tough," Flynn said. "For a human," he added as an afterthought.

My laugh choked off when shadowy figures appeared all around us. I surged to my feet and the others did the same. Looking around wildly, they reached for their weapons. They couldn't see what I could and they had no idea what had startled me.

"What is it, Lexi?" Mark asked. His gun was in his hand and he was ready to shoot at anything that moved.

"The ghosts are back," I said. They didn't look like they were going to attack, but it was still a shock to be surrounded by the dead.

"How many are there?" Kala asked. "Is it all five this time?"

"There's a lot more than five," I replied and did a quick headcount. "There's more like fifty of them." All of them were staring at me in a combination of hope and fear. I knew they wanted to communicate with me, but I didn't have any handy steam or a mirror to use this time.

"What do they want?" Mark asked and motioned for us to return to our seats. I was the only one who hadn't bothered to reach for my gun. Bullets were no use against spirits. The others put their weapons away. We sat down only moments before Margaret appeared with her trolley full of beverages and snacks.

Seeing my strained expression, she did a double take. "Are you feeling all right, dear? You look a little peaked."

"I'm fine," I lied. "My stomach is feeling bit upset." That was true. It was churning unpleasantly.

"I'll bring you some tea. I'm sure it will suit you far better than coffee," she decided without asking for my opinion. Kala made a face at the offer. She hated tea.

Mark waited for her to leave before he leaned in. "I have an idea, but it would be best if we waited until dark before we try it."

Somehow, I knew his idea was going to be something strange. "What's your plan?"

"I want to hold a séance."

My mouth dropped open at his reply. "Are you serious?"

"Deadly serious," he said and his expression was calm. "The spirits of this house clearly want to communicate with you. A séance would be our best chance to make that happen."

The ghosts turned to consult each other silently, then nodded and faded. My tension drained away as they disappeared. Margaret bustled inside and I waited for her to finish fussing over me and leave before I spoke. "The ghosts agree with your plan."

"What are they doing right now?" Mark asked. Even with all of his experience, he hadn't encountered ghosts before.

"They're not here anymore. They faded away after they all decided they liked your plan."

Kala mulled over our plight as she poured coffee for everyone but me. I picked up the only teacup on the tray. "A Ouija board might be a good idea," she decided. "That's how people usually communicate with the dead, isn't it?"

Mark had come to the same conclusion. "I'll drive to the nearest large town and see if I can locate one."

"You mean *I'll* drive," Reece argued. "You're in no shape to be behind the wheel."

"You two go, I'll stay here and protect the women folk," Flynn said solemnly. He grinned at the sour looks that Kala and I gave him. We were the last females who needed protection. Both of us were strong enough to dismember a human with our bare hands. Plus, we had guns and plenty of ammunition. If anyone needed protection here, it was the bad guys rather than us.

Finishing off their coffee, Mark and Reece left on their mini mission. Kala quickly grew bored. "I'm going to fall asleep if I sit around here for much longer. I'm going to go for a walk." Heaving herself to her feet, she ambled out through the front door, leaving Flynn and me alone in the parlor.

"Do you really think your Mom passed the ability to see ghosts to you?" Flynn asked.

"I have no idea. I was too young to remember her when she died and Dad rarely talks about her."

His expression was both sympathetic and melancholy. He'd been taken from his parents when he was a toddler. I might not remember my mom, but at least I knew my father. Reece, Kala and Flynn knew nothing about their families at all.

"Is a Ouija board really going to work?" I said to change the topic. Katrina was the last person I wanted to talk about. I had a superstitious notion that mentioning her would somehow conjure her up. It was daytime, so it was a stupid idea. Vampires couldn't leave their lairs until after dark.

"If a ghost can leave a message in a steamy mirror, a Ouija board shouldn't be a problem for them."

"I wonder if the ghosts have ever tried to contact anyone else?"

"If they have, I'd be willing to bet that person didn't survive long."

Coming to the notice of the coven was obviously a very bad idea. They hadn't been happy to discover that someone had tripped their wards and they'd reacted instantly. I didn't know what they'd planned to do if they found us, but I suspected it would be unpleasant.

Kala returned from her walk after about an hour and plonked down next to me on the couch. "Did I miss anything?" she asked.

"Margaret brought us some homemade chocolate chip cookies," Flynn said with a sly grin.

She surged back to her feet. "Why didn't you say so?"

"I just did," he said to her back as she darted into the hallway.

She returned with a plateful of cookies and a fresh mug of coffee. One thing I could say about Dawson's Retreat was that their food was fantastic. "I'd be the size of a house if I lived here," I mock-complained, holding a cookie in one hand and a cup of tea in the other.

"Nah," Kala argued with crumbs falling from her mouth as she spoke. "We burn off food too quickly to be able to put on much weight." That seemed to be true. I had to eat far more often than I ever had before just to stop myself from feeling hungry all the time.

Mark and Reece returned half an hour later. I'd had two cups of tea by then and had reached my limit. I politely refused Margaret's offer for a fresh cup when she appeared just as the agents sat down. I much preferred coffee to tea. I did accept her offer of lunch, though.

We made casual small talk until she returned with a gigantic plate of sandwiches. Some of the other guests had also returned for lunch. Sensing that we wished to speak in private, Margaret was kind enough to allow us to remain in the parlor.

"Did you manage to find a Ouija board?" Kala asked quietly when our hostess left. We'd be able to hear anyone approaching long before they could attempt to listen in.

Mark nodded. "It wasn't easy and we had to travel to another town before we finally located a store that sold them. I left it in the SUV."

That was wise. We wouldn't want Margaret or Edward to stumble across it by accident. They'd probably think we were crazy and would send us packing. Worse, they might call the cops. The local sheriff had to be beneath the coven's control. He or she would no doubt alert the witches and our cover would be blown.

Chapter Eleven

After lunch, we went our separate ways with the intention of coming back together again for dinner. Kala was taking a nap and Reece and Flynn had gone for a jog. Mark was also in his room, probably performing more research.

I spent a few hours sitting on my bed reading through the PIA archives. I'd stored a bunch of files that mentioned vampires on my laptop. The oldest one dated back to a time long before the Paranormal Investigation Agency had officially existed.

Roughly four hundred years ago, a priest in England had gathered a small group of people together to fight monsters. They'd slowly grown in number and had later spread to other countries. Now our organization was world-wide, if still unknown to the general populace.

The priest's name had been Thomas. He'd kept a detailed and illustrated journal of the strange things that he'd seen and of the monsters that he'd slain. I wished I could read his journal from start to finish, but each case had been split up into different categories. Fortunately, his notes had been translated from ye olde English into more modern terminology.

I'd already read the report of his first encounter with a master vampire and his nest. It was fascinating enough to read a second time. Quickly absorbed by the tale, I almost felt as if I was there as I read the account.

Thomas had received word from his base in London that a tiny, remote village had suffered a terrible tragedy. All twenty inhabitants had either been killed, or had gone missing. Curious, he'd decided to investigate.

People from the neighboring town had discovered and buried the bodies. They'd been interred for several weeks by the time he arrived on horseback. Being summer, their decomposition was already well advanced. He didn't allow that to stop him from investigating their wounds.

Thomas had dug up all eight of the corpses over the course of two days. While he hadn't seen a victim of a vampire attack before, the wounds indicated that one had most likely been responsible for their deaths. Closer examination determined that the bite marks were identical. He knew he was searching for a single culprit. Now that the creature had created a dozen minions, the number of vampires had risen to thirteen. It was an ill-omened figure.

Placing the corpses back in their graves, he rode to the neighboring town. The tavern was packed with frightened villagers. If he'd arrived after dark, they'd probably have attacked him with the wooden stakes they were trying so hard to hide.

Wary of strangers, at first they didn't want to discuss the doomed village with him. They were only willing to talk to him after he opened his scuffed travel bag and showed them his own crudely made wooden stake.

After that, he'd become an honorary member of their town. They told him of several more attacks on isolated farmhouses nearby. The nest hadn't moved on as he'd feared. Instead, they had a lair somewhere in the area.

Thomas asked if any of the townsfolk were willing to lend him a bloodhound. He was hoping the beast would be able to track down the fiends. One of the men had a farm nearby and agreed to his request. He offered the priest a bed for the night and Thomas accepted. Fearing to be out after dark, the pair travelled to the farm well before the sun had set.

The baying of several hounds greeted them as they arrived. Four dogs moved to surround their horses. They ran towards the house at the farmer's order. He wasn't willing to leave his dogs outside after dark. Vampires would eat anything if they were desperate enough. Their horses would have to fare for themselves, being too large to fit inside.

Stepping inside, Thomas saw that fortifications had been made. Wooden boards had been nailed over the windows from the inside and brackets had been added to either side of the door. The farmer, Harold, looked sheepish as he slid a thick wooden plank into place. It was doubtful that his precautions would work. At best, they would slow the undead monsters down for a few seconds. Braids of garlic hung from the rafters and wooden crosses had been nailed to every wall. They would provide much better protection.

After a sleepless night, the pair prepared themselves as best they could. Thomas gratefully accepted a necklace made of garlic cloves from his host. While it was pungent, he didn't hesitate to place it around his neck. Harold handed him half a dozen spare stakes and chose one of his dogs to accompany them.

They waited for dawn to arrive before commencing their journey. It took them longer than Harold anticipated to travel the distance and it was late afternoon by the time they arrived.

Several days had passed since the property had been attacked. It had rained since then and it took some time before the hound picked up the bloodsuckers' trail. Howling in distress, she rebelled against following the path they'd taken. Harold calmed her down eventually. Eyes rolling wildly, she reluctantly led them several miles to a cave.

Their horses balked as they also smelled the

vampires. Thomas and his companion rode back down the trail until their mounts calmed again. They tethered the horses to a tree and Harold ordered his hound to stay with them.

It was dangerously close to sundown when they approached the cave on foot. The entrance was mostly hidden behind a screen of half dead vines. Night would soon fall and Thomas knew they had to move fast. Miles from town or any other form of shelter, they had no choice but to put an end to the nest now.

Shifting the vines aside, just enough light filtered inside for Thomas to make out thirteen mounds of dirt on the cave floor. The creatures had buried themselves so they'd be protected from the sun.

Stepping over the mounds, the priest and the farmer knelt beside the grave at the back of the cave. It made sense to Thomas that the master would put his lackeys between himself and the entrance. Kneeling, he began to dig while his companion held a stake ready.

Unearthing the pale, handsome face of a man in the prime of his life, the priest reached for his stake just as the sun was going down. The fiend's eyes opened and latched onto his, instantly draining him of his will. The thing spoke, instructing him to remove the necklace of garlic. Helplessly ensnared, Thomas obeyed. If it hadn't been for his companion, he'd have become a meal for the monster.

Petrified, yet steadfast, Harold held his stake in

both hands and dropped to his knees. The sharpened wood pierced the vampire's chest and black, viscous blood sprayed from his mouth. Snapped out of his befuddlement, Thomas was splattered by the noisome fluid. Fearing he'd become infected, he frantically wiped his face with his sleeve.

Bellowing in rage and agony, the master vampire called forth his minions as Harold did his best to hold him down. Twelve men and women burst from their graves, intent on saving their creator. In desperation, Thomas lunged forward to add his weight to the stake. Together, they dug the weapon in deeper and deeper until it exited from the vampire's back. With a final gurgle, the creature died.

Not much had been known about the undead back then. Thomas mistakenly believed that taking down the leader would kill his lackeys. Instead, they'd been freed from their bondage. Ironically, setting them free saved the priest and the farmer's lives.

With their master dead, the fledglings went crazy. Wailing and shrieking, most fled into the night. Only two remained. They were too caught up in their internal turmoil to struggle as stakes were pounded into their hearts.

Harold's horse had broken its tether and had bolted in terror. Thomas' horse still remained. He stood with his head down, eyes rolling and shaking in reaction. Cowering in the bushes, the bloodhound crept out from hiding when her master called her.

Sharing the horse, they headed to town. Their eyes

scanned the area, expecting an attack at any moment. Dawn was nearing by the time they reached town. Disheveled and pale from their ordeal, they staggered inside the tavern the moment it opened.

By midday, everyone in town was aware of what had transpired. They agreed that they couldn't allow the nest to keep picking off farmers. They resolved to band together to eradicate the vampires. In pairs, the townsfolk spent the next few days riding out to isolated farms to warn their neighbors.

On the fifth day, another attack was discovered. All six family members had been drained of their blood. Hurrying back to town, the two men who'd made the grisly discovery spread the word. Thomas called a meeting and nearly everyone in town attended. In short order, they reached agreement to use the bloodhound to track the creatures to their new lair.

Thomas and his newly recruited partner agreed to lead the hunt. At dawn, the posse gathered and rode to the decimated farmhouse. The hound had to be persuaded to follow the trail, but she did her duty.

The nest's new lair was in an abandoned house. Floorboards had been torn up and fresh graves signified where they'd buried themselves for the day. Shovels were found and the vampires were hauled from their resting places.

Out of sheer curiosity, Thomas dragged one of the creatures outside. He wanted to see what would happen when they were exposed to the sun. He discovered that it wasn't a pretty sight.

As soon as the light touched the creature, he woke. Steam erupted from his clothes and blisters appeared on his skin. Screaming shrilly, he tried to claw his way back to the cover of the house. Silver flames burst from him before he managed to crawl more than a couple of feet. In seconds, the vampire was reduced to ash. Only his clothing remained.

The rest of the nest was dragged outside as well. It was sickening to witness their demise, but killing them in this method meant there was no mess to clean up afterwards.

Harold couldn't return to his life as a farmer now that he knew that monsters were out there. He and his faithful hound had travelled to London with Thomas. The priest had gained a new member of his slowly growing band. He'd also gained a best friend who would stand by him for years to come.

Chapter Twelve

Closing down the file, I shook my head in amazement at how descriptive Thomas' journal was. He'd been a very brave man. Armed with crude weapons and unflinching faith, he'd taken on monsters of all sizes and descriptions.

I vividly remembered reading his tale of facing and banishing a demon. It still occasionally gave me nightmares. After reading that account, my most fervent wish was never to have to face a demon. Considered to be the worst of the worst, they couldn't be killed and could only be banished back to their fiery domain.

The other files that I'd saved to my laptop seemed almost clinical after reading the priest's tale. Each PIA agent who'd come up against vampires had all recounted the same thing. The nests were usually fairly small, with anywhere from five up to fifteen minions. The master always had absolute control over the nest. Cruel and quick to punish, they used their servants however they pleased.

Loyalty was a foreign concept to the undead. Lackeys squabbled constantly and plotted against their masters. Unable to actually lift a finger against their creators, their plotting was usually in vain. The only way they could kill their overlords was to convince a human to do the job for them. They then showed their appreciation by draining the human to death so they couldn't rise and turn the tables on them.

It was both fascinating and horrible to read about the creatures that I was so close to becoming. Vampires were made by draining a human's blood over several days. The final step was to force them to drink the blood of the monster that'd drained them. Once that happened, their bodies expired and they were reborn the next night as the undead.

Vampires were bound to their master until either they, or their creator, died. They were similar to shifters in that they rarely remained alone for long. I wasn't sure why, but it bothered me that we had something in common with the undead.

There was one main difference between us. We were rarely able to control ourselves when we turned. We'd eat anything that moved. Vampires, on the other hand, retained their human intelligence. They didn't need to kill their victims. They chose to inflict pain and suffering on their meals. In essence, it was their conscious choice to be evil.

The undead were always hunted down once the PIA became aware of them, but shifters weren't automatically killed. We usually only became a target if we made the mistake of feeding on a human. Once that happened, we effectively signed our own death warrants. Apparently, humans tasted a little too good to our kind. One small snack was enough to make us want more.

A knock came at my door, startling me. I'd been so engrossed in the files that I hadn't been paying attention. I'd dimly been aware of someone climbing the stairs, but didn't realize they were heading for my room. I quickly closed the laptop when I remembered that I hadn't locked the door.

"Yes?" I called. The scent that wafted through the door told me that it was Edward on the other side. I relaxed again. Even if he'd rudely barged inside, he wouldn't have known what I was researching. To a civilian, it would look like I was reading a fictional story.

"Dinner will be ready in five minutes," he replied.

"I'll be right down," I said loudly, then bit back a yelp when the boy appeared beside me. As solemn as always, he pointed at my laptop. Staring at him blankly, I shook my head in puzzlement. He pointed from it, to me, then back again. "I don't get what you want me to do with it," I said in frustration. I'd been reading for hours. Why did he choose to appear when

I'd just closed the device?

Throwing his hands up, he stuck his tongue out and disappeared. "Little brat," I muttered as I stood and headed for the door.

My friends weren't the only ones in the dining room. Several couples were seated at the other tables. We received curious stares when we sat together since we clearly weren't related to each other. Edward and Margaret wheeled our meals in on trolleys. Our table was the last to be served. My stomach was rumbling embarrassingly by the time a dish of fish and salad was placed in front of me.

Nerves began to roil in my stomach shortly after I took my first bite. They grew worse as the meal progressed. I was pretty sure it wasn't food poisoning. I felt anxious rather than nauseous.

Reece picked up on my emotions and slid sidelong looks at me. I had the niggling sense that something was about to happen, but I didn't know what it was. Mark had to say my name twice to drag my attention back to him. "Lexi, are you feeling all right?" he asked.

"Not really," I replied and pushed my half eaten meal away. The others had demolished theirs. "Something weird is going to happen soon." I sounded as nervous as I felt and the others couldn't hide their concern.

"What are you sensing?" Mark asked.

I was silent for a long moment as I assessed the strangeness that was rapidly growing closer.

"It's the dead," Reece answered for me, reading the thought directly from my brain. "They're converging on the building."

"We should leave," Flynn said uneasily. "We don't want to be trapped in here if a bunch of zombies are about to attack."

"It's not the undead that are coming," I said before everyone at the table could scatter. "They're the true dead." I received blank stares. "Ghosts," I elaborated.

"We should go somewhere private," Mark decided.

The little boy materialized beside me again and pointed upwards. "You want us to go upstairs?" I asked.

He shook his head and held his hands a foot or so apart, miming carrying something. Feeling dumb, I shook my head. "I don't know what you mean." In a very modern gesture, he rolled his eyes and pretended to type. "Oh, you want me to get my laptop."

"That's really creepy," Kala said when she realized that I was talking to a ghost. Thankfully, none of the other diners were aware of what was going on.

I lifted my eyebrow in enquiry to Mark and he nodded. "Grab your computer."

Reece was reluctant to let me travel to the third floor alone. He was worried that the ghosts might be able to hurt me. They'd shown no signs of aggression towards me so far. I was pretty sure they couldn't cause me any physical harm.

Apart from when the ghost had drawn the message on the mirror, none of them had even tried to interact with us on the physical plane. "I'll be fine," I said to him before he could volunteer to accompany me. "I'll meet you all at the SUV."

I took the stairs up to my room and snatched the laptop off the bed. I was careful not to move too quickly as I locked the door again and jogged back down the stairs. I trotted past the kitchen where Margaret was washing up. Humming softly, she didn't even hear me leave through the backdoor. I hurried over to the SUV where everyone was waiting.

The boy popped into sight on the driveway and beckoned. "I think the kid wants us to follow him," I said to the others as I reached them.

Debating the wisdom of travelling to an unknown destination, Mark finally nodded. "You'd better take the front seat."

Flynn obligingly slid into the middle seat in the back while I took Mark's usual seat up front. I didn't want to analyze why it felt so right to be sitting beside Reece. It probably had something to do with being an alpha.

Chapter Thirteen

"Go right," I directed as we reached the road and Reece silently obeyed. Disappearing and reappearing intermittently, the small boy led us towards Bradbury. To our relief, he directed us to take one of the smaller roads when we were about halfway to town. Maybe he knew that crossing the town line would be too dangerous for Mark. He'd already lost too much blood and it wouldn't be healthy for him to suffer another nosebleed.

After a few minutes of driving, we turned onto a dirt track. The boy led us through a complicated series of paths through the woods. I wasn't sure that the residents even knew about some of the overgrown roads that we took. I was impressed with the little boy's knowledge of the area when we eventually emerged onto a road and saw the lights of

Bradbury in the distance.

The kid pointed away from town and we continued on. A short while later, we turned onto another rutted track. This one led us to the last place I wanted to visit after dark; a cemetery.

A dilapidated old church crouched beside an untended boneyard. The entire cemetery looked as if it had been abandoned decades ago. The gravestones were mossy and the inscriptions were worn and illegible.

Other specters began to appear as the child pointed at the small wooden building. Materializing by the dozens, they watched as Reece parked on the overgrown driveway. Flynn shivered as he climbed out and it wasn't from the cold. I was pretty sure he was sensitive to the phantoms' presence.

Mark carried the Ouija board beneath one arm and held a flashlight in his other hand. I carried my laptop cradled in my left arm. My right hand was ready to draw my gun, not that it would prove useful if it came down to battling ghosts.

"Do we really have to go in there?" Kala asked plaintively when I took a step towards the church.

"That's where they want us to go," I replied. I didn't want to enter the building any more than she did. It was marginally better than having our séance in the middle of the graveyard.

Reece took point and tested the first step that led to a tiny porch. Rotten from being out in the weather, it almost buckled beneath his weight. He stepped up onto the porch rather than risking any of the steps. The door opened inwards and it was stuck fast. He put his shoulder to it and it grudgingly gave way with a squeal of protest.

Mark's flashlight lit up the empty room. Pews had once graced the church, but they were long gone. The altar was gone as well. Any decorations that had once hung on the walls were missing and all of the windows had been smashed. I wasn't sure if vandals or the weather were responsible for the destruction.

The roof sported holes and a few boards were missing from the walls. It was a wonder the structure was still standing at all. Dirt and leaves covered the plain wooden floor. The boards were spongy, but they didn't give as we crossed to the center of the room.

Mark knelt and placed the Ouija board on the floor. He grimaced at having to sit in the filth and I shared his distaste. "Form a circle and hold hands," he instructed us.

I sat across from him with Reece on my left and Kala on my right. Flynn sat between Kala and Mark.

"I call on the spirits who wish to communicate with us," Mark said. As far as ceremonies went, it was pretty lame. I'd expected candles, black robes and chanting. He could have at least used a more dramatic tone.

Despite his lack of flair, it worked and the church was suddenly crowded with apparitions. All were attractive and were in their early twenties. Their clothing dated from roughly two centuries ago right up to modern day. Some of the older ghosts were far more transparent than the younger ones. Some of the fresher ones looked almost real and were only slightly see-through.

"Did it work?" Kala asked uneasily. Her shoulders were hunched and I imagined that her hackles were rising. She might not be able to see them, but she could sense their presence now that we were surrounded.

"Yep," I croaked. My skin was crawling at having so many spirits gathered in such close proximity. They'd left a small space around us, but the closest ones could have reached out and touched us.

"How many are there?" Reece asked. His grip was almost tight enough to be painful. My grip was just as tight as his and I could hardly complain.

"Hundreds," I replied. "The room is packed and I can sense more of them outside."

"Put your fingers on the planchette," Mark told me.

Reece released my hand and Mark reached forward at the same time as I did. As soon as our fingers touched the heart shaped pointer, it lurched into motion. The arrow briefly came to a rest on a dizzying number of letters. It moved so rapidly that I couldn't keep up with it.

"What did that just spell out?" Kala asked when the arrow went still.

"I couldn't quite follow it," Mark confessed.

"It said something about the coven, but it moved

too fast for me to get it all," Flynn said.

Mark sighed wearily. "This is going to take a while." His plan had been a good one, but it wasn't working out quite as well as he'd hoped.

The small boy appeared beside me and I started hard enough to make the planchette skid across the board. He pointed at the laptop then at me and mimed opening it. Finally getting what he wanted me to do, I almost flushed at my thick headedness. "Uh, I think they want to use the laptop," I said.

"Ghosts can type?" Kala said incredulously.

"I guess we're about to find out." Starting up the computer, I was glad I'd closed the files I'd been reading about vampires. I'd also taken the precaution of hiding them in an innocuous file that didn't look suspicious at a casual glance.

Opening a blank document, I waited for something to happen. Nothing did and I glanced at Mark for further orders.

"Put the computer on the Ouija board and join hands again," he instructed. I didn't know how he knew what to do, but it worked. I put the laptop down and as soon as our hands were touching again, words began to appear on the screen.

I didn't see anyone typing, but the keys were rapidly depressed. A short message appeared on the page. The heavy weight of dozens of dead eyes was on me as I read their warning out loud. Kala and Reece leaned over to read it silently. "It says, 'To destroy the coven, you must find the source of their power. They have hidden the talisman well and it will be perilous to search for it. If you come to their notice, you will be doomed to join our ranks.'"

"Gee, that's not at all ominous," Kala muttered with a small shudder.

With their message imparted, the ghosts faded until only the small boy remained. He put his hand on my shoulder and his expression was sorrowful. A bone cold chill seeped into my flesh from his insubstantial touch. It lingered for a few seconds after he also faded away to nothing. Pulling my hands free from Reece's and Kala's with a shudder, I rubbed my upper arms for warmth.

Flynn leaned forward and spun the laptop around so he and Mark could read the message. "Couldn't they just tell us where the talisman is instead of being so cryptic?" he complained.

"I don't think they know where it is," Mark said. "If they did, I'm sure they'd have informed us of its whereabouts."

"Do you think they're all victims of the coven?" Kala asked.

I nodded, still chilled. "They all matched the profile, so I guess they must be."

"How are we supposed to find the source of their power if we don't have any idea what it is, or where it's hidden?" Flynn said.

"I'll have to do some more digging," Mark decided. "There has to be something I can find to assist our search."

I hoped so, because otherwise we could be here for a very long time. The full moon wasn't far away now. None of us wanted to be stuck in Dawson's Retreat when that happened. We'd have no choice but to head to our closest compound, wherever that was.

Chapter Fourteen

We returned to the bed and breakfast following the same complicated route that we'd used to reach the cemetery. If we hadn't had the GPS to guide us, we'd have become lost in the woods.

Edward was kind enough to bring us a pot of coffee when we gathered in the parlor. The other guests had dispersed and our team would have some much needed privacy to discuss our mission.

I followed the old man into the hall. Waiting until he'd almost reached his and Margaret's private quarters at the back of the house, I caught his sleeve. I had a question for our host and I didn't want anyone to overhear me.

He turned around with a smile, but it withered at my question. "What do you know about the little boy who haunts this house?" I asked.

Bushy gray eyebrows rose in surprise. "I know very little, I'm afraid. I might be old, but he died long before my birth."

"There's nothing you can tell me about him?" I was curious about the kid. It was disappointing that he couldn't shed any light on how he'd died.

Edward hesitated, then reluctantly told me what he knew. "I believe the child was illegitimate, which was quite a scandal back then, you understand."

"Do you know how he died?"

"I am not sure of the actual cause," he said with a grimace. "But rumor has it that his own mother was the culprit."

Edward bade me goodnight, then stepped into his inner sanctum and closed the door. Sorrow for the child welled within me and I glanced down when coldness made my hand ache. The boy stood beside me with his head bowed and his hand in mine. I couldn't feel him, but the contact seemed to give him some comfort. "We'll get justice for you," I promised.

He lifted his head and smiled sadly, as if he wanted to believe me, but couldn't quite manage it. I didn't know why I made that promise. His mother would be long dead by now. I didn't have the tools to resurrect her just so I could send her back to hell again.

Mark was busy with his tablet, searching information about our targets when I returned to the parlor. Unlike my laptop, his tablet came equipped with the ability to access the PIA network from anywhere in the country. I'd left my computer beside

Kala on the couch and he pointed at it. "I've found some interesting information on the coven. I've just sent it to your laptop."

I placed the computer on the table and switched it on. I sat beside Kala and Flynn shifted his chair beside me so he could lean across and read the screen. Reece moved to stand directly behind me. His breath feathered my hair when he leaned in closer. His eyes were good enough to easily be able to read the ancient news article. He didn't need to lean in and I sensed that he felt the need to be close. I was pretty sure it was because we were bonded rather than because he felt an irresistible attraction for me.

A copy of the photo on the wall upstairs came up on the screen. It was from an ancient newspaper article. The names of the six coven members were typed beneath the picture. The woman from the café was called Talitha and the man was Malachi. Neither had aged a day since the photo had been taken.

The other girls were called Ophelia and Eunice and the men were called Jeremiah and Jonathan. They all shared the same surname of Dawson, which meant that my guess was right. They were siblings, or at least close cousins.

"The coven founded Bradbury," Kala read out loud in surprise.

"They also built this house," Flynn said after scanning the article. "Why did they build this place on the outskirts of town?"

"They'd have used this place to practice their spells

and to work their hexes in private," Mark replied. It was rare when he didn't have some kind of answer for our questions.

Kala put a hand on my arm when I shuddered at the thought that we were staying in the same house where evil magic had been conjured. "They performed their sacrifices here, didn't they?"

"It's very likely," Mark said after a short pause. He wanted to spare me from any unpleasantness, but I was one of his agents now. It was important for me to learn the truth. Remaining ignorant of the horrible things that were out there and the atrocities that people were capable of wouldn't help me to learn and grow.

"Why did they abandon this place?" Reece asked. "Why don't they still use it to perform their dark rites?"

"Maybe they can't now that they've set wards around the town," Flynn guessed. "Their magic only seems to work within the boundaries of Bradbury."

Mark nodded. "You're probably right. While they needed privacy to practice and perfect their spells, they eventually had to move closer to the epicenter of town. They have to stay close to be able to keep the populace beneath their power."

"We need to locate their homes and search for the talisman," Reece said.

"That might not be so easy to do," Mark warned us. "The coven owns nearly every home in town. It will be difficult to determine where they actually live."

"Are you saying that everyone who lives in Bradbury is renting their homes?" I asked.

"Nearly. The coven is raking in millions of dollars each year," Mark replied. "They own this town and everyone in it." His pronouncement dampened our mood even further. "Unfortunately, I'm not going to be able to assist you with the search. If I were to step across the town line again, the coven will undoubtedly become aware of my presence. I imagine they'd react swiftly and decisively."

"We'll have to go in on foot and avoid being spotted," Reece said. With Mark out of the picture, he was in charge. He was comfortable and at ease with the role. As an alpha, he didn't have any problems ordering the rest of us around. Kala and Flynn didn't mind, but I wasn't a fan of being told what to do. At least not by another shifter. It grated on me like fingernails on a chalkboard.

"Agent Levine," Mark said when I frowned. "Do you have a problem?"

Kala leaned forward to study my face. "She doesn't like the idea of Reece giving her orders."

"Is that true?" Mark asked.

I shrugged in response and felt Reece draw away a little. "I'm not a huge fan, but I'll follow my orders."

"I almost wish you two hadn't bonded," he said. "This is going to make things very difficult if neither of you can establish dominance."

"Dominance has already been established between us," Reece said with supreme confidence.

My ire flared and I turned to face him. "Really? When exactly did this happen?"

He flashed a mental picture of when he'd taken my virginity and I'd been helplessly pinned beneath him. My face flushed crimson that his memory of that event had been restored and that he could recall it in such vivid detail. In retaliation, I flashed a picture of me riding him in the back of the car. I'd been in control then and he'd been the helpless one.

Cocking his head, Reece nodded grudgingly. "Hmm. You have a point." Confused looks were exchanged by the others at our silent communication. "Maybe we haven't quite worked out which of us is in charge yet," Reece confessed.

Flynn had a simple solution to our problem. "Do you want to lead the team?" he asked me bluntly.

"No," I replied immediately.

"Then it's settled, Garrett is in charge."

Reece crossed his arms as he waited for me to acknowledge his leadership. "Fine," I said. "You're the boss and I'll do whatever you say."

Kala elbowed me in the ribs. "Don't give Rex any ideas." Her grin was sly and red stained my face again. Reece's grin was lazy and bordering on triumphant. Being in charge was far more important to him than it was to me. I guessed I just wanted to be classed as an equal rather than someone to be subjugated to his will.

His smile faded as he picked up that thought. "You are my equal, Lexi," he said. "But only one person can be the boss during our missions."

If we'd been just a normal pack of shifters, he and I would be alpha mates and we'd have both ruled the pack. Instead, we were two lone werewolves, a cougar and a snake. Our job was to hunt down and eradicate evil creatures. It was a waste of time to squabble about it. "You're right," I said and dropped my eyes. "Sorry for being such a pain."

Flynn patted me on the shoulder. "You can't help challenging Reece's authority. It's part of being an alpha."

Mark had taken in our exchange with interest. I wondered if he'd type up notes on what he'd witnessed since there was so little on file about our kind. "Now that that's settled, I suggest you head out and try to locate the coven," our boss ordered.

Kala and I already had Talitha and Malachi's scent and we all knew what the coven members looked like. It would just be a matter of searching the town to find their houses. Instinct told me that we wouldn't simply be able to walk up to the talisman and destroy it once we found it. A price would have to be paid first. The only question was which of us would be the one to pay it.

Chapter Fifteen

With stealth in mind, we changed into black clothes and dark sneakers. Mine had once been white, but had faded to a dingy gray with age. They didn't have any reflective patches and would be suitable for clandestine snooping.

We didn't have a printer handy to reproduce copies of the town map. Mark cut the only map he had into quadrants. Reece chose the north section and assigned Kala to the east. Flynn had the south and I was given the west side.

I was a little surprised that Reece was willing to allow me to search alone. After a moment of concentration, I delved into his thoughts. I picked up his intention to allow me to gain valuable field experience. He was far from happy about the prospect of me going solo, but he couldn't coddle me forever. He planned to keep watch over me through our bond.

Mark was grumpy about being left behind, but he kept his complaints to himself. He drew me aside before I could slip out through the backdoor. I'd put my hair up into a ponytail and I was aware of how young it made me look. "If you encounter any of the witches or warlocks, run," he advised me quietly. "If you can't run, shoot them. Don't hesitate, just pull the trigger."

Kala had another suggestion for me as she slipped past us. "If you can't get to your gun in time, just rip their heads off with your bare hands. That works for me every time," she said flippantly.

"How many heads has she ripped off?" I asked Mark.

"You don't want to know," he said heavily. "To this day, I don't understand why shifters take so much pleasure in rending limbs from their enemies."

"Because it's fun," Kala called back over her shoulder as she reached the guys.

"Is it fun?" he asked me skeptically.

"I have no idea," I shrugged. "I'll let you know when I actually tear something off someone." Horribly, a small part of me was looking forward to seeing if I could rend someone apart. I had yet to test my strength to its full capacity.

Leaving Mark behind, I joined the others. We sprinted along the side of the road towards Bradbury. We were ready to disappear into the trees if a car came along. My Beretta and spare ammunition were in the pockets of my cargo pants. My section of the map was in another. It was a cloudy night, but we had no need for flashlights even with the lack of moonlight. Our night vision made even the darkest of nights startlingly clear.

Reece decided to move to the center of town before splitting up. It was still early enough for people to be out and about. We ducked into the shadows before any pedestrians or motorists could spot us creeping through the streets.

Kate's Kafé was our starting point. We gathered into a small circle in the alley behind the building. Reece checked his watch and the rest of us automatically copied him. "Give me an update every fifteen minutes, unless you find one of the Coven's houses or run into trouble."

"Righty-o, guvna," Kala said in a truly awful British accent and saluted him mischievously. His stare wasn't quite as withering as Mark's and it did little to dampen her mood. She was just happy to finally be hunting our targets.

As we split up, we inserted the earpieces that would allow us to remain in constant contact. The town was small enough that the range almost stretched from one side to the other. If we did move out of range, we could always use our cell phones.

Nervous and excited to be on my own for once, I headed westward and stopped at the next street to consult my map. Being methodical was the only way

I'd be able to search all of the buildings in my quadrant.

Flynn's section bordered mine, but I didn't see him as I neared the first house on my list. He had far more training with surveillance and covert tactics than I did. He was adept at staying out of sight.

Vaulting over the low fence, I entered the yard and snuck up to the window where I could hear a TV playing. A small family of two adults and one child were watching a sitcom. I mentally crossed the house off my list and continued on to the next one.

My excitement waned within the first twenty minutes of searching and I quickly became bored. I hated to admit it, but I could now identify with Kala's lack of attention span when it came to this part of our job. Methodically searching every house in town was going to be a long, drawn out process.

Sidetracked by my increasing boredom, I forgot to check in with Reece the second time fifteen minutes came around. I was reminded of my lapse when he spoke. "Are you still alive, Lexi?" he asked. I shivered at hearing his voice in my ear. My body reacted as it always did, with a flare of heat.

"I'm alive," I whispered back.

"Sheesh, don't scare us like that," Kala said. I was supposed to report in first. The others had been waiting for me to speak.

"I haven't spotted any of the targets yet," I reported, flushing in embarrassment at forgetting to update Reece.

Flynn snorted out a laugh. "You're Philip Levine's daughter all right," he said. "No other girl your age would think of people as targets."

"I don't think of the coven as people at all," I countered as I leaped over a six foot fence and landed in a crouch on the other side. Coming face to face with a Rottweiler, I froze. His hackles rose and he bared his teeth in an almost silent growl.

Before he could lunge forward and tear out my throat, my instincts kicked in. My upper lip lifted in response and my return growl was menacing. We had a staring match and I knew that if I blinked, I'd soon be sporting a fresh set of teeth marks somewhere on my body.

After a few long, intense moments, the Rottweiler whined in capitulation. He dropped down and rolled over to expose his belly. It might be a struggle to hold my own against Reece, but at least I could dominate a normal dog without too much trouble.

"What was that?" Kala asked.

"A Rottweiler just challenged me when I entered his yard," I said.

"Who won?" Reece asked dryly.

"Me, of course." I petted the dog on the belly and he instantly became my friend for life. He shadowed me as I crept up to the window and peered inside. A young couple sat at the dinner table eating a late meal. Neither of them were coven members.

With the dog still at my heels, I moved to the fence. He whined when he realized I was about to leave.

"Good boy," I said and gave him a final pet on the head before jumping the fence into the neighboring yard. I had the strange feeling that the dog was bored and that he wanted someone to play with.

During my search, I learned that rabbits and guinea pigs were terrified of me. They went still and hunkered in their cages, desperately pretending they weren't there until I moved away. Cats hissed in spite before fleeing. Dogs either challenged me, or automatically accepted me as their superior. None tried to bite me, thankfully. Harming animals who were just trying to defend their property wasn't on my agenda.

After roughly an hour of searching, Flynn spoke a couple of minutes before it was time to check in. I sensed Reece coming to full alert and I paused to listen in.

"I've found one of the warlocks." Flynn spoke so quietly that I could barely hear him even with my enhanced senses. "It's Jeremiah."

Their names were archaic, which somehow made them even more sinister. They changed their names to more modern ones, but we were still referring to them with their original names. "He's asleep on the couch and it doesn't look like he's going to wake up anytime soon." Flynn debated for a few seconds then came to a decision. "I'm going in."

As soon as he made that pronouncement, a ghost appeared in front of me. It was the handsome young man who had written the message on the bathroom mirror. He shook his head frantically. "Wait!" I said.

"Why?"

"What's going on?" Kala said at the same time.

"One of the ghosts just appeared and he doesn't want you to enter the house." The ghost nodded and seemed relieved. "Can you show us where the coven lives?" I asked him. He nodded again and pointed in the direction of the B&B. "You want us to return to Dawson's Retreat?" He nodded a third time. Flapping his hands at me, he was growing more frantic by the second. "Uh, I think we need to get out of here," I warned the others.

Reece didn't waste time asking me any questions. "Return to the B&B," he ordered and I turned to run.

Chapter Sixteen

I managed to take two steps before I bounced off an invisible wall. With a muffled, "Oof!" I hit the ground and rolled over onto my back. Talitha stood over me wearing an expression of pure malevolence. Her eyes narrowed as she recognized me.

Remembering Mark's advice, I went for my gun. Invisible ropes pinned my arms to the ground before I could grab my weapon. Lifting her hands, the witch began to chant. Pain erupted inside my body from my head to my toes. I tried to scream and a wave of her hand silenced me.

"Lexi?" Reece called through the earpiece. He became alarmed when I didn't respond. "Alexis! What's wrong?"

I could only manage a pained gurgle. My vision began to turn black. Desperate to survive, I mentally grasped for assistance. On the edge of passing out, I brushed several minds that didn't belong to humans. *Help me,* I screamed silently. A moment later, the night was shattered by howls, yips and menacing growls.

Talitha's spell faltered momentarily when the first dog padded into view a few seconds later. The little white terrier lowered its fluffy head threateningly, growling in warning. Its yap was shrill enough to hurt my ears. I recognized it as the dog I'd seen being walked by her owner just before Mark's nose had begun gushing blood.

"How cute," the witch said and turned her attention back to me. "The itty bitty puppy is trying to save you!" Her laugh was cruel and held real amusement. She clearly enjoyed making people suffer. This was probably the highlight of her day.

The pain had faded enough for me to catch my breath. Behind her, the street rapidly filled up with dogs of all shapes and sizes. The Rottweiler stood at the head of the pack. He was growling so low that only I and the other dogs could hear him. His face was bloody from bashing his way free from his yard. The scrapes gave him an even more frightening appearance.

"I don't know who you are, or what your plan was," Talitha said menacingly, "but you made a very grave mistake coming to Bradbury. Your death will serve a purpose you couldn't even begin to comprehend." Her arrogance was stunning to behold.

Baring my teeth, I smiled at the witch. "I comprehend plenty, you psychotic weirdo." She drew in an affronted breath and I mentally urged the motley pack that was creeping up on her to move faster. They responded by snarling, howling and sprinting towards her. "Get her!" I shouted out loud and they obeyed.

Mobbed by dogs both small and large, she screamed in rage and pain as teeth tore through her clothing and into her flesh. Her shock at being attacked only lasted for a short moment. Clapping her hands, she sent a shockwave of air outwards in a circle.

If I hadn't already been lying down, I would have been sent flying. Some of the smaller dogs cartwheeled through the air with yelps of pain. Scrambling to their feet, they went straight back on the attack. Sending me a look that promised retribution, the witch fled.

Released from the invisible bonds, I sat up with a pained wince. I called the dogs back before they could be injured worse than they already were. Most of their wounds seemed to be superficial, mainly scrapes and bruises.

The Rottweiler trotted over and sat beside me. A bloody swatch of fabric that he'd torn from the witch's skirt dangled from his mouth. "Good boy," I said and stroked his head with a shaky hand. "You just saved my life." He grinned widely and I had the uncanny feeling that he'd understood me.

Chapter Seventeen

I felt Reece approaching long before he sprinted into view. Our bond had alerted him that I was in danger. It had then told him that I was okay. He came to a stop with his hands on his hips, wearing a strained smile. "I see you've made some new friends," he observed.

The pack had formed a protective circle around me. They all cringed away from him. Most rolled onto their backs to display their stomachs in acknowledgement of his superiority. The Rottweiler bared his teeth and leaned against me. He was willing to defend me even from a being that was alpha to him.

"It's okay," I said to the dog and scratched him behind his ear. "Reece is a friend." The canine relaxed and closed his eyes in enjoyment.

"I hope I'm more than that to you," Reece said in the low tone that made my stomach clench in reaction.

"Please," Kala's voice broke in before I could respond. "Spare us your burning passion for each other." She and Flynn jogged into view from opposite directions. Now that we were in close proximity, we removed our earpieces and switched them off.

"Is there a dog convention that we weren't informed of?" Flynn asked as he eyed the pack that surrounded me.

"I told you two to head back to base," Reece said. His frown was disapproving.

"Lexi was in trouble," Flynn said in self-defense. "Did you really expect us to just leave her?"

Reece shook his head after a moment of internal debate. "No. I'd have come to her rescue as well."

"What happened?" Kala asked as she helped me to my feet. With a thought, I sent the dogs back to their homes. Hanging their heads in disappointment, they loped off into the night.

The ghost appeared again. He was even more frantic than before. Waving at us to leave, he looked over his shoulder as if he knew someone was coming. "I'll tell you when we get back to base," I said. "We'd better get out of here before the rest of the coven arrives."

Without bothering to ask me first, Reece scooped me into his arms and took off at a full sprint. My weight didn't slow him down at all as he streaked through the night. We moved far too quickly for humans to make out more than just a vague blur.

Once we reached the outskirts of town, he slowed down enough for me to catch my breath. "I can walk, you know," I said tartly.

He deigned to glance down at me. "Carrying you is faster," he argued. I had to admit it was nice being in his arms, but I felt like an idiot being carried around. It was pointless to argue with him and I bore the indignity as well as I could. To be honest, I was still feeling shaky. I wasn't sure I'd have been able to run anyway.

Kala took her cell phone out of her pocket and called Mark. "Hey, boss."

"What's wrong?" he asked, instantly assuming that there was a problem.

"We had to abort the mission."

"What happened? Is anyone hurt?"

"Lexi had a run-in with one of the witches." She glanced over at me to assess the damage. "She's a little banged up and there might be some internal injuries."

"I'll call a doctor," he said.

"No!" I protested loudly enough for him to hear me. "I'm fine. The pain is already fading."

"How far away are you?" he asked.

"We'll be there in a couple of minutes," Kala replied.

"I'll see you soon," he said and hung up.

He was waiting for us at the backdoor when we

arrived a short while later. "Bring her to my room," he ordered Reece.

Margaret was still bustling around in the kitchen. We snuck past without her realizing we were there. Edward was in the parlor, reading a newspaper from the sound of crinkling paper.

We filed into Mark's room and the small space seemed cramped with all of us inside. "How badly are you hurt?" he asked.

"Not that badly," I replied. My entire body ached and my organs felt tender. I didn't think there was any internal bleeding from whatever the witch had done to me. "It hurt like hell, but I don't think there's any permanent damage."

Reece sat me down on the bed. Kala plumped a pillow and put it behind my back. I eased back against it and grimaced as residual pain made my insides cramp. Reece flinched in sympathy and clenched his fists in futile rage. "Calm down," I told him. "I'm fine." He sank down onto the only chair in the room. Flynn and Kala sat on the foot of the bed.

Mark opted to stand and crossed his arms tightly. "Tell me what happened."

I recited my search, starting from when I'd first come face to face with the Rottweiler. I ended my report with the pack responding to my call.

Kala gave an incredulous laugh. "Are you saying that the dogs saved your life?"

"You saw them," Reece said. He was just as disturbed by my tale as she was. "It looked like they were guarding her."

"No dog would ever come to my aid," Flynn said. "All animals hate me." He thought about it, then amended his statement. "Except for snakes, of course."

"Cats love me," Kala said. "But I've never had one try to save my life before."

"Maybe you've just never needed their help badly enough," I pointed out.

Mark had a theory, of course. "They came to your aid because you're an alpha. You'd already established dominance over them when you'd entered their yards." Now that he'd mentioned it, all of the dogs had come from the yards that I'd searched.

Reece asked the most pertinent question. "How were you able to call them?"

Everyone turned to look at me and I didn't have an answer for them. "I don't really know. I was desperate and in agony. I just kind of reached out with my mind." I shrugged to indicate that was the best explanation I could give them.

"You said that the ghost can help us find the witches' houses," Mark said, thankfully diverting the attention back to our problem and away from my weirdness. I was glad to have the focus shifted to a slightly less uncomfortable topic.

"Yeah. I guess I should get my laptop." I didn't try to inject any enthusiasm into the thought of having to move.

Kala waved at me to stay where I was. "Give me

your key and I'll get it for you."

I fished the key out of my pocket and handed it to her. She was back in less than a minute and gently placed the computer on my thighs. As I switched it on, the ghost who'd warned me to flee from Bradbury appeared. He'd been extremely helpful so far. We'd have probably all become sacrifices if it wasn't for him.

"Thanks for saving our butts," I said to him. He nodded solemnly in return. "I'm going to bring up a map of Bradbury. Can you point out where the witches and warlocks live?" He nodded again and I brought the map up. Through trial and error, I zoomed in on the areas he pointed to. He pinpointed six different locations.

"Are there any other buildings we need to be aware of?" Mark asked. He directed the question in the general direction of the ghost, missing him by a couple of feet.

Shaking his head, the spirit faded and disappeared. "He said no," I replied to Mark.

Sitting on the bed beside me, he took the laptop and shrank the map down so the whole town fit on the screen. One of the houses that the ghost had identified was the one where Flynn had spotted Jeremiah. That meant the other locations were probably accurate as well.

"Hmm," he said as he studied the map. "I can see a pattern." He used a program that I hadn't even known existed to draw a diagram over the map.

"Is that what I think it is?" Kala asked uneasily as she watched over Mark's shoulder.

"It's an inverted pentagram," he confirmed. Five of the coven members lived at each point of the pentagram. The sixth location was in the center. Somehow, I wasn't surprised to see that Kate's Kafé was the final building. It had an apartment above it where she presumably lived.

"The coven must be aware that I'm not just a normal person now," I said. "They'll be waiting for us to make our move."

"Undoubtedly," Mark agreed. "That means we'll have to be extremely careful from now on."

I hoped he could come up with a plan that wouldn't result in my insides being scrambled again. Once had definitely been enough.

Chapter Eighteen

Feeling decidedly unwell, I allowed Reece to help me up to my room once our meeting was over.

"Thanks," I said and tried to close the door.

He put a hand out to catch it. "Do you realize how close you came to being captured by the coven?" he said too quietly for the others to hear him. "You know what they would have done to you." We both knew that I would have become the next sacrifice.

"I'm well aware," I replied wryly. "This isn't the first time I've been in danger. Greed came very close to choking me to death, then burning me into a crispy critter," I reminded him.

"You shouldn't have to be put in situations like this." He was anguished and I sensed he also felt guilty for dragging me into his life.

"Do you think I'd have been in any less danger if

I'd become a soldier as I'd planned?"

He shrugged, but I read his thoughts. If I'd remained human, I wouldn't have to face monsters. "Ordinary people can be just as monstrous as witches, psychics, vampires, shifters and every other type of creature we hunt down," I said.

"You could never have been a stay at home mom, could you?" he asked with a half-smile. It did things to my libido that I really wasn't feeling up to at the moment.

"I doubt it. I'd probably go crazy if I tried."

Leaning in, he planted a soft kiss on my cheek. "I'll see you in the morning, Lexi." He walked to his door and unlocked it. Aware that I was watching him, he turned, winked and stepped inside.

Snapping out of my daydream of following him into his room and stripping him naked, I shut and locked my door. I took a long shower and was exhausted by the time I'd finished blow drying my hair.

Changing into my usual sleeping attire of a thin singlet and tiny shorts, I lay down and pulled the light blanket up to my chin. It took me a long time to fall asleep. When I did, I replayed my encounter with Talitha. This time, the dog pack didn't arrive in time to save me and the witch tore me apart from the inside out.

I was relieved when my alarm finally woke me the next morning. My sleep had been broken due to a succession of bad dreams. I'd started awake too many times to count. Cautiously rising, I found that my internal pain was gone. I was fully healed again and I was famished when I met the others in the dining room for breakfast.

Three couples were eating at the tables around us. None were close enough to overhear us as long as we spoke quietly.

"How are you feeling?" Mark asked.

"Hungry," I replied as I took a seat next to Kala. I was the last to arrive.

"Are you experiencing any residual pain?"

"Nope. I feel fine."

Kala poured me coffee from the pot. "Remind me not to get too close to the witches. I'd prefer not to have my insides microwaved."

"It wasn't a fun experience," I agreed. Our conversation cut off as Margaret appeared with a trolley full of food. Again, we had a wide range to choose from. I opted for bacon, eggs and toast. It wasn't particularly healthy, but it would fill the hole in my stomach.

"I think we should move in and search the buildings as soon as it gets dark tonight," Flynn suggested after Margaret had finished serving us and had moved to the next table. "They won't be expecting us to return so soon."

"Yeah, because it would be stupid to waltz right back in there when we know they're on to us," Kala said and rolled her eyes.

"Exactly," he grinned. "They'll expect us to cower

in hiding, praying they don't find us. What kind of idiots would voluntarily return after discovering that they can subdue us so easily?"

"It will be extremely dangerous," Mark cautioned. "They might not be expecting you to return tonight, but they will still be wary."

"We'll be more careful this time," Reece said and flicked a meaningful glance at me. He was having second thoughts about allowing me to gain some much needed field experience. It was embarrassing that I'd been the only one to get caught. I obviously had a lot to learn about stealth.

"I can't take sitting around in this parlor all day," Kala said. "Can we get out of here for a few hours?"

"Good idea," Mark agreed. "I'm sure Margaret could use a break from serving us coffee and cake."

We piled into the SUV and drove for an hour or so. We ended up in a small town about the same size as Bradbury. It was as good a place as any to while away our time. We spent a few hours sitting in a café drinking coffee and snacking on an assortment of cookies. It wasn't much different from being in the parlor, but at least we had different scenery to look at.

People were less suspicious in this town, but we still drew attention. Kala and I received a few interested looks from young men as they walked past. Reece and Flynn were just as popular with the ladies. Even Mark was worthy of a second look from the more mature women. Kala winked at the cuter guys, but the rest of us ignored their scrutiny.

"Mmm," Kala said when she was halfway through her third cookie. "These are really, really good." For once, she wasn't expelling crumbs with each word that she uttered. The cookie was nearly the size of her head, or had been before she'd started devouring it.

"Imagine how god-awful it would have been if you'd made it," Flynn teased her slyly.

Her happy smile changed to a scowl. "Like you're a master baker," she retaliated.

"It's Mark's birthday tomorrow," he reminded Reece. "Are you still going to bake him a cake?"

"Of course," Reece replied. I saw and sensed no signs of panic from him at the prospect of baking a cake. "We should pick up the ingredients on our way back to Dawson's Retreat."

Mark tried and failed to suppress a sigh. It was clear that he expected the cake to turn out badly. I had the feeling that celebrating birthdays and holidays wasn't something they did very often. Maybe they were making an exception lately because I'd joined their team. They were doing their best to behave like a normal family, which was a stretch considering that we were agents of the PIA.

Kala instantly smirked at the reminder. "I almost forgot about that. It's going to be fun watching you crash and burn." The cake she'd made me for my eighteenth birthday had been an abomination that I wished I could wipe from my memory forever. I could vividly remember the horrible taste of the charred lump that I'd choked down.

Catching that thought, Reece hid his smile. "I'll have to search the internet for a recipe," he said.

Flynn tapped his forehead. "Don't worry, I have the list of ingredients that you'll need stored up here."

"Do you have a photographic memory?" I asked.

"Nope. I just really like chocolate cake."

"It's always been your favorite," Mark said with a nostalgic smile.

They all shared a grin, leaving me feeling like an outsider. No matter how much time I spent with the team, I'd always be the newcomer.

We stopped at a grocery store after lunch to buy the ingredients that Reece would need. Flynn did indeed have a good memory. I was pretty sure the list was complete when we left the store. Even if he'd forgotten something, Margaret would no doubt have it in stock.

She appeared in the kitchen door when we trooped in through the backdoor rather than through the front. She took in the bags that Reece was carrying and raised her eyebrows.

"Would it be possible for me to borrow your kitchen tomorrow?" he asked. "It's Mark's birthday and I'd like to bake him a cake."

"I can make that for you, dear," she said, totally won over by his politeness, or possibly by his hotness. She might be old enough to be his mother, but I'd seen her checking him out a few times.

"Reece promised Mark that he'd make it," Kala said charmingly. "All by himself," she added for good measure so our hostess wouldn't be tempted to assist him.

"I'll make sure he doesn't set anything on fire," I reassured her when she wrung her hands in worry. She seemed to trust me more than the others when it came to cooking and nodded. She had good judgment. I'd been taking care of myself every time my father was sent on a mission ever since I'd turned thirteen. I'd never yet set the kitchen on fire and I had a pretty good track record when it came to baking.

"Would you like coffee?" she asked.

"We'd love some," Mark responded.

Truthfully, I wasn't sure I could drink more coffee just yet. Apparently, neither could Kala. "Why don't we take a walk?" she suggested and linked her arm through mine.

"Stay out of trouble," our boss ordered.

"Yes, Dad," she replied in a long-suffering tone. It made me smile, but it also brought a stab of pain as I was reminded of the rift that had grown between myself and my father.

I waited until we were outside and out of hearing before I spoke. "Do you really think of Mark as your father?"

She cut a glance at me and shrugged. "Sometimes." She was silent while she put more thought into it. "I can't remember my parents at all and I have no idea if I have any siblings. Mark and the guys are my family as far as I'm concerned."

"Have you ever tried to find your parents?"

"Mark tried to find out who our parents were and what happened to them," she said. "He couldn't find any records of missing children who matched any of our descriptions."

It sucked having a vampire for a mother, but at least I knew who both of my parents were. It must have been awful not knowing what had become of their families. If the organization that had snatched them was anything like I suspected, their families would be dead.

The PIA wasn't the only agency that knew about supernatural creatures. A rival organization had performed experiments on Reece, Kala and Flynn when they were toddlers. They'd injected them with various viruses that had turned them all into shifters. Their intention had been to keep the trio prisoner. They were going to document the changes that happened to them as they grew older.

Mark had saved them from that fate and had become their guardian. Knowing him, he'd probably kept records of his own while he'd been raising the kids. It made sense not to waste the opportunity to learn more about our species.

"If someone could wave a magic wand and change your life, would you choose to be just a normal person?" I asked.

This time, her silence lasted longer before she answered me. "I've never known what it's like to be normal," she said at last. "Mark raised us with the knowledge that we were different. He prepared us for what would happen when we turned fifteen."

"How did he know that you'd shift then?"

"He read it in the archives. Any children conceived by shifters become shifters as well. Their first transformation always happens on the first full moon after their fifteenth birthday. No one knows why. Mark's theory is that we turn then because we've passed through puberty, but haven't quite reached adulthood yet. In cases of people who are turned, like you, it's more painful. The transformation becomes more traumatic the older they are when they're turned."

In that case, I was glad I'd only just turned eighteen when Reece had marked me, because it hurt like hell when I transformed. I wished I'd had someone to guide me through the process. I hadn't had any warning that I was going to turn into a monster. One day I'd been a normal teenager, and the next I was hunting wild animals down and eating their intestines.

"I don't think I'd have changed anything," Kala said introspectively. "Instead of going to college and getting a degree that I'd probably never even use, I'm out there fighting the bad guys and saving the humans from being eaten."

"By creatures like us," I said and we shared a rueful look.

Chapter Nineteen

Hearing a car approaching us from behind, we ambled over to give it room. We both turned when it sped up. Kala realized that the driver was going to run us over a split second before I did. She dived at me and pushed me out of the way. I heard a crunch and she shouted in pain when the car clipped her. We tumbled to the grass in a tangle of limbs.

Landing on top, I rolled Kala onto her back, fearing the worst. Her golden eyes blazed in fury and pain, but she was alive. Her cargo pants were torn at the knee and blood was soaking into the fabric. "How badly are you hurt?" I asked.

"I'll live." She didn't try to get up and I wondered if she'd sustained any other injuries that I couldn't see.

The car had come to a stop and the driver looked out the window to check on the damage that he'd caused. A sour stink came off him that was part sweat and something that I couldn't quite define. Maybe it was malevolence.

His happy grin revealed stained and broken teeth. Limp and unwashed, his shoulder length hair was a dirty shade of light brown. His rusty pickup truck was devoid of a license plate on the back. Pulling his head back inside, he put his foot down on the gas and my rage flared. He'd tried to kill us and now he was just going to drive away. I wasn't about to let that happen and I scrambled to my feet.

"Go get that guy," Kala hissed and I began to run.

I had a disconcerting moment of double vision as Reece realized something was wrong and reached out to connect with me. *That truck just tried to run us down,* I said to him with my focus on the truck. *Kala's hurt. She might need medical attention.*

We're on our way, he thought back at me.

If the pickup truck had been new rather than ancient, the driver might have gotten away. Since it wasn't, I caught up to it easily. Wrenching the door open, I dragged the guy out. The truck kept going for a few yards before stalling.

Not much taller than me, he had a slim, malnourished build. Cursing in fright and anger, his putrid breath washed over me as I drew my hand back to punch him. I saw the knife in his hand as it sliced towards my stomach.

Only my uncanny reflexes allowed me to step back in time. If I'd still been human, my intestines would have spilled out onto my feet. I grabbed his arm in mid-swing before he could take another stab at me. I'd been warned that I was much stronger than a normal teen now, but I was used to sparring with my fellow shifters. This was the first time I'd gone hand to hand with a human and I wrenched his arm a little too hard.

With a wet, tearing sound, it came loose from his shoulder. We both stared down at the limb that was now in my hands. For a moment, my attacker was too shocked to react as blood spurted from his stump. It splashed on me, coating my face and clothes in thick, red liquid. Regaining his voice, he shrieked and backed away.

His screams of terror and agony startled birds from their nests. Kala limped over to survey my work. I was glad to see her already up and moving around. Maybe she wasn't hurt as badly as I'd feared.

The driver would die quickly from blood loss, but I wasn't sure I could stand to listen to him screaming for that long. "Hold this for a second," I said and handed her the arm. Drawing my pistol, I put a bullet between his eyes. It was a relief when his shrill scream cut off after my shot rang out.

Mark, Reece and Flynn arrived moments later. Reece had watched the exchange through my eyes and our bond had led him straight to us. We gathered in a loose circle around the body. Mark grimaced at the sight of Kala holding the arm.

"Don't look at me," she said and handed the limb

back to me. "This one was all Lexi's."

I took it, then didn't know what to do with it.

Mark took a photo of the corpse with his cell phone. "Let's put him in the back of his truck," he decided. "I've already called the Cleanup Crew, but it will take them an hour to get here." He knew us well enough to guess that the man would be dead before they arrived to back us up. He'd planned ahead.

"We can't leave the truck on the side of the road," Reece said. "We'll have to move it before anyone reports it to the cops."

Trying to avoid the blood splatters, Reece and Flynn picked up the body while Mark unfolded a piece of tarpaulin he found in the back of the truck. They wrapped the corpse inside and I tucked his arm in as well. The knife that he'd tried to eviscerate me with was still clutched in his fist. That saved me from having to search for it.

Mark gestured for me to follow him as he climbed into the dead man's truck. The others gave me sympathetic glances. I figured I was about to receive a stern lecture. They drove off in the SUV and we followed.

"So," Mark ventured. "Was it fun?"

Surprised by his question, I was lost for a second before I grasped his meaning. "Pulling his arm off?" He nodded and I put some thought into it. It had happened so fast that I hadn't really felt anything, except for a sense of satisfaction. I'd been strongly linked to Reece at the time. It had been hard to tell if the emotion came from him or from me. "Not really. I didn't mean to rip his arm off. It just sort of happened."

"You don't seem upset about it," he observed.

"Should I be?" I asked curiously. "He was planning to murder us. He's just as bad as Officer Mallory, but at least this guy didn't try to rape me first."

His eyes left the road long enough to glance at me. "I was advised by my police contact in New Orleans that the detective had gone missing. I take it you were responsible for his disappearance?"

"Reece did the honors," I admitted. "I'd have killed him myself, but he beat me to it." I'd been meaning to tell Mark about the dead cop so the families of the girls he'd murdered could be notified. "Why are so many people evil?" I asked tiredly.

"I wish I knew," he replied. "Sometimes, it's hard to remember that most people are inherently good. We see so much malice in our line of work that it would be easy to begin thinking of humans as monsters."

He went quiet and I waited for him to give me a dressing down. He didn't and the silence started to get to me. "Aren't you going to lecture me?"

His expression was mildly surprised. "Lecture you about what? Stopping an attempted murderer from getting away? While I'm not thrilled with your methods of killing him, I'd be far more upset if you'd allowed yourself to come to any harm."

"Oh." I frowned in puzzlement. "Then why did

you want me to ride with you if you're not going to yell at me?"

"I just wanted to make sure you were all right."

It was such a fatherly thing to say that it brought tears to my eyes. I suddenly realized how much I missed my dad. Mark might be able to accept the fact that I was a supernatural being who had the tendency to kill anyone who wished me ill, but could my father do the same?

Sensing my misery, he patted my arm. "It'll be okay, Lexi," he said softly. "I won't allow you to turn into a monster."

Pressing my lips together, I held in the bitter words that wanted to spill out. Didn't he realize that it was too late for that? I'd just torn a man's arm off and had finished him off by putting a bullet into his brain. I'd felt no remorse or guilt at all, but instead had felt satisfied and possibly even a little pleased. Wasn't that the very definition of a monster?

My fellow agents were the only people who would ever be able to accept me now. To anyone else, I was a freak who should be hunted down and destroyed. A small part of me wondered how my father truly felt about me now that I was no longer fully human. If he ever came face to face with me when I was a werewolf, would he be tempted to shoot me? I prayed that we'd never have to find out.

Chapter Twenty

Mark followed the SUV off the main road and onto one of the smaller tracks. He nudged the truck into a dense copse of trees. It would be hidden from sight until the Crew could retrieve and dispose of it.

Branches boxed me in. I had to shove the door hard to get it open. Twigs scratched me as I fought my way free.

Trapped inside, Mark futilely attempted to push his door open. "A little help?" he called.

Shaking my head in pity at his feebleness, I battled through the branches and forced his door open. It seemed ironic that I was half his size, yet I was far stronger than he was. "There you go, boss," I said as he squeezed through the narrow opening.

He nodded his thanks and followed in my wake as I forged the way through the trees. We were both covered in scratches by the time we reached the SUV. Mine faded almost instantly, but Mark's would have to heal naturally. He'd shielded his face and most of the marks were on his hands. Our clothes were torn in a few places. Mine were stained with blood and were ruined anyway, so it wasn't a great loss. Mark had plenty of backup suits in his wardrobe.

Flynn powered his window down. "I hope you're not thinking of riding with us with your clothes in that condition." He pointed at the blood that coated me. "It'll ruin the upholstery."

I pulled my shirt away from my chest. I was sticky and the smell wasn't particularly pleasant. "I'll run the rest of the way," I told him. God forbid I should ruin the leather.

"Good idea," Mark replied. "We'll be right behind you."

I took off and easily beat them back to Dawson's Retreat. Edward was nowhere in sight and I could hear Margaret in the kitchen when I arrived. I quickly ran upstairs, locked my door and took a long shower. I rinsed as much of the blood from my clothes as I could, but they'd still have to be thrown out. Changing into a fresh white t-shirt and jeans, I met the others in the parlor.

Coffee and snacks were waiting. I bit into a slice of cake and chewed enthusiastically. It was coffee cake, one of my favorites.

"I see ripping that guy's arm off didn't affect your appetite," Reece observed with a half-smile.

"He had it coming," Kala said in my defense. She'd changed as well and was showing no signs of being in pain. Her injuries had already healed and she was none the worse for wear.

"He certainly did," Mark agreed. "I ran a search on him while you were in the shower. His name was Randy Tidwell and he was wanted for suspicion of murder."

"I'm shocked and surprised," I said and Kala snickered. "It sounds like I did the world a favor by blowing his brains out."

"Why did you shoot him?" Reece asked curiously. "He would have died from blood loss in another minute or so."

"He was screaming like a little girl," Kala replied for me. "It was pretty annoying. If Lexi hadn't shot him, I would have."

Well used to how callous we sounded, Mark wasn't disturbed by our conversation. We didn't have the same mindset as humans. Randy Tidwell had been a threat, not just to us, but to anyone who went for a stroll along the roadside. To our kind, I'd done the practical thing by killing him before he could kill me.

Kala raised a question that was far more difficult to answer. "Why do you seem to be a magnet for the bad guys? I've never met anyone who has so many people trying to kill her. It's uncanny."

"It's just my bad luck, I guess," I muttered. Maybe I was cursed. Bad things did seem to happen to me with great regularity lately.

"Now this is how a cake should taste," Flynn said, changing the subject abruptly. "See how it isn't the consistency of rock?" he said to Kala then shifted his attention to Reece. "I hope you're taking notes, bro."

"You have no faith in my abilities," Reece said. He crossed his arms, which made his biceps bulge. I looked away before I could be caught staring like a love struck fool.

"I've just been left disappointed too many times," Flynn said with a sad shake of his head and cut a glance at Kala.

Every time it was her turn to cook turned out to be a disappointment. Mainly because she didn't cook at all. Her idea of preparing a meal was to heat up a frozen pizza.

Scowling, the object of our discussion bit into her cake. "So what if I can't cook?" she said after she'd chewed it into a congealed wad. "I have many other far more useful talents."

"That's true," he conceded. "You can torture information out of someone faster than any of us."

"That's because I'm a cougar," she said with a sunny grin. "We love to play with our victims." Real cougars usually ate their prey afterwards. In her case, I was pretty sure she just killed them.

We went silent when Margaret appeared to refill our mugs.

I should probably have been disturbed to learn that the squad sometimes resorted to torture, but I wasn't. After reading through some of the files, I'd come to realize that there were many strange and horrible creatures out there. Our team would do anything necessary to complete our missions. That apparently included holding people against their will and causing them harm until they coughed up vital information.

We whiled the rest of the afternoon away then had an early dinner. The other guests began to arrive and Margaret was kept busy serving them as well. We were the first to finish our meals and we gathered outside next to the SUV to discuss our plans.

"I'll go in alone this time and scout the area," Reece said. "I want to make sure it's safe to enter. For all we know, the coven might have altered their wards now that they know we aren't fully human."

It made sense and no one argued with his plan, although we weren't happy about him going in alone.

"I'm going with you," Mark said. He held up a hand to stop us from voicing our protests. "I won't enter Bradbury. I just want to be close in case you require a quick exit. I might not be able to assist your search, but I can at least man the wheel."

"You might as well drive us there then," Reece said and handed the keys over.

Glad to have something to do, Mark drove us towards Bradbury. He stopped short of the town line. Climbing out, we stayed at a safe distance as Reece approached the invisible barrier. I tensed up in expectation of pain as he extended his hand past the sign.

Nothing happened, so he cautiously entered the

town. It might have been my imagination, but I could almost see a shimmer in the air when he walked across the town line.

He waited for a few moments, then turned to Mark. "It's seems to be safe." He directed his next words at the rest of us. "I'll contact you once I know the area is clear."

He loped off and quickly disappeared. Flynn waited for a few minutes, then turned to me. "Can you see through Garrett's eyes?"

I'd been tempted to try, but I hadn't wanted to intrude. Kala and Flynn were both as anxious as I was. Mark was also worried, but he hid his concern better. Closing my eyes, I reached out and tentatively touched Reece's mind. *Flynn asked me to look through your eyes,* I said. I didn't want him to think I was just being nosy.

Go ahead, he replied and relinquished a tiny part of his brain that allowed me to see what he saw. We were both careful not to pry into each other's thoughts. Our personal issues would have to wait until after our mission was finished.

"Reece just reached the center of Bradbury," I told the others. "He's approaching Kate's Kafé." I studied the building through his eyes and saw the entire coven gathered together through the window.

The café was closed to the public and they'd dragged a couple of tables together. They were leaning towards each other as they discussed something earnestly. I presumed they were talking about us. "The coven is holding a meeting," I informed the others. "Reece is too far away to hear what they're talking about."

I'm about to rectify that, he thought and moved in closer.

Reece hunkered down between two cars that were parked on the street outside the café. He could smell a human inside the trunk of the lead vehicle. From their deep, even breathing, the person had probably been put to sleep by a spell. Attempting to break them free would alert the coven and he didn't want to risk discovery. Raising his head, he peered through the window again.

"We don't know how many of them are hunting us," one of the warlocks said.

"I'm not just going to sit here doing nothing," Talitha replied, frustration evident in her tone and posture. "I say we should turn the tables on them and hunt them down."

"We don't even know who they are," one of the other women said. I heard fear in her tone and smiled as I recited their conversation to the others.

"Who cares who they are?" Talitha snarled. "We'll kill them, just like we've killed everyone else who discovered what we are."

"We're still performing the ritual tonight, right?" another male voice interjected.

"Yes, Jeremiah," the first warlock said with exaggerated patience. I was pretty sure it was Malachi. His back was to Reece and the men sounded very similar, so I couldn't be sure. "We might as well get it over with now. I highly doubt the intruders will be stupid enough to return tonight."

"Are they from a rival coven?" Ophelia wondered. "That girl has to have some kind of magical abilities to be able to control dogs like that."

Talitha shook her head. "I don't know what she is, but she isn't like us."

"The next time you encounter her, or any other strangers, make sure you do a better job of detaining them than our dear sister did," Malachi informed the group as they stood. She sneered, but said nothing. That was one question answered. They were definitely siblings.

I shivered as I relayed this to the others. I'd already had a taste of Talitha's power and I didn't want a repeat performance.

Reece ghosted away from the café and into the shadows as the six witches and warlocks left the building. Talitha locked the door and they climbed into the two cars that were parked out front.

This is the perfect opportunity for us to search their homes, Reece thought at me. *I'll follow the coven while you three split up and search two houses each. I'll warn you when they've finished their ritual.*

Okay, I replied and opened my eyes. "The coven are about to sacrifice another human," I told the team. Now I knew why there was a person in the trunk and what they planned to do with them. "Reece wants us to move in and search the properties while they're distracted."

We pulled our map pieces out of our pockets to consult them. "I'll take the one towards the east and the one in Reece's section," Flynn said.

"Do you remember where it is?" Kala queried doubtfully. Reece had the northern section of the map. Flynn only had the east quarter.

"I'll be able to find it," he said confidently.

"I'll take these two," Kala said and indicated the house to the west and one to the south.

"I guess that leaves me with this house and the café," I pointed at the final two properties that were marked on my map. Two of the houses weren't far from where we stood now. It wouldn't take long for Kala and me to walk there.

"I'll wait here," Mark said. "Call me if you run into any trouble."

"You couldn't help us even if we do," Kala reminded him as kindly as possible. "You'd hemorrhage and die before you could even reach us."

He gave a frustrated nod. "Be careful."

"Aye, aye, Captain," she snapped him a salute and Flynn and I copied her. He cracked a worried smile and we took off into the darkness.

Chapter Twenty-One

Kala stopped at the street that would carry her to the first house on her list. "Watch your back this time," she warned me.

"I will." I wasn't about to make the embarrassing mistake of being caught so easily again.

Knowing that the witches and warlocks were currently busy working their black magic helped boost my confidence. Still, I approached the first building on my list cautiously and stopped to inspect it for telltale signs of a ward. Not that I really knew what to look for.

The house looked like all the others in the street. Nothing about it stood out from the other properties. It didn't have a sign proclaiming that a witch lived inside. Just as I was about to step through the gate, I felt a surge of unease coming from Reece.

Drawn to his mind, I concentrated and caught a glimpse of what he was seeing. I picked up that he was in a park somewhere to the north. Moving slowly and quietly, he pushed his way through a copse of trees to the edge of a clearing.

Six robed figures stood in a circle around a struggling man. They'd woken their victim from the spell so he would be aware of what they were doing to him. It seemed like an unnecessary cruelty, but it didn't particularly surprise me. The coven weren't exactly humanitarians.

Reece shuddered in reaction to the miasma of evil that pulsed from the siblings. Blood already stained the bare ground where grass refused to grow. Hundreds of men and women had already died in that clearing and yet another was about to join them. He would shortly become one more ghost that was bound to Bradbury. Unless we could destroy the coven, he'd be doomed to exist as a spirit for all eternity.

Hurrying into the witch's yard, I stood in the shadows of a tree so I wouldn't be caught trespassing. My curiosity had always been strong and this time was no different. I wanted to witness the ritual as it transpired rather than hear about it secondhand.

I closed my eyes so I could concentrate on the scene more clearly. The shrouded figures drew my attention first. Their robes were dark blue and their hoods hung low enough to cover their faces. A pentagram had been painted in the dirt. The skull of a goat lay between the victim's legs. There was something satanic about the pentagram and the skull, but I didn't think the coven worshipped the devil. They just used a similar setup as Satanists to get what they wanted. Apparently, eternal youth was their goal.

The man lying in the center of the pentagram was young, handsome and completely naked. His arms and legs were spread and were tied to large metal spikes that had been driven deep into the ground. His eyes were wide and terrified and his screams were muffled by a gag.

One of the warlocks began to chant in a low voice. I assumed it was Jeremiah, since it was his turn to perform the ritual. He spoke in an ancient, foreign language that was unfamiliar to me. Drawing a dagger from beneath his robes, he knelt beside the sacrifice. His chant grew louder and more frantic, then he plunged the dagger into the man's heart.

Reece cursed beneath his breath when the young man shrieked in agony. He thrashed for a few moments, then mercifully passed out. Limp and unaware, blood ran down his side to stain the ground.

Jeremiah knelt in the spreading red pool, patiently waiting for his sacrifice to expire. He didn't have to wait for long. I let out a soft gasp as an insubstantial mist floated up from the corpse. Jeremiah chanted a few more words and the mist was drawn to him. It hovered near his face and was sucked beneath his robe as he breathed it in.

Throwing his head back, his hood slipped off to

reveal his ecstatic expression as he spread his arms open wide. His body jerked backwards and forwards as he absorbed the victim's life force. He dropped the knife and one of the others scooped it up from the ground.

Sagging in exhaustion, Jeremiah fell forward. He barely managed to put his hands out in time to catch himself from sprawling on the corpse. Glazed and unseeing, the sacrifice's eyes reflected the agony and horror that he'd just suffered.

Moments later, his spirit formed and stared around in confusion. Instead of being naked, he wore jeans and a t-shirt. Apparently, ghosts were clothed in the outfits they'd last been wearing before they died. Seeing the body on the ground, a look of abject sorrow came over him. Wailing soundlessly, he turned and fled from the sight of his own dead body.

"It is done," Jeremiah said and staggered to his feet. That seemed to end the ritual and the circle broke apart. None had seen the ghost appear. They hadn't seemed to be aware of it at all.

Flipping his hood back, Malachi surveyed the bound man. "Help me get rid of the body," he instructed the other two warlocks. Together, all three dragged the corpse over to a darker patch of ground near the trees. He lifted a cleverly hidden trapdoor and they pushed the corpse through the opening. I heard a thump a second later and surmised that they'd dug out their own private graveyard. I didn't even want to know how many bodies were interred inside the pit.

"Something is wrong," Talitha said. "I can feel someone watching us." Still hooded, her gaze swung towards Reece. He melted back into the trees before she could pinpoint his location.

They know we're here. Abort the search, he instructed me. *Tell Kala and Flynn to run.*

Okay, I responded. *We'll meet you back at the SUV.* He gave me a mental nod. "Kala, Flynn," I said, knowing they were wearing their earpieces and that they could hear me. "The ritual is finished and the witches are already on their way back to their homes."

"Damn it," Kala replied. "I was just about to break into the first house." I shared her frustration. I was only steps away from the home that I'd intended to search.

"We'll have to try again tomorrow night," Flynn said. He was more philosophical about our failure than Kala and I were. We wanted to get this done now, not postpone it yet again.

Turning to run, I stumbled to a stop when I felt a surge of confusion from Reece. Again, my mind was drawn to his and I saw through his eyes.

Waiting for the coven to leave, he'd almost made it out of the park when he felt someone watching him. A woman was standing in the shadows across the road. She looked so much like me that he was momentarily puzzled. He should have been able to sense me, but he couldn't.

Before I could warn him to flee, she moved. In the

blink of an eye, she was standing right in front of him. She'd moved so quickly that not even he'd been able to track her movement. Only one creature could move that fast; a vampire.

Capturing him with her gaze, he instantly became immobile. "So, you are the creature who has stolen my daughter away from me," she said. I didn't know how Katrina had managed to track me to West Virginia. I hadn't sensed her hunting me this time. Maybe because I wasn't her intended victim.

Mesmerized, Reece could only watch as the woman who resembled me so greatly circled around him. Her spell held him still as she placed a razor sharp fingernail on his chest. "I'm going to carve out your still beating heart and feed it to you." Her smile was beautiful, yet twisted. "No," she said as she changed her mind, "that would be too quick, too easy and far too painless. I have a much better idea."

Her smile was malicious and I knew what she planned to do to him. He tried to back away from her when he felt my panic, but was held immobile by her will. I'd begun to sprint towards the park as soon as I'd realized she was there. I knew I wouldn't make it in time to save him. "Garrett's in trouble!" I shouted, hoping Kala and Flynn were still wearing their earpieces. If they were, I'd probably just shattered their eardrums.

Gripping Reece by the back of his neck, Katrina ripped his shirt open to give her unobstructed access to his flesh. She savagely sank her fangs into his right shoulder. Pain and befuddlement transfixed him and he opened his mouth in a wordless scream.

Guided by our bond, I ran as fast as I could. I spied Reece and my mother ahead and prayed that I could reach him before it was too late. Even as I watched, he sank to his knees. My leech of a parent bent over him with her mouth still fastened to his flesh. I heard the sucking noises as I closed in.

Absorbed in feeding, I was on her before she even realized I was there. Grasping Katrina by the hair, I tore her off Reece and tossed her aside like a rag doll. Snarling, she scrambled to her feet. Blood smeared her face and dripped from her elongated teeth. "You dare to defy me?" she hissed. "Your own mother?"

"You're not my mother," I said coldly and drew my gun. "You're just the reanimated corpse of the woman who gave birth to me." Her outrage changed to alarm when I pulled the trigger. Moving with shocking speed, she dodged the bullet. It only grazed her arm rather than piercing her heart. I'd known that killing her wouldn't be easy and she was proving me right.

Kala and Flynn sprinted into view and Katrina hesitated. With a final snarl of rage, she spun around and ran.

"Was that what I think it was?" Flynn asked uneasily as they reached me. She'd fled before they could get a good look at her.

"If you were thinking it was a vampire, then yes, it is what you think it is," Kala confirmed. Concern flickered across her face when she saw Reece on his knees. "Please tell me she didn't bite him." The fear in her voice worried me almost as much as the attack itself had.

We moved in to surround him. Blood still oozed from the nasty wound on his shoulder. "We have to get him back to Mark asap," Flynn said. "I'll go get the SUV."

"What happened?" Kala asked when he darted off into the darkness.

"I sensed that Reece was in danger. I reached him just as the vampire was biting him," I explained.

"How did she manage to get so close to him? He's too smart to just let a bloodsucker walk up to him and start chowing down."

I avoided her gaze and shrugged, but I knew exactly what had happened. Katrina had confused Reece because she looked so much like me, or I looked so much like her. Then she'd been within striking distance and he'd fallen beneath her spell. I didn't know how she'd found us, but she clearly had a vendetta against him. With Reece out of the way, she probably thought she'd be free to convert me to her side. That was my guess anyway.

Flynn returned with the SUV and pulled up as close as he could to the park. Kala and I carried Reece the short distance and gently placed him on the backseat. I climbed in and pillowed his head on my shoulder as Kala grabbed the first aid kit from the back. She slid in on his other side and did her best to stop the bleeding as Flynn drove us back to Mark.

Our boss climbed into the front seat. His worried look did nothing to dispel my fears. "Let's get him back to Dawson's Retreat," he said quietly. Flynn sped off, driving almost as recklessly as Reece usually did.

It didn't surprise me that no one had come running to investigate the gunshot. Bradbury was so heavily beneath the coven's spells and hexes that it was a wonder any of the inhabitants could function at all.

We parked close to the house then Flynn, Kala and I carried our teammate up to the third floor and placed him on his bed. Reece's head lolled towards me and I put my bloody palm against his cheek. He was deeply unconscious, still beneath the vamp's spell. "When is he going to wake up?" I asked. A heavy silence was my only reply. I glanced up to see the team staring at me in pity. "What?"

"Alexis," Mark said gently, "I'm afraid Reece isn't going to wake up."

"What do you mean?"

Kala rubbed a hand across her mouth, as if she tasted something bad. "Not many people know this, but vampires are toxic to shifters. We always end up dying painfully and horribly when they bite us." I could tell she didn't want to add that last part, but felt she had to. She didn't want me to hold onto false hope.

My face drained of blood. "I don't understand." I'd been bitten by both supernatural beings and I was fine. More or less.

"There's some kind of venom in vampire saliva that reacts badly to our blood," Flynn explained. "Once bitten, we have no chance of survival."

"That isn't completely true," I replied in a low voice. "I survived."

Comprehension dawned and Mark leaned forward to take me by the shoulder. "Is that what happened to you in New Orleans? Were you bitten by a vampire?"

I nodded unwillingly and astonished glances were exchanged. "She messed with my memory, but I'm pretty sure she drank from me twice."

Mark sank back in the chair. He was almost as pale as I felt. "That's the battle that's going on in your spirit," he realized out loud. "The voodoo priestess knew you'd been bitten by a vampire." He frowned as he realized the timing wasn't right. We'd seen her shortly after we'd arrived in the city. Katrina hadn't bitten me until several nights had passed. He shook his head in the futility of worrying about it. "I don't know how you managed to survive, but I'm afraid Reece isn't going to be so lucky."

I'd clamped down on the bond so tightly that I could feel only a flicker of the pain that Reece was suffering. Opening the bond wider, I blanched at the avalanche of agony that assailed him. He was burning up from the inside. Our bond was also rapidly growing weaker. He was slipping away from me both physically and mentally. "There has to be something I can do," I said helplessly.

Kala and Flynn shared a long look then Kala turned to me. "There is something you can try."

I looked at her hopefully. "Name it."

"You can attempt to strengthen the bond between you," she said. "It worked for you when you were getting weaker and weaker. Maybe it'll work for him, too, since he's linked to you so strongly."

Mark seized on the idea and hope lit his face. "I know you despise being tied to Reece, but would you be willing to try it?"

"I don't despise being tied to him," I replied. "I just hate the fact that we didn't have a choice about being stuck together permanently. If we'd never met Lust, none of this would have happened."

I couldn't hide the bitterness at the memory of Reece being forced to have sex with me on the night of a full moon. It was the worst possible time for a shifter to engage in intercourse. Our instincts were very hard to resist during those crucial hours. He'd bitten me and I'd in turn bitten him a month later. We were so tightly entwined now that we'd never be able to cut each other loose.

"I'm not so sure that this wouldn't have happened eventually," Kala said. "I think this was supposed to be."

"Did you turn into a mystic when I wasn't looking?" Flynn asked incredulously.

"Think about it," she said with a hint of impatience. "Philip Levine just happened to be out of the country when we needed an expert sniper and

Lexi was the next best person available. She was at loose ends because she had to wait until she turned eighteen before she could sign up to be a soldier. Major Levine gave Mark his permission for his one and only child to join the TAK Squad, putting Lexi within Reece's reach." She lifted her hands in the air as if that explained it all. "Doesn't this seem to be just a bit too coincidental?"

Mark looked thoughtful and nodded. "It did seem almost too easy to convince Philip to allow Lexi to join us." He gathered himself and frowned at Reece. "If this was meant to be, then there is a chance that Alexis can save Reece." He looked at me and met my eyes. "Are you willing to try?"

Staring down at Reece, I could feel the heat draining out of his skin. He was dying and I was the only one who had a chance of saving him. "I'll try," I said softly.

"Let's give them some privacy," Kala said and herded the other two out of the room.

Chapter Twenty-Two

Knowing what I had to do, I delayed the inevitable for a few seconds by locking the door. I could feel Reece slipping further and further away from me with every second that passed. To save him, I was going to have to get naked with him yet again. If I did nothing, he would die. I wasn't about to let that happen.

A tingle of excitement spread through me, warming me from the inside out. The other guests on our floor had left. It was just us two up here now. We had about as much privacy as we could get without being in one of the soundproof rooms at our compound. It still wasn't private enough for me. Kala and Flynn would both be able to hear it if we made too much noise. To restore the bond, I'd have to get very physical with Reece. We both had a tendency to get vocal when we were in the moment.

Putting my modesty aside was difficult, but necessary. We didn't have any time to waste. I stripped down to my skin and placed my clothes on the chair beside the bed. Reece didn't even twitch when I removed his clothes. He lay inert and unresponsive when I straddled him.

He was flawless. Muscles bulged everywhere and it was hard to choose my favorite feature. Starting at his abs, I ran my hands up the contours of his body to his chest. His face was handsome even when he was unconscious. Male models would kill to have his cheekbones. His dark brown hair was kept short at the sides with a mini Mohawk. He looked very young and vulnerable. My heart beat faster at the thought of losing him.

Leaning down until my face was only inches away from his, the bite mark on his right shoulder caught my eye. It wasn't showing any signs of healing yet. It occurred to me that we now had the exact same bite marks on our shoulders. My mother had bitten us both on the right side and we'd bitten each other on the left. We were a matched pair.

Acting on instinct, I leaned down until our chests were touching and sank my teeth into him. I bit him directly over the mark that I'd left a few weeks ago. Reece reacted to the pain instantly and his back arched. Holding on with my teeth and hands, I smashed through the flimsy mental shield that was between us.

What's happening? He was understandably groggy

and confused. His veins were on fire as his body battled the vampire toxin that was killing him.

It was quicker to show him than to explain. Watching the barrage of images, he grasped the fact that he was dying with calm equanimity. "It's for the best," he rasped out loud, shocking me into sitting up and glaring down at him. Even though he was in agony, his eyes dropped down to my chest and he smiled slightly. "At least I'll have a memorable sight to take with me when I die."

"You're not going to die," I ground out.

"I've been bitten by a vampire." His voice faded in and out and he was on the verge of blacking out again. "There is no hope for me."

The fact that he was awake at all gave me hope. Mark had been certain Reece wouldn't regain consciousness at all. I shook him hard enough for him to wince in pain. "Mark thinks I can save you with our bond."

He lifted a brow in doubt. "Why would he think that?"

"Because it saved me," I replied and sent him a mental picture of my mother biting me. I hid her identity from him and just thought of her as a rogue vampire. He was already weak and I didn't want to shock him into getting worse.

Understanding rose and he shook his head in disapproval. "You should have told us you'd been bitten," he admonished me.

"Save your disapproval for later. Let's worry about

saving your hide first."

"What do you have in mind?" His hands went to my hips and he slowly smoothed them down my thighs. Burning up from the inside, his body was still capable of responding to my nakedness. Men were truly mystifying creatures.

"I'm thinking you should bite me, then we can have sex," I said bluntly. Seduction wasn't in my meager sexual repertoire yet. Frankness was more my style.

Blinking in surprise, he lifted his left shoulder in capitulation. That caused a fresh rill of blood to flow from his wound. I astonished us both by leaning down and licking the blood away. He made a noise of pleasure, then tilted my head aside and brushed my hair out of the way. Holding the back of my neck gently, he pulled me in close and bit down on my shoulder. It should have been painful, but I felt only pleasure as he sucked my flesh. He gained strength from my blood and the bond also grew stronger.

I was on the verge of ecstasy already and he'd barely even touched me. He made a sound of disappointment when I pulled away. It changed to a groan of sexual torment when I bit him again. His hands cupped my hips and pulled me against his groin. I was more than ready for him when he guided himself inside me. I sank down onto him and moaned at the sensation of completeness that I'd been longing for.

"Don't stop," he urged and I bit him again, much deeper this time. He shuddered when I sucked the blood from the wound, then he flipped me over onto my back.

Bracing myself just in time, I muffled my cry of pleasure with my hand when Reece bit me. A small flood of blood poured into his mouth and he drank it down. Heat built inside both of us, replacing the fire in his veins with a different type of flame.

My legs went around him and he began to move faster, piercing me deeper each time our bodies came together. I locked my hands around his neck, holding him in place as he sucked at the wound that was already closing. His tongue probed at the torn flesh, wringing another cry from me.

When the bite healed completely, he levered himself up onto his elbows. Our eyes locked and he paused for a second as his pain receded. The toxin had been dampened by the infusion of my blood and our bond became stable again.

His mind was open and I felt his pleasure at being inside me. He also felt my enjoyment at being taken. Reece knew what I wanted and he was happy to comply. Our mouths met and he plunged inside me deeply. His kiss muffled my moans as he relentlessly drove me towards the edge. It didn't take long before my body jolted in intense pleasure, clenching on the inside and causing him to follow me into climax.

The heat between us flared almost hot enough to ignite us both before it finally receded. Instead of being painful, it left us feeling invigorated.

Reece shifted to lie beside me and took my hand.

"Thank you for saving me, Lexi. I know that can't have been easy for you."

It had been surprisingly easy, physically. Emotionally, I was awash with conflicting emotions. How could something that felt so right cause me so much anguish? I shut down the bond before he could glean my thoughts.

Reece thought I didn't want to sleep with him, but he was very wrong about that. In all of my eighteen years, I'd never enjoyed anything as much as being in bed with him. My dilemma was that he didn't feel the same way about me. Not to say he didn't enjoy himself, but for him it was purely physical. He didn't care for me the same way that I did for him. I was nothing more than a burden that he felt responsible for.

"How are you feeling?" I asked and tried to hide how empty I felt.

"Much better," he replied.

Pulling the sheet up to cover myself, I rolled onto my elbow and peered at his wounds. His had healed and so had mine. "I thought it took a while for bites from other shifters to heal."

He shrugged. "Our rapid healing must have something to do with our bond." He was regarding me with a neutral expression. He was hiding his thoughts from me as hard as I was masking mine from him.

"Well," I said and looked longingly at my clothes. "I guess we should tell the others that you've clawed your way back from death's door."

"As I recall, you were the one doing the clawing," he replied with a grin. I saw what he meant when he stood and I caught a glimpse of his back. Quickly fading furrows marred his skin. "I'm going to take a shower," his smile was strained this time and our awkwardness built.

I waited for him to walk into the bathroom, then quickly scooped up my clothes and dressed. I scurried next door into my room and locked the door before taking a shower of my own.

Battling tears, I wished that I could feel good for once rather than horrible after being naked with Reece. It just didn't seem right that our bond should cause us so much mutual misery.

Chapter Twenty-Three

Reece was waiting for me in the hallway when I emerged from my room. Kala and Flynn would have heard at least some of what had happened between us. They knew that Reece was alive and they were anticipating our arrival.

"I told you it would work!" Kala crowed softly even before we appeared in the doorway of the parlor.

Flynn grinned fiercely and gave her a high five. "For once, I'm glad you were right."

Mark's relief was palpable when he saw his agent looking so well. "How do you feel?" he asked as Reece took the seat beside him. I sat on the other couch next to Kala.

"I feel great," he replied. "It's hard to believe I was bitten at all."

"What did you have to do to restore the bond?" Kala asked. Her expression was curious rather than lecherous for a change.

"There was some biting, blood drinking and, uh, nakedness involved," I replied.

Flynn pressed his lips together as he tried to hide his smirk. Kala was less successful and snickered. Mark sent them both a heavy frown. "I take it your bond has been restored?" he asked.

We both nodded and Reece pulled his t-shirt aside so they could see the now healed wound on his right shoulder. "I've never seen a vampire or shifter bite heal this quickly before," he said.

Mark leaned in close to examine the wound and flicked a glance at me. I read the knowledge in his eyes as he mentally compared our scars. He knew we'd been bitten by the same creature. "Alexis, is there something we need to know about the vampire that attacked you both?" he said evenly.

I looked away as tears welled and spilled over. I couldn't hide the truth from them any longer, but there was someone else I had to talk to first. "I need to make a phone call," I said as I used my sleeve to wipe my tears away. I'd been dreading this conversation, but I couldn't put it off any longer.

I retreated to my room before taking my cell phone out of my pocket. I dialed my father's personal number and hoped he had his phone switched on. He answered far more quickly than I'd expected.

"Lexi?" he said anxiously. "Are you all right?"

"I'm fine, Dad." The connection was startlingly clear and I had a feeling he was no longer overseas. "Where are you?"

"I'm home, honey," he replied and I heard weariness in his tone. "I just arrived a few minutes ago. I was going to call you after I'd had a few hours' sleep."

I felt guilty that I was about to snatch his ability to sleep away. Then I reminded myself that he'd been lying to me almost since my birth. He was the one who should be feeling guilty here, not me. "There's something we need to discuss." My tone went slightly chilly.

He drew in a sharp breath and I couldn't blame him for his automatic concern. The last time I'd called him on an urgent matter, I'd had to break the news that I was a werewolf. This discussion was going to be just as bad. "What is it this time?" he asked tightly.

It was best to just get to the point rather than drawing it out. "Mom didn't die when I was a baby, did she?" I said. "Well, I guess she did die, just not completely." I wasn't handling this well. Taking a deep breath, I held it for a couple of seconds then let it out again. "Why didn't you tell me that she's a vampire?" Silence met that statement, but I sensed it wasn't a shocked silence. "Don't tell me you didn't know that she wasn't murdered by a human."

"I knew," he confessed and sighed quietly.

I was already aware that he'd been hiding this from me, but it still hurt to hear him admit it. A realization hit me and I put a few things together. Mark had looked at me as if he knew me when we'd first met. He'd also hinted that the scar on my shoulder hadn't been from a dog bite.

"Mark knew, too," I realized out loud and a sense of betrayal rose. I'd been played by the two men I trusted the most. They'd been keeping secrets from me, ones that had affected my entire life.

"Don't jump to any conclusions, Alexis," my father ordered. "You need to know the full story before you can judge our actions."

Very tempted to throw my cell phone at the wall, I paced backwards and forwards as I tried to get my temper under control. For the first time, I was thankful that Reece had been training me to learn how to rein in my rage. "What else have you kept from me?" I ground out.

"I need to speak to Agent Steel," he said, evading my question. "Put him on the phone."

"If I see Mark right now I'll probably tear his head off," I replied honestly. I now knew just how easy it was to dismember someone. "I don't want to see, or speak to either of you until I manage to calm down."

With that, I hung up and tossed my phone onto the bed. Leaving by the stairs would bring me into close proximity with the others and I didn't want to risk my anger spilling over. Crossing to the window, I shoved it upwards and dived through headfirst. Falling three stories, I landed on my feet with uncanny agility and started running.

Taking to the woods, I ended up in the last place I'd have chosen as a refuge if I'd been thinking straight.

My steps slowed when I reached the cemetery on the far side of town. I sat on the damp ground in the middle of the boneyard and was soon surrounded by ghosts. They looked even gloomier than I felt. Drifting a few inches off the ground, they mournfully stared at the grave markers of long dead people.

None of these spirits had a grave to call their own. Their bodies had been unceremoniously dumped in pits and left to rot. How they must envy the dead who had managed to move on to wherever they'd been destined to go. These poor souls were instead trapped in perpetual limbo.

I didn't know how long I'd been sitting there before the boy appeared beside me. He stared at me forlornly. I was decades too late to save him, but maybe I could offer him some small comfort. I opened my arms and he sat down on my lap.

Coldness sank into me as I tried to wrap my arms around him. My mother had done her best to see me dead and his mother had succeeded in killing him. That made us kindred spirits in my book.

As if thinking about her had conjured her up, a spectral finger ran down the back of my neck a few minutes later. The ghosts roused from their misery and turned to confront the undead woman who I so closely resembled.

"We are alone at last, my darling daughter," Katrina

said. Her teeth were still stained with Reece's blood when she smiled.

"We're not alone," I pointed out. "We're surrounded by spirits." I noticed that she was staying a safe distance away from the church grounds. That had to mean it was still hallowed ground after all this time.

Looking beyond me, Katrina concentrated. Her eyes widened when the ghosts became apparent. She waved a hand negligently. "They are but fragments of the past and are of no consequence."

The boy in my lap turned to look up at me. "You matter," I said to him. "You all matter," I told the dead who crowded around me protectively. "My friends and I will find a way to put you to rest. If my mother doesn't kill me first," I said as an afterthought.

Katrina studied me with a small smile. "Is your mate dead yet?" she asked sweetly. "He was very…tasty."

She licked her lips and I made a sound of disgust. "Reece is still alive and he'll hunt you down and rip your head off if you touch me," I threatened her.

She uttered a childish giggle that raised the hairs on my arms and gave me gooseflesh. I wasn't sure at what point she'd lost her mind, but I was pretty sure she was totally insane. "No shape shifter has the strength, or the speed to kill me," she declared.

I struggled to my feet, numb with cold from having the ghost child cradled in my arms. The spirits crowded closer. Some were beginning to look menacing as Katrina drew closer to the edge of the graveyard. As long as I stayed inside the boundary, I'd be safe.

"Come, daughter, it is time for you to succumb to your destiny and join me." She held out her hand and I made the mistake of looking into her eyes.

While her link to me was muted thanks to the holy ground, she could still control me with her will alone. Now that I was caught in her snare, I was irresistibly drawn to her. The boy shook his head and tried to stop me, but I stepped through his insubstantial form. Cold shocked me for a moment, then I continued on.

Realizing their only hope of salvation was about to be snatched away, a transformation came over the spirits. Their benign, human forms were replaced with figures out of a horror movie. Clawed, fanged and hideous, their flesh melted away to reveal their bones. Their hair grew long and tangled and their clothes became tattered black shrouds.

The hairs on the back of my neck rose as I heard their hollow moans of anguish. They converged on Katrina, rushing towards her en masse. A flicker of fear spread over her lovely face. She blanched as the first ghost lunged at her and entered her body. Screaming in pain, she thrashed as if she'd been electrocuted. It passed through her and exited from her back. Before she could recover, another spirit invaded her.

Broken from her spell, I backed away as my undead

mother was hounded by the protective ghosts. They drove her away from the cemetery until she turned tail and ran. Only the small boy had retained his normal guise. He lifted a hand and waved at her, smiling nastily as she disappeared.

One by one, the other spirits returned to their natural forms. My heart was thundering in my chest and I wondered if they would turn on me next. The kid looked up at me sadly, then patted me on the leg and disappeared.

"Did I just see what I think I just saw?" Kala said as she jogged into view. Her eyes were wide and she was shaken. She'd seen many weird and horrible things during her job as an agent, but this was apparently something new.

"What did you see?" I asked her curiously.

"The vampire being driven away by something invisible," she replied and shivered.

"It was the ghosts," I told her. "Be glad that you couldn't see them." A shudder wracked my entire body.

With the threat of a vampire hanging over us, she searched the shadows. "Are you okay?"

I tried to nod, but it came out as a shake instead. "This has been a really crappy day." I came close to embarrassing myself with a sob.

Kala's hug was comfortingly warm when she put her arm around me. She kept her other hand free, ready to defend us both with her Colt. "Your father is on his way here. He'll be here soon."

I pushed away from her, angry all over again at the secrets my dad and Mark had kept from me. I'd been in the cemetery longer than I'd thought and dawn wasn't far away now. At least we'd be safe from Katrina once the sun came up. "I guess we'd better get back," I said with a sigh. It had been a smart move to send Kala to retrieve me. I wasn't sure I'd have been able to hold my temper if any of the guys had come to get me.

"She's your mother, isn't she?" Kala said as we started back towards the B&B. I shot her a cautious glance, expecting to see anger but not finding any. "You look just like her," she explained. "Apart from the fangs, extreme paleness and utter insanity, that is."

Her solemnness made me smile, then we were both laughing. I didn't know why I found that so funny. I attributed it to stress and a lack of sleep.

"Yeah, that's my Mom," I said when I had myself under control again. "I must have the strangest family in the world."

"Let's see," she started counting off on her fingers. "Your Dad is a crack sniper, your mother is a vampire and you're a werewolf. I'd say that qualifies as being pretty strange."

We shared another giggle and I could only imagine that she was as tired and stressed as I was. We might not all share a bond, but we were a pack, if a rather strange one. What impacted on one of us impacted on us all. "I should have told you guys," I admitted.

"I can understand why you didn't," she said and

slung her arm around my shoulder. "No one would want to admit that their mother is a murderous, bloodsucking, crazy vampire."

"Thanks, Kala," I said dryly. She grinned, willingly admitting that she completely lacked tact.

Chapter Twenty-Four

We took our time walking back to Dawson's Retreat to find that my father hadn't arrived yet. Margaret was already up and she was surprised to see us gathered in the dining room. She offered to make us an early breakfast and Mark accepted.

We heard a car arrive just as breakfast was being served. A couple of minutes later, Edward escorted my father into the dining room and pointed at our table. The gesture was unnecessary since we were the only people in the room. "Your party is just about to begin their breakfast, Major Levine. I'm sure they'll be delighted for you to join them."

"Thank you, Edward," my dad said politely and strode across the room. With Margaret standing right there, he had to pretend that everything was normal. Tension had seeped into me and my back was rigid.

"Oh," our hostess exclaimed when she realized she had another mouth to feed. "We have another guest! I take it you all know each other?"

"We do," Mark confirmed. "I'm glad you could join us, Philip." His expression was guarded. He wasn't sure what reaction he'd receive from the soldier. My father's visit to our compound in Colorado had been decidedly strained.

I knew my father well and he was tightly controlling his emotions. I refused to meet his eyes and shot a glare at Kala when she moved over, leaving the seat beside me vacant. My father didn't hesitate and sat next to me. "I'm glad to be here," he said with what sounded like sincerity.

Margaret was delighted to offer him breakfast from the trolley she'd wheeled in. He accepted a plate and she piled it high with bacon, scrambled eggs and hash browns. When we'd all been served, we concentrated on eating. By mutual agreement, we ate in silence.

Finishing my breakfast, I pushed my plate away and started when the boy appeared beside me. He looked from me to my father and back again. He pointed at us both and raised his eyebrows in query.

"Yeah, he's my Dad," I confirmed. Concern crossed the child's face and he moved in front of me protectively. "He'd never hurt me," I told the child. "He loves me."

My father had paused with his fork halfway to his mouth when I'd first started to speak. He was staring at me like I'd gone crazy. "Who are you talking to,

Lexi?"

"This house is haunted," Kala responded for me. Her tone was nonchalant. "Five ghosts live here and she can see them all." I could also see every other ghost that was tied to this area, but it would feel a little too much like bragging to mention it.

Astonished to hear that news, my father put his fork down. "How long have you been able to see ghosts?" he asked me.

"Since my undead mother bit me when we were in New Orleans and tried to turn me into a vampire," I replied bitterly.

"The vampire is your mother?" Flynn said in disbelief. He looked around to see that no one else was surprised by this knowledge. "How come I'm the only one who didn't know about this?"

"I only found out when she bit me," Reece said. His hand went to the fresh scar on his right shoulder.

"I figured it out when I went to get Lexi and saw the vamp being driven away by invisible ghosts," Kala said, drawing a shocked silence from everyone. "The resemblance between them is uncanny. They look more like sisters than mother and daughter."

"How about you, boss?" Flynn asked. "How long have you known that Lexi's mother is a vampire?"

"I've known about Katrina for eighteen years," he replied calmly.

Both Kala and the ghost put their hands on me when I tried to leap to my feet. I didn't know why the boy wanted me to stay, but the ghosts had saved my life and I was willing to follow their guidance. Crossing my arms, I scowled down at the table rather than meeting anyone's eyes.

"Maybe you'd better start at the beginning," Reece said. His tone was cool and I felt his annoyance that we'd all been kept in the dark for so long. This secret had impacted on more than just me. The entire squad had been in danger once we'd come to my mom's notice. Their excuse for not telling us about her had better be a good one.

A young couple entered the dining room, accompanied by Margaret. "If you've all finished eating, we should take this discussion somewhere more private," Mark said.

Kala stuffed a final piece of toast in her mouth and stood. "After you," she said to Flynn and he shook his head in mock disgust at her mangled words.

I was the first to the door and Reece was right on my heels. My father hung back, knowing I wasn't ready for him to speak to me directly yet. It was rare for me to become truly angry. My emotions were far more unstable now and he didn't know quite how to take me.

Reece unlocked the SUV once we emerged through the backdoor and I climbed into the back. Mark explained where we were going to my father as Kala, Flynn and Reece took their usual seats. With a nod, my dad strode over to a dark blue hire car. It was a nondescript sedan that would blend in with other traffic easily. It was automatic for him to think in terms of stealth. I just wished he'd passed that trait on to me.

He followed us to the abandoned church and his car bumped along the rutted, untended roads. It wasn't as equipped for rough terrain as our SUV, but it made the journey without breaking down.

The church was the one place nearby where we knew we wouldn't be disturbed. As always, it was empty when we arrived. Not even the ghosts were here this time and we had the place to ourselves. The decrepit old building suited my mood perfectly as I leaped over the saggy stairs.

We'd left the door open and I entered first. I came to a stop in the middle of the room and crossed my arms. I still couldn't look at Mark or my father. It was hard to say if my anger or disappointment in them was stronger. My teammates moved to surround me with Kala on my left, Flynn on my right and Reece at my back. I didn't find it strange that they were siding with me rather than with our boss. We were all feeling betrayed and we wanted answers.

Mark gestured for my father to tell the tale. Standing at attention, my dad clasped his hands behind his back and addressed me. "I met your mother in Romania when I was deployed on my first overseas mission."

I risked a glance at him to see him lost in his memories. He hardly ever spoke about my mother and I'd rarely asked him questions about her. I always figured her disappearance was too difficult for him to speak about. I knew she'd been born somewhere in Europe. Having Romanian genes explained my dark hair and eyes and almost exotic features.

"Her family was poor and she was near starving," he reminisced. "They lived in a small town near where I was stationed. I snuck away as often as I could, meeting Katrina in secret. We were young and stupid and we fell in love." He smiled sadly. "I told her I'd make her my wife if she came back to the US with me and she agreed."

I wondered if Katrina had truly loved him, or if she'd just used him to escape from poverty. "I had to call in some favors to bring her home, but we were married within a month."

I met his gaze and saw his pain. They couldn't have been married for very long before she'd been snatched away from him. He'd loved her so much that he'd never remarried. As far as I knew, he hadn't even dated anyone.

"You were only a week old when I was transferred to the army base near New Orleans. Your mother feared and hated the city from the moment we arrived. Her family were superstitious folk. They raised her to believe in what I thought was nonsense about zombies and vampires. It bothered her that there were so many cemeteries right there in town. I think she had a touch of clairvoyance because she sensed that something bad was going to happen to her. She told me she wanted to leave, but my superiors wouldn't have been happy if I asked for a transfer so soon."

He shook his head in weary regret that he hadn't listened to her instincts. "Nearly four months after we arrived, Katrina began to change. She became withdrawn, moody and sullen. She'd always been pale, but she looked anemic, sickly and far too thin. I woke up several times to find her missing from our bed. One night, I went searching for her and found her in the nursery."

Our eyes locked and I couldn't look away from him. "She was cradling you to her chest and the look on her face was…" He searched for a description and the one he came up with made me shudder. "Monstrously hungry."

"Didn't you see the bite marks on her?" Kala asked. She was anguished that I'd had to go through such a horrible ordeal when I'd been so young.

He shook his head. "She wore shirts and dresses with high collars and refused to let me near her. I didn't get a chance to see her up close," he explained. "Besides, how could I possibly have known that she was being drained by a vampire? As far as I knew, they were just a myth."

"When did you figure out what she was?" Reece asked. He was standing close enough behind me for his chest to brush up against my back. His presence was more comforting than I was willing to admit even to myself.

"A couple of days later," he replied. "I came home from work the next afternoon to find Alexis screaming with hunger. She hadn't been tended to all day as far as I could tell."

Kala and Flynn pressed in close beside me and Reece's hands went to my shoulders. Mark flicked me a sympathetic glance, then returned his attention to his old friend.

"I called out to Katrina, but she didn't answer me. I searched the house and she wasn't there. There was no note and no sign of a struggle." He drew in a breath and held it for a few seconds before letting it out again. I sensed he was struggling against tears, which shocked me. My father had never cried in front of me before.

"I notified the police that she was missing and took the day off work to take care of Lexi," he continued. "The cops came to search the house, but they didn't find anything useful. Then a federal agent showed up, asking strange questions about my missing wife."

All eyes switched to Mark and he shrugged. "I'd heard there was a new vampire nest in New Orleans. Once I arrived, I heard rumors that Mrs. Levine had gone missing. I knew it would only be a matter of time before she reappeared."

"I told Mark about the changes I'd noticed in Katrina," my dad said. "I knew they rang alarm bells for him. He wouldn't tell me what he suspected had happened to her, but he warned me to keep a close watch on Alexis."

He dropped his eyes and his shoulders slumped. "I didn't listen to Mark's warning and I put you to bed in the nursery as usual." He was silent long enough for Mark to put his hand on his arm. "I heard a muffled cry in the middle of the night and sensed that something was wrong. I went to check on you and heard a horrible noise coming from the nursery." I didn't need to ask what the noise had been. I'd heard the disgusting sucking sounds for myself as she'd fed from Reece.

"I opened the door to see your mother holding you." He mimed holding a baby up to his shoulder. "At first, I thought she was just hugging you," he said to me. "Then I saw the blood on your clothes and realized she was biting you."

My chest hitched in a near sob and Reece's hands clamped down on my shoulders hard enough to hurt. The pain helped me to focus and to drive my grief away, at least for the moment.

"I'd been keeping a watch on the house," Mark said. "I saw a woman sneaking in through the nursery window. I was about to go in after her when Philip entered the room. He was armed and his reputation as a crack shot was already well established. I stayed outside to provide backup if it was required."

"I didn't want to admit to myself what Katrina had become," my dad said. The tears in his eyes almost broke my heart. "But I couldn't let her kill you, even if that meant I had to kill her to keep you safe."

"You shot her in the head," I said, remembering the faint scar on Katrina's forehead. I'd had a dream about being snatched out of my cradle by a monster and my father coming to my rescue. It hadn't been a dream at all, but a memory of the night my mother had tried to drain me.

He nodded in confirmation. "It didn't kill her like I'd hoped, but it hurt her. She staggered back and dropped you. I caught you just before you hit the floor." He looked down at his hands as if he was picturing me as a baby again. "There was so much blood and you were so tiny." He shook his head, unable to go on.

"Your mother was gravely wounded," Mark explained. "I'd only been in the PIA for a couple of years by then and she was the first vampire that I'd encountered. I knew that a single gunshot to the head wouldn't kill her. I dragged her out through the window and saw she was already starting to heal. I'd brought along a stake just in case she showed up."

"I take it you didn't get a chance to use it," Reece said dryly.

"No," he admitted. "She knocked my hand away before I could stake her. She escaped into the swamp and it would have been suicide to follow her. Her maker and the rest of their nest were somewhere close by. I couldn't take on that many vampires alone and hope to survive."

"I saw Mark drag Katrina out the window and figured he knew she wasn't human," my dad said. "He told me that she'd escaped and offered to call a doctor who was a friend of his. I couldn't take you to the hospital. How could I possibly explain what had happened to you?" It was a rhetorical question and I didn't try to answer it. "I agreed to his plan. The doc stole some blood from the hospital where he worked. He gave you a transfusion and stitched up your wound."

"Did you go after her?" I asked, already knowing the answer. He would have felt compelled to try to put an end to the woman he'd married. He wouldn't have wanted her to remain a bloodthirsty monster.

"We did," he confirmed. "But the entire nest had fled. Mark figured her master was too smart to stay in town after they'd been discovered. We searched for a few days, but couldn't find any sign of them."

It was all so clear to me now. Mark had introduced my father to the Paranormal Investigation Agency after he'd helped save my life. They'd stayed in touch all these years without me even knowing about it. Rather than telling me the truth after I'd learned that supernatural beings existed, they'd decided to hide it from me. They'd continued their deception even after I'd become a monster myself.

"Why didn't you tell me?" I ground out.

"I was going to," he replied. "I'd already arranged to take a vacation so I could tell you all this. Mark was going to give you a few days off when I returned home."

Mark backed him up. "It's true. I'd already booked you a flight back to Texas, but then this mission came up and we had to postpone your vacation."

"What else haven't you told me?" I asked them and

received blank stares.

"We've told you everything, honey," my dad said.

"Something else must have happened to me." I was frustrated and even the touch of my fellow shifters wasn't enough to calm me.

"What makes you think that?" Mark's question was cautious.

"Because I'm not normal!" I felt Reece flinch both in body and mind. He knew what I was talking about. I was different from him, even though we were the same species. "I've been bitten by both a vampire and a werewolf and I'm still alive. I can see ghosts and I can control dogs with my mind. God only knows what else I can do that I haven't discovered yet."

"Wait." My father held up a hand to stop me. "You can control dogs with your mind?" He was clearly stunned by that prospect. Kala snickered at his surprise and Reece glowered at her in warning. Now wasn't the appropriate time for her humor to surface.

Instead of disgust or fear, my dad shook his head in amazement. "What's so great about being normal anyway?" He opened his arms and I didn't hesitate to launch myself at him. He caught me and held me tightly. I had to swallow back sobs of relief that he still loved me even though I was a freak.

Chapter Twenty-Five

It was embarrassing to have a mini meltdown in front of everyone. Considering the circumstances, I didn't think anyone would blame me. I sensed tension coming from the bond and couldn't decide if I was amused, or appalled when I realized the cause.

Reece was jealous of our closeness. His instincts were to protect me and someone else was standing in the way of him doing his duty. Being around an alpha could be very trying at times. It didn't help that I was apparently also an alpha.

Deciding to ignore Reece's grouchiness, I slung my arm around my dad's waist. He carried a handgun in the small of his back, hidden beneath his shirt. It wasn't the most comfortable place to carry a weapon, but it gave him quick and easy access.

"What exactly are we facing here?" my father asked.

It seemed that he'd decided he was going to assist us with our mission. No one protested. Frankly, we could use the help.

"Originally, we were investigating a coven of witches," Mark explained. "Now, it appears we also have Katrina to contend with."

"What did the witches do to deserve being hunted by the TAK Squad?"

"They've been killing young men and women for the past couple of hundred years," Kala said. She was eyeing my dad with interest, which made me highly uncomfortable. I knew she liked to play around and the thought of her with my father made me want to shudder. "They drain their life force to keep themselves alive," she explained.

"I take it we can't just gun them down in cold blood?"

I rolled my eyes at his simple solution. "They'd already be dead if that was an option," I said. "The ghosts told us that we can only kill them if we destroy some kind of talisman first. They've wards set up around the perimeter of Bradbury that are designed to warn them if any humans who are aware of their existence enter the town." I didn't know much about spells, but it seemed very sophisticated and complex. It would take a lot of power to set them up and maintain them.

"I guess this means you and I can't directly assist the squad in this mission," my dad said to Mark.

"Entering the town would be deadly for us both,"

he confirmed. "We need to think of a way to lure the coven out of town. We'll only have a short time to search the building where the talisman is probably being kept."

Reece figured it out before the rest of us did. "You think it's in the center of the pentagram. Either in the coffee shop, or in the apartment above it."

"It makes sense that it would be at the center of their town where the most power is concentrated."

"I'll search the café," I volunteered, surprising everyone with the offer.

"No," Reece argued immediately. "It's too dangerous. I'm not going to let you go in there alone." Our gazes locked and neither of us were about to back down this time.

"Why should you be the one to search the place?" my father asked, giving me the opportunity to look away without actually conceding defeat.

"The ghosts can scout the area for me and warn me if the witches are coming," I said. "I can also call on the dogs, if I need to." I was reluctant to do that. It would undoubtedly draw unwanted attention if the café was surrounded by a pack of canines.

"Can you explain how you can control dogs?"

"When we were looking for the witches' houses, I ran into a few of them," I explained. "I had to establish dominance over them so they wouldn't bark and give away my presence. That seemed to have formed a brief link to them. When one of the witches attacked me, I sort of reached out with my mind and called on the dogs for help. They came to my rescue and drove her off before she could kill me."

He paled at how close I'd come to dying. Sadly, I was starting to get used to my close encounters with death. It was turning out to be an occupational hazard. "I take it the ghosts have been helpful so far?" he asked.

I nodded and automatically glanced around to see if any of the spirts were here. They weren't and we were still alone. "They warned us to get out of Bradbury, then one of them pinpointed where each of the witches' houses were. They attacked the vampire when she came for me in the cemetery." It hurt to think of her as my mother and it was easier to refer to her as impersonally as possible.

"I couldn't see the ghosts, but they did a good job of scaring the bloodsucker away," Kala said with a smirk.

"How did they manage that?" Mark asked. He was itching to take notes, but didn't reach for the tablet that was in an inner pocket of his jacket.

"It was pretty scary," I said. "They changed from normal, benign spirits into these hideous, clawed monsters."

"It sounds like they turned vengeful," he mused. "I wonder why they don't turn against the coven?"

At his question, the handsome young man who had helped us out several times appeared. He shook his head anxiously at the mere suggestion that they might turn against the people who'd killed them.

"I don't think they can attack the witches directly," I said and the ghost nodded. "Would it harm you if you tried?" I asked and he nodded again. "If we were to kill them, would it set you guys free?" I didn't know where that notion had come from, but it was a good guess. He smiled, inclined his head for a third time and reached out to pat my arm.

Everyone was looking at me strangely at my apparent one sided conversation with an invisible being. "I think I know why the ghosts are willing to help us now," I said, trying not to pull away as the coldness seeped from him into my flesh. "The witches have some kind of power over them. It's keeping them here instead of letting them move on."

As I spoke, the old church began to fill up with spirits. "If we can destroy them and their talisman, then the spirits will be free." The longing on their faces was poignant enough to almost bring tears to my eyes.

"So," my father said, "all of these ghosts are young men and women?" I nodded and he frowned. "Then who is the boy? What part does he play in all this?"

It was a good question and one that none of us had considered. The child in question appeared and stared up at me forlornly. I crouched down in front of him so we were face to face. A horrible suspicion hit me and I voiced it. "Is your mother one of the witches?"

He screwed his face up and he silently began to cry as he nodded. Just like I had with my father, he flung himself into my arms. His sorrow was almost enough

201

to make him corporeal. The usual deep chill sank into me as I did my best to soothe him.

The young man stepped forward and drew the child away. Flynn helped me to stand and put his arm around my shoulder. He rubbed my arm to give me some warmth. Reece glared at Flynn in automatic jealousy. Kala's lips twitched and I sent her a narrow stare. This routine was already starting to get old.

"How are we going to lure the witches out of town?" my father asked, bringing our focus back to the task at hand.

Mark had a solution, but it would be risky. "I think the best way would be to trip the wards again." Our whole team rounded on him in protest. He held up his hands to stop us before we could unleash our complaints. "It's the only way we can draw them out long enough for Lexi to search the café."

"What if we tripped it in more than one place?" my dad said. "That'll force them to split up. Dividing their forces will help add to the confusion."

It was a sound idea, yet I was far from happy that he was volunteering to put himself in danger. It was bad enough that he faced human enemies on a daily basis. Now he was taking on people who possessed unpredictable and uncanny powers.

"What if they've changed the wards so they can kill intruders rather than just warn them that someone is on to them?" I asked.

Mark hesitated, clearly he hadn't thought of that possibility. "I'll test the wards. If I just get a nosebleed again, then we can proceed with the plan."

"And if you die?" Kala asked. For once, she was standing still rather than shifting from foot to foot restlessly. "How do you think we can go on without you as our leader?"

"Of course you can go on without me," he said, waving away her concern. "I've taught you everything you need to know. Reece can easily lead you in my place."

"Mark," I said and he looked at me warily at my sharp tone. "You might not be their biological father, but you're still their Dad. They won't be able to function if you die."

Their expressions backed up my warning and he blew out a sigh of acknowledgement. "I know," he admitted. "I just want to get this mission over and done with."

"Can we get help from another witch?" my dad asked. "A good one, if there is such a thing?"

Mark pondered the idea and eventually nodded. "I know someone who might be able to assist us. She lives in England, so it might take a while for her to reach us. I'll call her and see if she's available."

He moved away so he could speak as privately as was possible in such a small place. The rest of us huddled together. Wan daylight filtered through the holes in the roof, casting narrow beams of light through the gloom. The church was creepy even in the daytime. I wished we could find somewhere else to hold our meetings.

Mark returned after a few minutes with a somber expression. "Beatrice is willing to assist us, but the earliest she can get here is in three days."

"That's cutting it close to the full moon," Reece pointed out. "We'll only have two days left to carry out this mission."

None of us wanted to postpone this any longer than we had to. It wasn't just the coven that was a danger to us. Katrina was also lurking around and waiting to strike. She hadn't seen my father for eighteen years. I wondered how she'd react if she knew he was here. For all I knew, she might want to make him her husband in semi-death as well as in life.

Chapter Twenty-Six

We returned to Dawson's Retreat and Margaret met us at the door. She offered us morning tea, which Mark accepted, of course. We trooped inside and headed to the parlor.

"Since we have plenty of time to kill, how about you bake that cake you promised?" Flynn said to Reece as we all took a seat.

Reminded of what day it was, I turned to our boss. "Happy birthday, Mark."

He offered me a weary smile. "Thank you. I'm sure it will be a memorable day." It already had been and it wasn't even lunchtime yet.

"Don't let Margaret help you," Kala reminded Reece as he stood again. "Lexi, make sure he does this on his own."

Remembering the promise I'd made to Margaret

that I wouldn't let him burn down the kitchen, I stood as well. My father watched us in bemusement as we headed for the door. Our hostess arrived with a trolley full of coffee and tea before he could ask us what was going on.

"I'm going to utilize your kitchen for an hour or so," Reece told her.

Margaret shot a worried look at me and I patted her on the shoulder as I sidled past. "It'll be okay. I'll watch him closely."

"I bet you will," Kala murmured just loudly enough for us shifters to hear her. Flynn looked down at his feet, trying hard not to grin.

Following Reece into the kitchen, I sat on a stool while he searched for a cake recipe on his cell phone. The kitchen was gigantic, with a large island counter in the middle of the room. Pots and pans hung from hooks above the counter and cupboards were set beneath it. A massive stainless steel fridge stood next to the sink. A dishwasher had been added to the right of the sink. While the house was old, the kitchen had been modernized.

Choosing a recipe, Reece searched the cupboards for a mixing bowl and a cake tin. He retrieved the ingredients that we'd bought yesterday. Flynn's memory had been accurate and he had everything that he needed. Setting the oven to preheat, he proceeded to mix the ingredients together. Unlike Kala, he didn't simply dump everything into the bowl at once, but added them in the correct order.

I shouldn't have been surprised that he was adept at baking a cake. Kala was a disaster in the kitchen, but the rest of us were far more competent. She'd be devastated when his cake turned out so much better than hers. It would be one more sign that she was inferior when it came to cooking.

That reminded me of the other talents that she'd mentioned. "Who did Kala have to torture for information?" I asked while Reece slid the cake into the oven. He turned the timer on then began to clean up the mess he'd made.

Glancing around to make sure Margaret wasn't about to walk in, he handed me the spoon that he'd used to scoop the mixture into the cake tin. I licked the chocolate off it and his eyes followed the movement. Heat rose to my hairline as we both remembered using our hands and mouths on each other. I moved to the sink to rinse off the utensil.

Ignoring the tension that had just sprung up between us, Reece carried the bowl over to me. I took it from him and washed it by hand. "It was during one of our early missions," he said. "We were sent after a ring of sexual deviants who preyed on children." My expression reflected my disgust and he picked up on my wish not to know the details of their crimes. "We knew who most of the members were, but we didn't know who the ringleader was."

Plucking a dishtowel from a hook on the wall, he took the bowl from me and began drying it. "We captured three of the perverts and took them to the cells in our base to question them." It was news to me that our compounds contained cells. It just showed how little I still knew about our bases.

"Kala made her captive crack far faster than the rest of us," he continued and shook his head at the memory. I winced when he inadvertently sent me an image of a broken, bleeding human. "She has an aptitude for causing just enough pain to make someone tell her everything she wants to know."

"Why was the TAK Squad sent after a group of pedophiles?" We didn't usually track down that type of monster. They were undoubtedly evil, but of a different kind than we usually handled.

"It was a favor for one of Mark's superiors." He shrugged to indicate that he hadn't questioned his boss about the matter.

"I take it you found the ringleader?"

"Of course," he said with a small smile. "We're the ultimate hunters. No one can hide from us for long."

That was true. We had the means to find anyone no matter how hard or fast they ran. Mark's technological skills, coupled with our supernatural abilities, made us a formidable team. I almost pitied the creatures we were sent to hunt down and eradicate. Then again, they deserved everything they had coming to them.

With the kitchen put back to rights, we returned to the parlor. Margaret had taken a seat on the lounge next to my father. He looked far more relaxed than usual, but he was still alert and ready for action. At six foot four, he towered over our hostess even when sitting. She was captivated by his charm and looks. He had blond hair that was graying at the temples and light blue eyes. I could see nothing of him in myself at all. The only thing I'd inherited from him was my stubbornness and my prowess with firearms.

Flynn took a deep breath with his mouth open slightly, surreptitiously tasting the air. "The cake smells good," he noted. His eyes strayed towards the door, as if he was longing to sneak to the kitchen and gobble it down before it was even finished cooking.

"Of course it's going to be good," Reece said in a mock affronted tone.

Kala sneered from her seat next to the birthday boy. "*I'll* be the judge of that."

"Would you like tea or coffee, dear?" Margaret asked me. She leaned forward, ready to serve me from the selection she'd put on the coffee table.

"Coffee, please." That would always be my first preference. Reece indicated he'd like the same. With our hostess in attendance, we had to stick to topics that wouldn't make her run screaming in horror. It was a relief when the cake timer finally went off after nearly an hour of excruciatingly boring conversation.

"Are you going to supervise the frosting of the cake?" Reece asked me.

I could have kissed him right in front of everyone for giving me an excuse to leave the room. I was willing to do almost anything to escape by then. Margaret, Mark and my father were discussing politics, which was the swiftest way to put me to sleep.

"I'll help," Kala said and surged to her feet. She was even more bored than I was.

"I call dibs on the bowl," Flynn called to her back.

"I'll fight you for it," she grinned over her shoulder.

"Oh dear," Margaret said and wrung her hands in distress. "I hope they don't break anything."

"I'm sure they'll be careful," Mark told her as Reece and I loped after the other two.

We arrived just in time to see Kala removing the cake from the oven. She placed it on the counter and scowled down at it. My mouth was already watering at the chocolaty scent that permeated the room. "It's perfect," she said in a flat tone and shot him an accusing glare. "How come yours looks like this and mine looked like something a dog crapped out?"

"Because I followed the recipe," he replied with a shrug. We'd bought premade frosting rather than attempting to make one ourselves. All he had to do now was wait for the cake to cool then smear it over the top.

Unwilling to wait any longer than he absolutely had to, Flynn tipped the cake out onto a plate, then put it in the fridge so it would cool faster. I washed the cake tin while the others chatted quietly about our mission.

"I hate this part of our job," Kala complained. "Waiting around with nothing to do always gets to me." It was going to be extremely boring until Beatrice turned up and we could continue on with the mission.

"It wouldn't be so bad if there was a gym nearby," Flynn said. "What are we going to do for the next couple of days?"

"There must be something interesting to see in the area," I ventured and received three incredulous stares. "Don't you ever do any sightseeing?" I asked in exasperation.

Reece lifted a shoulder, then let it fall. "We're usually too focused on the job to think about anything else."

It made me a little sad that they didn't take the time to enjoy life. They spent all of their time either hunting the bad guys down, or training. Only Kala was interested in watching TV. Flynn sometimes watched a movie with us, but none of the agents had any hobbies or interests. If I didn't have my books or the archives to read in my downtime, I'd have been bored out of my mind.

Mark wandered into the kitchen a few minutes later, presumably to check up on us and to make sure we weren't fighting over the cake. "What's the verdict?" he asked. He was only showing a slight case of nerves. He was a brave man, but facing another disaster like the cake Kala had baked for me would make anyone flinch.

"It looks pretty good," Flynn replied and removed the cake from the fridge. It was now cool enough for Reece to frost it.

We watched him carefully smear the chocolate

mixture over the top. The finished product looked like it could have graced the front page of a food magazine. "Is there anything you can't do?" I asked him in mock disgust.

"Not that I know of," he said with a small grin.

Kala rolled her eyes and pulled a knife out of the block sitting on the counter. "Let's see if it tastes as good as it looks." She handed the knife to Mark. "You can do the honors, since it's your birthday." It was gracious of her to let him cut his own cake.

Mark cut into it and Flynn leaned forward to breathe in the scent of the still slightly warm center. Margaret and my father appeared and our hostess handed out plates to everyone. She was almost as fastidious about keeping the kitchen clean as Mark was.

"My goodness, that is a beautiful cake," she beamed at Reece. He took his plate with a modest smile, which deepened Kala's scowl.

Since it was Mark's birthday, he took the first bite. He made a sound of pure enjoyment and flicked an apologetic glance at Kala. "It's really, really good," he said with his mouth full. He lifted his plate just in time to catch a few crumbs.

"Jeez, Mark, I thought you had better manners than that," Kala said facetiously. She bit into her cake almost savagely. She chewed, swallowed and shot a sour look at Reece. He raised his eyebrows in innocent enquiry. "It's edible, I suppose," she said grudgingly.

Flynn took a bite, closed his eyes and chewed slowly. "I don't even have words to describe how good this is," he said sincerely when his mouth was empty.

Reece and I both took a bite at the same time. The cake was moist, fluffy and damn near perfect. Margaret also had a piece and looked at Reece in surprise. "This is a very good cake, young man. Have you ever thought about entering a baking competition?"

Stuffing the last piece of her cake into her mouth, Kala muttered something and stalked off. Her mouth was too full to be able to understand her, which was probably a good thing.

My father ate his cake in silence. A single nod at Reece was his only acknowledgement that he liked it. For him, it was high praise.

Once everyone dispersed, I cleaned up the mess. To my surprise, Reece lingered to help me. "Is that the first cake you've ever baked?" I asked.

He nodded and reached up to put the plates back in the cupboard above the sink. A flash of tanned stomach showed and I clenched my fists to stop myself from reaching out and touching him. "Being the only female, Kala always felt like she had to prove herself to us," he explained. "It's a real blow to her ego that she can't cook."

"Do you think she'd let me give her some lessons?"

"I'm not sure," he shrugged. "It's hard to say with Kala. Her moods can be pretty changeable."

That was the cougar in her. One minute she could be playful and affectionate, then she could be moody and want to be alone. I'd try to catch her in one of her better moods and ask her if she'd like my assistance. I'd have to wait until we were back at one of our compounds before I made the offer. I doubted that Margaret would be very happy if Kala destroyed her kitchen.

Chapter Twenty-Seven

We spent the next couple of days playing board games in the parlor. Margaret had kept them even after her kids had outgrown the games. Both of her daughters were now married with children. They lived in nearby towns, but not in Bradbury itself. I didn't know them, but I was glad they hadn't been caught up in the coven's spells and hexes.

I wasn't at all surprised to find that Reece, Kala and Flynn were highly competitive. I was just as bad. None of us liked to lose and our games tended to get quite heated. If Mark and my father hadn't been there to act as referees, we'd have probably come to blows a few times. At least we weren't bored while we were squabbling.

After dark, we spent a few hours scouting Bradbury from afar. My father had suggested to Mark that we keep our eye on the town to make sure the coven wasn't planning anything.

The night before Beatrice was scheduled to arrive, I paired up with my father to patrol. We circled the town on foot, being careful to stay outside the wards. Now that I was aware of them, I recognized the faint shimmer in the air that was invisible to humans. It was apparently also undetectable to other shifters. I was the only one who could see it and I kept the ability from the others. It was just one more strange thing about me that made me different from everyone else.

"How are things between you and Agent Garrett?" my father asked, startling me with the unexpected question.

I could have fabricated a lie, but I'd always been honest with him. I wasn't about to start telling him untruths now. "Kind of awkward most of the time," I replied. "The bond is holding us both prisoner and neither of us is happy about it."

He studied me as best as he could in the darkness. "I wouldn't say that he's unhappy about being bonded to you," he said mildly. "He seems very protective." Reece had been hovering close to me ever since my father had arrived.

"It's an alpha thing," I explained. "He feels a sense of ownership over me. He doesn't like anyone else encroaching on his turf, not even if that someone is my father."

He laughed quietly. "That isn't just an alpha thing,

honey. All men feel that way when their girl's attention is taken away from them."

I goggled at his description. "I'm not Reece's girl!" I said it a little too loudly. A dog barked in warning and I sent it calming thoughts. It quietened immediately with a submissive whine.

"Lexi, like it or not, you're bound to Reece." His tone was stoic, but I sensed his unhappiness. "You two are going to be together until death, or so Mark believes."

A small shudder wracked me. He slid his arm over my shoulder and hugged me to his side. "Sometimes, I almost wish I'd never gone to Colorado with Mark," I said. "I should have been enlisted in the army by now. Instead of being a soldier, I'm a secret agent for an organization no one has ever heard of."

He squeezed my shoulder comfortingly. "Life doesn't always go the way we plan it, sweetheart. Sometimes it throws us for a loop. We either have to go with it, or let it overwhelm us."

He'd been thrown one hell of a loop when my mother had been turned into a bloodsucker. He hadn't let that tragedy ruin our lives. My dad had done his best to provide me with a stable and loving home. I could either spend my free time whining and being miserable, or I could suck it up and attempt to be the adult I was supposed to be. "You're right," I said. "I need to make the best of this situation."

I might not be a soldier, but I was still saving lives and taking down the bad guys. If it also meant that I occasionally had to share Reece's bed, then so be it. It wasn't like I didn't enjoy it when we were naked together. On the contrary, I enjoyed that part very much.

"Do I even want to know what you're thinking about?" my father said dryly. "I don't think I've ever seen you smile quite like that before."

I made my smug, self-satisfied grin disappear and replaced it with an innocent look. Or as innocent as I could make it.

As we skirted the edge of town, I sensed a dog approaching and grabbed my father's arm to stop him. He became alert and drew his gun. "What's wrong?" His eyes probed the shadows, searching for a target.

"Nothing's wrong. We're just about to have some company and I didn't want you to be startled."

The Rottweiler who had broken free from his yard to come to my rescue emerged from the shadows. He trotted over and sat at my feet. He'd lost weight and his ribs were showing.

"What are you doing here, boy?" I asked and hunkered down to pet him. He whined and licked my hand. His collar was gone and I wondered if he'd run away from home. Delving into his mind, I found that he'd been searching for me. It seemed that he'd switched his loyalties from his previous owners to me. "Uh oh," I said and stood.

"Is this one of the dogs who saved you from the witch?" my father asked as he slipped his gun into the small of his back again. A holster would be a dead giveaway that he was armed in the off chance that we were spotted creeping around the edge of town by anyone.

"Yep. He led the pack."

He knelt and offered the animal his hand. After a suspicious sniff, the dog licked his fingers. "Good boy." My dad thumped him on the flank a few times and the Rottweiler's tongue lolled in happiness. "You should send him back to his owners before they miss him," he suggested.

"That's the thing," I said uneasily. "He thinks I'm his owner now."

Looking up at me in surprise, he rose to his feet. "Are you saying that you can read his mind?"

"Sort of," I shrugged. "I can pick up the sense that he left his home to search for me. Now that's he's found me, he has no intention of leaving."

Putting his hand on my shoulder, he smiled widely. "Congratulations, Lexi. You're the proud new owner of a Rottweiler. You finally have the puppy that you've always wanted."

We both looked down at the 'puppy'. When standing, his head came to my waist. He probably weighed more than I did.

We'd walked our section of the perimeter of town with the dog following at my heels. He passed through the magical barrier without setting it off or suffering any ill effects. I could sense Reece on patrol a short distance away. I had the feeling he wasn't going to be happy with this new addition to our team.

"What are you going to call him?" my dad asked.

I scanned the dog for his name and came up empty. With his collar missing, I had no idea what his former owners had called him. "Zeus," I decided. It seemed to suit him with his size and overall menacing appearance.

We continued our circuit until it was time to call it a night. Reece and Flynn were waiting for us at the appointed meeting place. Reece looked at the animal that was trotting along happily at my side. "Do I even want to know why that dog is following you?" he asked with his hands on his hips and his eyebrows raised. Flynn was just as surprised and eyed the dog warily.

Zeus growled low in his throat, knowing that neither of the men was human. They hadn't exactly had a chance to become acquainted after Talitha had tried to kill me. I stroked the Rottweiler's head to calm him. He was so big that I didn't even need to bend down to reach him. "Zeus decided that he belongs to me now," I explained.

Reece rolled his eyes, but he didn't bother to argue. Even with both of us clamping down on the bond, he could read enough of my emotions to know that it was a done deal. "I'm sure Mark is going to be ecstatic about this," he muttered. "We've never had a pet before."

Zeus was far more than a mere pet, he was also my guardian. He was already a loyal companion and he'd only been with me for a couple of hours.

Dawn was nearing and it was time to head back to our base. We met up with Mark and Kala at the SUV where it was parked a short distance from the edge of town. We hadn't spied any of the coven members during our patrol. As far as we could tell, they hadn't set any traps for us. Hopefully, Beatrice would be able to tell for sure.

Kala smelled Zeus before he trotted into view and she sent me an accusing stare. While she could tolerate werewolves, she really didn't like dogs. Dogs liked her even less. My new friend's hackles rose as he pinned her with his stare.

"Why is that dog with you?" Mark asked.

"Zeus is mine now," I said simply. "He refused to return home even when I ordered him to."

Instead of being angry, he was thoughtful. "Is he likely to attack any of us?"

"He's not too thrilled with Kala," I said, "but he won't attack unless I tell him to."

Kala was glowering at the animal in annoyance. "Can you tell him to stop growling at me?"

Zeus' upper lip was curled back, baring his teeth. His whole body vibrated with a nearly inaudible growl. "Sit," I said and he complied. "Kala is a friend," I said both with my mouth and with my mind. The dog whined and looked up at me in confusion. I sent him a picture of a human, three dogs, a snake and a cat living together. He didn't like the idea at all. In his mind, all felines were enemies.

He was even less sure about adding a snake to the picture.

I gestured for Kala to approach and she did so warily. Zeus cocked his head to the side when we linked arms. His expression was so comical that we both burst out laughing. Picking up that we cared about each other, my new companion reluctantly accepted that she was a member of our pack. He wasn't thrilled about Flynn's presence either, but he would put up with him for my sake.

Chapter Twenty-Eight

Zeus followed me to the back of the SUV and leaped inside when I opened the door for him. Kala opted to ride with my father in his rental car rather than to be confined in a small space with a large dog. She was having a harder time adjusting to this than Zeus was.

Flynn sat sideways so he could keep a wary eye on my guardian. Zeus hunkered in the back of the vehicle. Mainly watching me, he occasionally glanced out through the tinted windows. He'd only been with me for a short time, but he already loved me. It was hard not to return such unwavering affection.

Having an animal depending on me was a new challenge. Our job would most likely take us all over the US. I wasn't sure if I was going to be able to keep Zeus with me at all times. He whined as he picked up my concern and leaned over the back of the seat to lick my cheek.

"Gross," Flynn complained. "It smells like dog breath in here now." Following my direction, Zeus swung his head towards Flynn and huffed out a low bark. Blanching, Flynn waved the stench away with a scowl. "I should have kept my mouth shut."

"I highly doubt Margaret and Edward will allow an animal to stay inside the house," Mark turned around to say as we pulled up in the parking lot at the back of Dawson's Rest. "What are you going to do with him?"

It was clear that Zeus was my responsibility and I wasn't about to shirk my duty. "He hasn't eaten for a couple of days, so I'll need to buy some food for him. I'll ask him to stay out of sight and guard the property while we're sleeping."

Reece met my eyes in the rearview mirror. "Why ask him? You're the boss, just tell him what to do."

"I'd rather have Zeus as a friend than a lowly minion."

Sensing that I was defending him, Zeus leaned over and rested his head on my shoulder.

"Can he understand everything you're saying?" Flynn asked.

"Only if I project my thoughts to him."

Reece seemed relieved. "So, he isn't linked to you in the same way that I am?"

My nose wrinkled at that thought. "No. We're not bonded. We can just sense each other's thoughts if we try hard enough." Zeus and I were linked, but not in the same way that Reece and I were. It took conscious effort for me to portray what I was thinking to the animal.

"I'll take you to buy some pet food," Reece offered. He didn't trust me to be alone, not even during the day and with my guard dog with me. So far, Katrina hadn't made any further attempts to kill Reece, or to turn me. She was lying low, waiting for her chance to strike. At night, I could feel her hovering at the edge of my senses. She was close enough to keep tabs on me, but stayed far enough away that we wouldn't be able to find her easily.

I nodded and climbed out to take Mark's place up the front when he left the SUV.

Zeus alternated between staring at me forlornly from the back of the vehicle and glowering at Reece for getting to sit beside me as we headed to the next town. I had plenty of money, thanks to my generous government salary and lack of bills. I'd barely spent any of the pay that I'd earned yet, mainly because we'd been so busy hunting the bad guys.

Reece parked out front of a pet store and I told Zeus to stay in the SUV. I pitied anyone who tried to steal the car with the Rottweiler still inside. It was a cool day, so he wasn't in danger of overheating.

Dressed all in black, Reece and I looked like we were playing dress up as a SWAT team. I made my way to the counter and the clerk's eyes widened when he saw me up close. Aware that many men found me to be attractive, I tried not to roll my eyes. Reece's shoulders moved as he laughed silently at the clerk's stunned reaction.

"Can I help you?" the man squeaked.

"I need some dog food."

"What kind of dog do you have?"

"He's a Rottweiler."

"How old is he?" On familiar ground, the clerk ignored Reece completely and focused his attention on me.

I stared back at him blankly. How was I supposed to know how old Zeus was? I doubted he even knew the answer to that question.

"He's about two years old," Reece said.

"You'll need both wet and dry food," the clerk decided and hustled off to search for what we needed.

"How do you know Zeus is two years old?" I asked.

Leaning against the counter, Reece shrugged. "It was just a guess. He's not a puppy, but he's also still fairly young."

The clerk returned with a bag of dry food that had to weigh half what he did. "I'll be right back with the rest," he puffed and disappeared again. Blinking at the massive bag of food, I could now see why my father had never wanted a dog. I had no idea they required so much food. The clerk came back with an armful of cans and dumped them on the counter. "That should be enough food for a week," he pronounced.

"A week?" I said. My voice went up a few octaves higher than usual.

"You should have researched what you were getting yourself into before you bought the dog," the clerk said with a complete lack of sympathy, not realizing that I hadn't had a choice about it. "Food and water bowls are over there."

Following where he was pointing, I saw a shelf crammed with bowls of all shapes and sizes. Keeping Zeus' size in mind, I chose two large stainless steel bowls for food and water and returned to the clerk. He rang up the items and I handed over my credit card. Reece hefted the bag of dry food over his shoulder and I carried the rest of the items.

"I hope I'll see you again soon," the clerk called as we left his store.

"Not likely," Reece muttered.

His jealousy was starting to get out of hand and I sent him a frown. "Can you stop glowering at every male who looks at me sideways?"

"No," he replied evenly as he opened the back of the SUV to dump the food inside.

"Why not?"

"Because I'm an alpha and you're my mate."

"You make it sound like I belong to you," I complained.

Taking the bag from me, he placed it next to the dry food then turned to face me. "You do belong to me, Lexi." His stare was compelling and his tone was very nearly seductive. "Just as I belong to you."

I frowned and looked away to see a pair of young women staring at Reece. They were around his age, only a couple of years older than me. He chuckled when he felt a flare of jealousy from me. "It might not have been our choice to bond with each other," he said reasonably, "but it's done now and we just have to live with it.

Unfortunately, neither of us knew the slightest thing about what it meant to be bonded. There was nothing about it in the PIA files and we just had to stumble through this on our own.

Zeus had obligingly moved aside to give us room to stash the packages. He could smell the dry food even through the plastic bag and started salivating. The poor thing was starving. I couldn't make him wait another half an hour to return to our temporary base to eat. I ripped the bag open and poured some food into one of the bowls. Zeus leaped down and gobbled up the biscuits, then looked at me hopefully.

"I have no idea how much I should give him," I said. I'd only had him for a few short hours and I was already feeling overwhelmed and not up to the task.

Reece bent over to read the instructions on the bag and the two women giggled. They were staring at his butt, which was admittedly impressive. I stepped in front of him to block the view. My glare effectively killed their laughter and they scurried away with spiteful whispers aimed at me.

"Down, girl," Reece said silkily into my ear.

"Sure thing, 'Rex'," I replied and he scowled. Rex was the nickname Kala had given him when they'd been kids. He'd always hated it.

"Watch it, or I'll start calling you Rexina," he threatened.

"Fair enough," I conceded in defeat. I didn't want, or need a nickname like that.

"You can give Zeus another handful of dry food, but no more until later this evening," he instructed.

Licking his chops, my new companion barely waited for the food to land in the bowl before he devoured it. "That's all you're getting," I told him when it was gone. "Back in the car."

Slightly disappointed, Zeus obeyed me and leaped inside. Much happier now that he was no longer starving, his tongue lolled in a doggy grin as I closed the door. At least one of us was happy, I thought grumpily. Being alone with Reece was bringing out feelings in me that I was desperately trying to avoid thinking about.

Chapter Twenty-Nine

We returned to the B&B and I let Zeus out after checking that Margaret and Edward were both inside. He followed me over to the faucet at the side of the house and watched with interest as I washed his food bowl, then filled the other one with water. I carried it over to the tree line that bordered the property and placed it behind a bush where it would be out of sight of the house.

Hunkering beside him, I scratched his ears and he closed his eyes in enjoyment. "I need you to stay out of sight and to let me know if any strangers approach the house," I said to him. He acknowledged my request with a lick of the back of my hand and disappeared into the shadows.

Shaking his head in disbelief, Reece followed me inside the house, carrying the gigantic bag of dry food. I had my arms full with the cans. "Will he actually be able to warn you if one of the witches shows up?"

"Yep. He knows there's something different about them. He can tell them apart from normal humans," I replied quietly. We weren't the only ones up and about and we didn't want anyone to overhear our conversation.

Taking the stairs quickly, I unlocked my door and moved aside to let Reece in first. He knelt and placed the bag on the floor, then slid it under my bed. It wouldn't be pleasant having the smell of dog food permeating my room, but I didn't have anywhere else to stash it. "Thanks," I said.

"I'm glad I'm not sleeping in here," he replied, wrinkling his nose at the smell. He left and entered his room next to mine to wash up before breakfast. I hid the food bowl and cans next to the dry food, then spent a couple of minutes in the bathroom.

Margaret was serving an early breakfast when I joined everyone in the dining room. It had been hours since I'd eaten. I devoured my cereal and followed it up with four pieces of toast. The coffee was hot, strong and wonderful.

Tired from spending the night on patrol, we headed to our rooms to sleep for a few hours after we'd eaten.

Zeus woke me with a mental bark when a car arrived. Groggy from sleeping during the day rather than at night, I walked to the window and peered out.

A car parked in the lot behind the house. Zeus confirmed that the woman who climbed out was a witch, but she wasn't from the dark coven.

Mark appeared below and jogged over to help her with her suitcase. He planted a kiss on her cheek, which confirmed my suspicions that she was Beatrice.

Taking a quick shower, I was more alert when I joined the others in the dining room downstairs.

Beatrice wasn't what I'd expected at all. I'd been picturing an ugly old crone with pure white hair, possibly dressed in a black robe. Instead, she had shoulder length brown hair, wore jeans and a man's chambray shirt with the sleeves rolled up to her elbows. She carried a large brown purse on one shoulder.

I was the last to arrive and her back stiffened when she sensed me. When she turned around, I saw that she was in her late forties. There were a few lines on her forehead and at the corners of her eyes, but she was still quite pretty. Or she would have been if her hazel eyes hadn't been wide with fear.

I looked behind me to see if the ghosts had materialized, but I was alone. When I turned back, the witch was smiling. She gave no sign that she'd just been staring at me like I was going to tackle her to the ground and start gnawing on her entrails. "You must be Alexis," she said and extended her hand.

Taking her hand in mine, I shook it gently and noticed her cringe away slightly. "Is there a reason why you're so afraid of me?" I asked her curiously.

"I'm not planning on biting you, you know." Not yet anyway, the full moon was tomorrow night, so theoretically, it could happen.

"Are you aware that you're…different from normal shifters?" she asked as delicately as possible as I brushed past her and sat beside my father.

"I'm well aware," I replied dryly. "I've been bitten by both a vampire and a werewolf, which I understand should have killed me."

"Oh, it will," she said and received stares of consternation from everyone. "I mean, it will eventually if you don't take steps to stop the taint from spreading."

Margaret bustled into the room, pushing a trolley with tea, coffee, the remainder of Mark's chocolate cake and enough cups for everyone. We'd slept through lunch and would have to settle for afternoon tea instead. Our hostess was pleased to see that we had another guest. With the addition of Beatrice and my father, she had a full house again.

Mark waited for her to leave before he leaned forward, beating my father to the question. "What can you tell us about Lexi's condition?"

Kala leaned against me in support at hearing that I now had a condition. I thought strengthening the bond with Reece had fixed the problem. Obviously, I was wrong. It was distressing to hear that I was tainted.

"I can see her aura and it's obvious that her soul is in torment." Beatrice was looking at me, but her focus wasn't on my face. It was on my aura that no one else could see. "There are two forces battling each other for supremacy. If the vampire side of you wins, you'll become the undead. If that happens, nothing will be able to bring you back."

Before we could take in that shock, she turned to Reece. "Your soul is also under siege. I'm afraid that you will also eventually turn if you don't kill the vampire who is responsible for your taint."

"So," I said, drawing all eyes to me. "We have to hunt down the vamp that bit us both and stake her through the heart."

"Neither of you can kill her," she said in alarm. "You know what will happen if you do." We'd die, of course. Reece and I nodded our understanding of the danger. "Killing her will help, but ultimately, it won't save you," Beatrice went on. Her British accent sounded quite posh to me. "She mustn't be a master vampire." At our enquiring looks, she explained further. "If she was, you'd be undead already. She's just a lackey, which is why it's taking so long for the taint to take you over."

Mark grasped what she was hinting at. "Are you saying that we need to kill the master who created the vampire that infected both Lexi and Reece?"

Her nod was crisp. "That's exactly what I'm saying. The vampirism originally came from him, assuming her master is male. In order to stop the taint from spreading and to have a chance of reversing it, you have to destroy both of these creatures."

"I didn't see the master vampire," Mark said to my dad. "I have no idea who he is."

"I can't help you find him, but I might be able to help you to locate the vampire who bit your two agents," the witch said. She bent to rummage around in her bag. Pulling out an ancient book bound in cracked and faded red leather, she flicked through the yellowed pages. I caught a glimpse of handwritten notes and intricate illustrations before she settled on a page. The book reminded me of the journal that Thomas the priest had penned.

Placing the book flat on the table, she pointed at a passage that was written in archaic English. "This spell should help. All we need is an item that belonged to the vampire. Then I can cast the spell and the item should be able to track her back to her nest."

As far as I knew, I didn't have anything that would help. The only item I had that even reminded me of my mother was a silver locket that had a picture of us both inside. Now that I was a werewolf, touching any form of silver was extremely painful. Ingesting it could kill me outright. I kept the locket in a pewter jewelry box. It was currently at our base in Colorado.

"I have an item that belonged to her," my dad said. At Beatrice's raised eyebrows, he explained. "The vampire was my wife, Katrina. She was also Lexi's mother." He was talking about her in the past tense, even though she wasn't quite dead. Maybe she already was in his eyes.

The witch turned to me and her fear turned to compassion. "Oh, my dear, I am so sorry."

I shrugged off her pity. It couldn't help and would only make me feel worse. "I just want her to finally be at peace." That wasn't exactly the whole truth. After watching her savage Reece and being at her mercy a few times, I kind of wanted to see her suffer before we sent her and her maker to hell. She might have been my mother once, but she'd lost any hope that I'd be able to love her when she'd tried to kill me as a baby.

Reece knew what I was feeling and sent me a knowing look. He wanted her dead just as much as I did. The feeling had intensified now that he knew we were both at risk of turning into vampires. If it wasn't for our bond, we'd already be dead. Our link had simply postponed the inevitable.

"What else do you need to perform the spell?" Mark asked.

"A few ingredients that should be easy enough to find," she said. "The question is, do we focus on the vampire, or on the coven first?"

"The witches are our main mission," Mark decided. "We'll deal with them first."

Beatrice radiated concern and shifted in her seat, as if she wanted to speak, but was unsure we wanted to hear what she had to say. Mark nodded at her to voice whatever was on her mind. "It is worrisome that the vampire has tracked Alexis down across several states. They aren't usually this persistent."

"She wants us to be a family again," I explained with an attempt at a smile that failed miserably.

Her expression became even more grave, if that was possible. "It sounds like she has fixated on you. I fear she won't give up until she gets what she wants."

"Wow, Lexi, you're so popular," Kala smirked. Flynn elbowed her in the side hard enough to make her wince.

"Behave," Mark admonished them both. "We'll focus on taking down the vampire after we've taken care of the coven."

My father nodded his agreement with the plan, but I knew he was more concerned with my welfare than in taking down the six witches. If he even caught a glimpse of my mother, he'd put another bullet through her forehead. This time, he'd follow it up with a stake through the heart. I only hoped that I would be there to hand him a hammer to drive it home.

Chapter Thirty

"I hate driving in America," Beatrice complained. "You people insist on driving on the wrong side of the road. I almost died three times on the way here from the airport. Someone will need to drive me to the closest grocery store. I should be able to find the ingredients I'll need for both spells there."

I'd had the mistaken belief that a spell would involve exotic components rather than something that could be purchased at a supermarket. Sometimes it was good to be wrong. We wouldn't have to waste time searching for rare ingredients.

"Agent Garrett, I'm sure you won't mind being Beatrice's chauffeur," Mark said.

Reece flicked a look at my father and received a nod of acknowledgement that he would watch over me. They both ignored the disgusted look I gave them. Thanks to the training that my teammates had given me, I could now take care of myself to a certain extent. Plus, I was much stronger and faster than any normal human.

Glumly, I realized that speed and strength hadn't helped when Talitha had cast a spell on me. She'd had no trouble overpowering me with her black magic. If the pack of dogs hadn't come to my rescue, I wouldn't have made it out of Bradbury. Maybe it wouldn't be such a bad idea to have someone watching my back after all.

Reece and the witch were gone for over an hour. Maybe it hadn't been quite so easy to find everything she needed after all. I knew they were on their way back when I sensed Reece drawing closer. Zeus announced their arrival with a mental picture of the SUV pulling to a stop in the parking lot. He was proving to be an effective guard dog. I petted him mentally and sensed him wagging his stumpy tail in delight.

Beatrice didn't join us in the parlor, but went directly to her bedroom on the second floor. She had some preparations to make before she could cast the spell. Our hope was that it would draw the coven out of Bradbury long enough for me to enter and search for the talisman.

Reece entered the parlor and sat on one of the armchairs. While we'd been waiting for the pair to return, I'd filled my father in on what had happened in New Orleans during our hunt for the Zombie

King. I had the feeling he was impressed that I was still keeping it together after coming face to face with walking corpses. I didn't have the heart to tell him that turning into a werewolf had changed me on a fundamental level. While I was still wary of monsters, I was well equipped to deal with them.

As the sun began to sink from the sky, we shifted to the dining room and pushed two of the tables together. Margaret arrived to take our dinner orders. Beatrice joined us shortly afterwards, looking weary and strained. She gave Margaret her order, then sat down. "The spell is ready to be cast," she said quietly. Two other couples had arrived and were sitting at the tables nearby.

"What happens next?" Kala asked.

"We need to wait for full dark, then find someplace secluded so I can perform the spell."

"Would an abandoned church be suitable?" Mark queried.

Beatrice nodded and poured a cup of tea from the fresh pot. "That would be perfect. If the ground is still consecrated, it will help to keep away any evil influences."

"It's still holy," I confirmed. "Katrina wasn't able to enter the cemetery."

"What effect will your spell have?" Mark asked. He also poured a cup of tea and I held my cup out for him to fill it as well. Kala made a face. She was prejudiced against the beverage.

"It will have three purposes, which is why it took

me so long to prepare it," she explained. "First, it will nullify any harmful hexes that may have been added to the wards. Next, it will trigger the wards in six different places. Hopefully, the coven will investigate each breach, which will split them up as per your plan. Thirdly, the spell will lead them on a merry chase, giving Lexi time to enter the town and search for the source of their power."

I was still in the dark about exactly what I'd be looking for. "Do you know what the talisman will look like?"

"It could be anything," she replied. "But I expect you'll know it as soon as you see it. I sense that you have an affinity for magical objects. I doubt you'll have any problems locating it."

Great, now I had an affinity for magical stuff. Kala's lips twitched in amusement, but she held back her comment at a warning look from Mark. I was growing very tired of being 'special'.

We ate our dinner quickly, then dispersed to get ready for our mission. I dressed in head to toe black again. It would be crucial for me to remain unseen this time. I was nervous at the idea of entering Bradbury alone, but it was necessary. The others would be following the witches as they chased after the red herrings that Beatrice's spell would unleash. Once I'd located and destroyed the talisman, the team should be able to move in and finish off the coven members. With the talisman gone, their unholy protection would be lost, leaving them vulnerable.

Carrying Zeus' food bowl to the kitchen, I emptied half a can of dog food into it, then hid the can at the back of the fridge where I hoped it wouldn't be discovered. Excited by the prospect of food, Zeus was waiting for me near the backdoor. He gobbled it down and licked the bowl clean, then looked up at me hopefully.

"That's all you're getting, greedy guts," I said fondly and his ears drooped despondently. They perked up again when he heard the others coming. I darted into the kitchen to wash the bowl and spoon and returned to my room just long enough to hide the bowl again.

We met at the vehicles and Mark motioned for us to gather into a circle. "Philip is going to drive you all to the town line and drop you off at your designated places. I'll borrow his sedan to take Beatrice to the church. I want you all to listen in on your cell phones while she performs her spell."

We all nodded and Mark turned to me. "Beatrice and I will then head for the final two locations. Once I give you the all clear, head straight to the café and try to locate the talisman. Call me the instant that you've destroyed it."

With the team spread out in a wide circle around the perimeter of the town, our earpieces would be less effective. We were going to rely on our cell phones instead. Reece still disapproved of me going in alone and sent me an anguished look.

"Lexi will be fine," Kala said, accurately interpreting his stare. "She has ghosts and a pack of dogs to warn her if any of the witches approaches the café."

Reece wasn't happy about taking the passenger seat rather than the driver's seat, but he wisely kept silent. He might be an alpha werewolf, but my father was a much older alpha male himself. Reece hadn't been quite brave enough to stop him when he'd snatched the keys out of his hand. I smirked at the thought of them both living beneath the same roof. Sparks would definitely fly if they were forced to spend too much time together.

I was already uncomfortable with both of them staying in the B&B. To make matters worse, my father had been given a room on the third floor. I was very glad that he hadn't been around when we'd renewed our bond. Thankfully, no one had brought that episode up in his presence so far.

One by one, the agents were dropped off until it was just my dad, Zeus and I left. I moved up to the front and my furry companion climbed through onto the backseat.

"Do you think this spell is going to work?" my father asked as we circled towards my designated spot.

"I hope so, because we're running short of time. If it doesn't work, we'll have to think of something else to get rid of the coven long enough for me to search the place."

He knew I was referring to the full moon tomorrow night. "What is it like when you change?"

he asked.

"Painful," I said and he winced in sympathy. "It was pretty bad the first time, but the process seems to be getting quicker. It doesn't hurt as much now." It still wasn't pleasant having my entire body transform into another shape, even if it was faster now.

"I'm sorry I allowed Mark to take you to Colorado, sweetheart," he said.

I sensed his grief that I was no longer the innocent young girl he'd left to go on his overseas mission. "None of this is your fault," I said sharply enough for him to glance at me in surprise. "Don't try to take the blame for something that was out of your control. If I hadn't agreed to assist Mark, more people would have died. I'd have had that on my conscience forever." Not that I'd have heard about the Seven Deadly Sinners and the havoc they'd wrought in Denver.

I was silent for a moment as I thought back over everything that had happened to me over the past few months. "I've always been willing to sacrifice my life to keep others safe." He acknowledged that statement with a nod. "It was my dream to become a soldier and I still am, in a way. I'm just a supernatural one now instead of a human one."

He spared me a quick look before returning his gaze to the road. "I'm always amazed at your maturity, Alexis. You make me proud to be your father."

It was rare to receive praise and my eyes filled. I blinked the tears away, hoping he'd always be proud of me and that he'd never be horrified at what I'd become. I sincerely hoped we could end this mission tonight. I wanted him to return to Texas before we were compelled to turn into our animal forms. If he saw me in my altered state, I doubted he'd ever be able to think of me as his little girl ever again.

Picking up on my morbid thoughts, Zeus leaned over and nudged my shoulder. I turned to pet him and my nose wrinkled at his breath. Partially digested dog food wasn't the most pleasant smell.

Reaching the sign that advised we were about to enter Bradbury, my father pulled over to let me out then powered down his window. "Be careful, Lexi. I love you."

"I love you, too," I replied then let Zeus out. We loped over to melt into the trees as my father hopped out and took up his station.

Mark had advised us all to call him at ten pm. I reached the spot where I would enter town and watched the minute hand of my watch click over. When it did, I made the call. Everyone else called at the same time and he connected us in a conference call. "I take it you're all in position," he said and we gave him the affirmative.

"There are so many lost souls gathered here," Beatrice said sadly in the background. I assumed the ghosts had assembled at the church to watch over her. I hoped some of them were still in Bradbury to keep their eye on me.

"You can begin whenever you're ready," Mark told

her.

She began to chant in a language that I knew was English, but was so archaic that it sounded foreign. Her voice rose and fell for a couple of minutes, then the air in front of me rippled as the ward was activated.

"That should have triggered the wards," Beatrice said wearily.

"It did," I confirmed. "I saw a ripple in the barrier."

"You do have an affinity for magic," the witch said into Mark's phone. "Do you sense if it is safe to enter the town?"

There was only one way to find out for sure, so I stepped across the invisible line. "It's safe," I confirmed.

"Did you even test it, or did you just walk through it?" Reece asked. He was on the far side of town, but I was still able to sense his annoyance.

"Does it matter? I'm still alive, aren't I?"

"We'll discuss this later," Mark said and I heard his disapproval that I'd risked my life. "Let's concentrate on the mission. Beatrice and I are about to head to our designated areas. Lexi, head to the café."

"Be careful," my dad warned me, then we all hung up. From now on, there would be phone silence until I'd found and destroyed the talisman. If anyone did use their phone, it would be because they'd run into serious trouble.

Chapter Thirty-One

With Zeus at my side, I jogged towards the middle of town. He wouldn't be able to keep up if I sprinted and I wanted to keep him close. His hearing and sense of smell were even sharper than mine. He'd sense the witches before I did.

Speaking of the devil, the Rottweiler tensed and growled when he heard someone approaching. I darted into an alley and he came unwillingly when I mentally called him. A woman ran past the mouth of the alley a second later. I only caught a glimpse of her pale, intense face. I was pretty sure it was Ophelia. Beatrice's spell had worked and the coven was investigating the multiple breaches in their wards.

I followed the alley to the end and cut through the back streets, avoiding the few pedestrians and cars that were on the roads. A pall had fallen over

Bradbury. The inhabitants were hunkered in their homes. They sensed that all was not well, but were unsure of the cause. If they had any brains, they'd stay inside until morning. Our mission would either be over by then, or we'd all be screwed.

Reaching Kate's Kafé, I wasn't surprised to see that it was closed. The lights were off and the closed sign was hanging on the door. Zeus was alert and gave no indication that he sensed anyone dangerous nearby. Talitha was off chasing magical shadows, leaving her business and the apartment above it empty.

We circled around to the back of the building and I checked the door for an alarm. It seemed to be clear, so I rammed it with my shoulder. The door squealed when it burst open and I waited for an alarm to blare. None did, so we entered and I shut the door behind us.

It was dark, but my eyes adjusted to the lack of light quickly. We were in a short hallway that ended in a T-junction. Walking to the end of the hall, I glanced both ways to see a longer hallway to the right and a set of stairs leading upwards to the left. It made sense that the talisman would be in the apartment upstairs. Talitha wouldn't want to risk any of her customers stumbling across it. We turned left and started climbing.

Apart from the clicking sound of Zeus' claws on the linoleum, the building was silent. At the top of the stairs, we found another long hallway with several doors branching off on each side. All of the doors were open, revealing a bathroom and three bedrooms. The final door at the end opened to a living room.

I felt a strong surge of power coming from the room and entered with my guard dog at my back. The furniture was inexpensive and unremarkable. In direct contrast to the plainness of the couch and coffee table, disturbing paintings hung on the walls. In each, blue robed figures performed their dark ritual. There were six, one for each of the witches and warlocks.

For a moment, I wondered if they were the source of the power. Then my gaze was drawn to a bundle of ivory colored sticks that dangled from a strange wooden chandelier in the center of the room.

Moving closer, I studied the chandelier and realized it was an inverted pentagram. The sticks hung just low enough for me to be able to reach them. I touched one and it didn't feel like wood at all. Turning the bundle around, I started back when I saw a small human skull. In horror, I realized that they weren't sticks at all. The skeleton of a small child had been cleverly pieced together with almost invisible wires.

Realization dawned that the coven's talisman was the long dead corpse of the boy who haunted Dawson's Rest. Sorrow and pity for the boy swelled when I saw that a large section of his skull was missing. Cracks radiated outwards from the wound. It appeared that his head had been bashed in by something, probably a rock.

The room was empty of other people, yet the hairs

on the back of my neck stirred. Zeus' hackles rose as well. He began growling silently as he sensed danger approaching. Realizing that one of the coven members was about to appear, I reached up to pull the talisman down.

A cold, male voice spoke in a foreign language and my body locked in place. I was frozen with my hands stretched upwards. They were only a few centimeters away from the talisman. I couldn't move no matter how hard I strained.

"I thought I might find you here," Malachi said. I recognized his voice by now without needing to see his face. He moved to stand in front of me and examined me with a smile that didn't touch his eyes. "It was clever to attempt to lure us away so you could sneak in here and steal the source of our power. Talitha has been frantic to find you. She has special plans for you, my sweet."

I tried to speak, but my vocal cords were just as frozen as the rest of my body. So much for the ghosts appearing to warn me of danger. Even Zeus hadn't been as much help as I'd hoped. Malachi must have cloaked himself from us both using his witchcraft.

Growling and snarling savagely, Zeus gathered himself to leap. I silently ordered him not to attack and his snarl changed into a puzzled whine. The warlock would just kill him and then I'd have no possibility of escaping from this trap.

Ignoring my companion completely, Malachi reached out and took my chin in his hand. "You are a pretty one. I'm going to have some fun with you before my dear sister arrives."

I had a feeling his idea of fun wasn't the same as mine. My stomach was churning in disgust and he'd barely even touched me yet. He stepped in close enough for his chin length dark brown hair to brush my face. As he bent to kiss me, Zeus ignored my order for him not to attack. With a menacing growl, he lunged forward and bit Malachi on the calf.

Cursing foully, the warlock kicked at the dog, but Zeus dodged out of the way. He lifted his hands to cast a spell and I mentally shouted at my guardian to run. Locked in place, I watched them from the corner of my eye.

Obeying me this time, Zeus dashed past Malachi just as another witch was entering the room. He crashed into her, knocking her into the door. My order for him to run was so strong that he didn't take the opportunity to bite her. Instead, he fled down the stairs before she could react to his presence.

I couldn't see her face, but I figured it was probably Talitha. "What was that dog doing in here?" she snarled and my hunch was proven to be correct.

"Our pretty little intruder brought a pet with her," Malachi drawled. Now that we had company, he'd thankfully postponed his intention of becoming better acquainted with me.

"We need to get out of here," his sister said and marched into view. Talitha didn't seem surprised to see me and sneered at my frozen state. "You really shouldn't have come back to town. Now that I have you, you'll tell me everything I want to know about who you are and where your friends are hiding."

Malachi grinned, then reached up to unhook the grisly skeleton from the pentagram. "I want some time alone with her before you torture her," he said. "They're always so messy afterwards. You know I like them to be clean. To start with anyway."

Talitha gave a derisive snort. "I am well aware of your perversions, brother dear," she said dryly.

"I know you are, sister dear," he replied then shocked me by grabbing her by the back of the neck and pulling her in for a lengthy kiss. I wanted to close my eyes and block out the sight, but unfortunately I couldn't control any particle of my body. I was looking right at the tiny skeleton and the pair that were locked in perverted passion.

Yet another horrid realization hit me and my stomach flopped over once more. Malachi wasn't just the boy ghost's uncle, he was also his father. The incestuous parents had killed their ill begotten son and had used his body to form their evil talisman.

Breaking apart at last, the siblings turned nearly identical stares on me. "Jeremiah just performed his sacrifice a few nights ago. I'll have to wait for at least two more nights before I can repeat the ritual," Talitha said. "We need to take her somewhere secure where her friends can't find her. I'll wring their whereabouts from her soon enough."

"We'll take her to the farm. She won't be able to

escape from the pit and they'll never be able to find her there," Malachi smirked.

I felt Reece's alarm when he realized that something was wrong. He'd chased after Jeremiah, but the warlock had realized that it had been a ruse. He was heading back towards town. *Did you find the talisman?*

Yes, but Malachi caught me before I could destroy it. He cast a spell on me and I can't move. I couldn't hide my panic and I didn't even try.

I had a sense of double vision when he looked through my eyes and saw that I was utterly helpless. *What are they going to do with you?*

Before I could answer him, Malachi's face came into view. "Sleep," he commanded and darkness descended.

Chapter Thirty-Two

I woke an unknown length of time later. Instant panic filled me, but I wasn't even sure why I was afraid. My mind was strangely foggy and I was having trouble concentrating. A nagging voice in the back of my head was shouting that something was wrong. It was telling me that I had to wake up.

Forcing my eyes open, I saw that I was lying on the ground. Dirt, dead leaves, sticks and round, smooth rocks had been my mattress for however long I'd been asleep. It was dark, musty and lightless.

I was lying on my stomach and my hands and feet were bound. To make it harder for me to escape, my feet and hands had been hogtied together. They'd been secured with the same plastic ties that cops used to subdue their captives.

My legs had been bent backwards for so long that

I'd lost all feeling in them. My hands were numb as well and my shoulders were aching. I must have been in this position for at least several hours.

Groggy and lethargic, I couldn't remember how I'd ended up in this prison, or who had captured me. I was on the verge of falling asleep again when a mind touched mine. Alarm at the invasion woke me up slightly.

My fright faded a little when I realized Reece was trying to contact me. I struggled to open the bond enough to allow his message to get through. He didn't use words, but instead sent me a frantic image of the full moon. My fright returned and it was much stronger this time. I was in an enclosed room and couldn't see the sky, but I could feel twilight nearing. The moon would rise in another couple of hours and then I would turn.

Feeling more awake by the second, I sent back the message that I was aware of the danger. I sent a picture of me being tied up and Reece growled in fury. He didn't know where I was and he couldn't help me to escape.

Remembering that Malachi had cast a spell that had put me to sleep, I figured it was also masking my location from the rest of the team. Even the bond wasn't going to be able to help me now. While I could feel Reece in my head, I had no idea where he was.

My eyes focused on one of the rocks and I frowned when I saw two holes that looked a lot like eye sockets. Looking around as best I could, I realized it wasn't a rock at all. It was a skull. The sticks weren't sticks, they were bones. I was alone and trapped in an underground grave. I was lying on the remains of men and women who had died to keep the dark coven young.

Refusing to give in to my horror and despair, I tried to pull my wrists apart and felt the plastic flexi ties stretching. Malachi still didn't realize what he'd captured. The plastic cut into my skin, but it parted and my hands and feet became free.

Rolling over onto my back, I waited for the feeling to return to my hands before I broke the bindings on my ankles. If I'd been human, I'd have lain there helplessly trussed, waiting to become the next sacrifice. I was probably only awake at all because I was a shifter. The spell had worn off sooner than it was supposed to.

Thankful for being a monster for a change, I rose and dusted myself off. It was impossible not to stand on bones. They were everywhere. The pit was around four meters square. I was surrounded by dirt walls and floor, but the ceiling was made of wood.

If this pit was the same as the one in the park, then the wood above me should actually be a trapdoor. Listening carefully, I couldn't hear anyone moving about up above. Throwing caution aside, I bent my knees and leaped upwards. My fists punched through the wood and I grabbed hold of the edge of the hole I'd just made.

Fresh air and a few leaves wafted in through the

opening. A few more punches knocked enough of the wood away for me to climb to safety. Brushing leaves and dirt out of my hair, I checked my pockets and discovered that my cell phone, weapon and ammo were missing. I turned in a circle and saw only trees. A narrow path caught my eye and so did Malachi's scent. His scent led me to the path and I followed it at a run through the woods.

I stopped at the edge of a clearing when I spied a farm house across a field. It was large, rustic and old. It appeared that extra rooms had been added to it over the decades. Smoke trailed listlessly from one of three chimneys. The lights were off and I couldn't hear anyone moving around inside.

A building to the left of the house had been converted from a barn into a double garage. The doors were open and it was empty. The scent of gasoline and oil was fresh enough to indicate that a car had been inside within the past twenty-four hours.

I needed to find a phone so I could call Mark. I hoped mine was inside the house, because his number was stored on it. I couldn't remember it off the top of my head. If my phone was inside, it was either switched off, or it was broken. Otherwise Mark would have tracked me using the GPS chip inside the device.

Something nudged the edge of my senses and it wasn't Reece this time. Tuning into the other mind, I realized it was Zeus. I felt his joy when he felt me in his mind. He'd tried to follow the witches when they'd kidnapped me and had lost my scent when their car had left town. He'd followed his instincts and was closing in on the farmhouse.

Hearing a car approaching, he flattened himself down on the side of the road. A brief sniff as it drove past told him that Malachi was behind the wheel. The warlock was no doubt returning to have some special time alone with me.

He'd made a terrible mistake bringing both me and the talisman to the same location. I could feel its power emanating from the farmhouse. With luck, there would be a phone inside. If so, then I could kill two metaphorical birds with one stone; destroy the source of his power and call for help.

I calculated that I had a few minutes left before the warlock would arrive and sprinted over to the building. The door splintered down the middle when I kicked it. Two more kicks broke it down and I strode into a large, square living room.

The floor was made of plain wooden boards. The room was devoid of furniture, which made it seem bigger than it really was. Just like in Talitha's apartment, paintings hung on the walls. A glance told me that they'd been created by the same artist. These were much worse and far more disquieting.

Instead of wearing robes, the coven members were naked. In each painting, they were paired together and were performing sex acts that boggled and disturbed my young mind. In others, they were torturing their sacrifices in inventive ways before stealing their life forces.

The coven had grown weary over time. They no longer bothered to play with their sacrifices now. Their rituals had become stale and boring. An unnaturally long life possibly wasn't quite as wonderful as they'd expected. They'd only been alive for a couple of hundred years. How jaded and cynical would they be in five hundred years? Or in a thousand? If I had my way, they wouldn't need to worry about it at all, because they'd shortly be dead.

Apart from the paintings, the only other item in the living room was a wooden altar. The talisman had been placed on it so that the skeleton dangled over the edge. It was positioned so it was looking down at the floor. The empty eye sockets seemed to be staring at the inverted pentagram that had been painted in the center of the room. This time, the goat skull lay in the middle of the diagram. An ancient evil seemed to fill the house, waiting for the opportunity to escape.

From the faded smears of long dried blood and a thick coating of dust on the floor, it seemed that the coven hadn't used this place to hold their sacrifices for a very long time. It was chilly and Malachi must have set the fire before he'd left. Coals still smoldered in the fireplace on the far side of the room. An old book sat on the mantelpiece. It was as dusty as the floor.

Like Dawson's Retreat, the farmhouse must have been outside the sphere of the coven's influence. I guessed that it was somewhere on the outskirts of Bradbury. If so, I might still have time to reach the others and find somewhere safe to be imprisoned before the moon rose.

Now that I'd found the talisman again, I had no idea how to destroy it. At that thought, the little boy appeared and pointed at the fireplace. "You want me to burn it?" I asked and he nodded solemnly. "Will this hurt you?" He shook his head and smiled. It was so pure and innocent that my heart ached for him.

I didn't have the time to treat his remains with reverence. Zeus was running for all he was worth in the wake of Malachi's car. He warned me that the warlock had almost reached the farmhouse. I could hear the car approaching now and knew I was out of time.

Snatching up the bundle of bones, I tossed it into the fireplace. Sparks flew, but the bones didn't catch on fire. A few pieces of charred wood were nestled in the ashes, but they wouldn't be enough to cause a blaze. I needed something flammable to fuel the fire with.

The book on the mantelpiece caught my eye again. Judging by the cracked black leather and title that was written in another language, it was probably a spell book. Without thinking about the possible consequences, I grabbed it. Ripping out a few pages, I screwed them into a ball and threw them on the coals.

Blue flames exploded to life, blinding me with their brightness. I lifted a hand to shield my face and backed away a few feet. The bones caught as if they were also made of paper. A car door slammed outside and Malachi let out a howl of pain and rage.

"Screw it," I muttered and threw the rest of the spell book onto the blaze. A blast of power was expelled as the talisman was destroyed. I staggered back from the burst of flames that shot out for several feet.

Malachi staggered into the doorway with an expression of abject horror as he saw the talisman burning. "What have you done?" he whispered.

"What have *I* done?" I retorted. "What have you and your sick, twisted brothers and sisters done?" As I spoke, ghosts began to appear. His eyes widened and I knew he could see them. Fear replaced his anger. "You've killed hundreds of innocent men and women to keep yourselves young." The spirits of the people he'd slain moved in to surround him. He backed away, then halted when Zeus growled to warn him that his retreat had just been cut off.

Lifting his hands, Malachi tried to cast a spell. I tensed, expecting pain, but nothing happened. "Your power is gone," I realized out loud. "You can't cast any more spells."

His handsome face twisted into a rictus of loathing and hatred. He reached into his jacket and pulled out my Beretta. "I don't need a spell to kill you. I'll use your own gun to do the trick. Then I'll carve your flesh from your bones and turn your skeleton into a new talisman!"

He started towards me, grinning with evil pleasure. The young male ghost who had written the message on my bathroom mirror appeared in front of me, shielding me from harm. Malachi stumbled to a halt. "You don't have the power to hurt me. You're just a pitiful, useless dead thing."

He couldn't have been more wrong about that. The spirits moved in to surround him as he backed out through the door and into the yard. Malachi's fear returned when they began to change. Their fingers lengthened into claws and their flesh withered and melted away to expose their bones. Their eyes grew milky and their hair turned long and scraggly. Their clothes turned into tattered black shrouds that billowed around their skeletal bodies.

I followed them to the doorway, staying at what I hoped was a safe distance. I watched on in horrified fascination as the spirits changed from benign beings into murderous wraiths. With hollow moans and howls of rage, they launched themselves at the warlock. This time, they didn't pass through him as they had with Katrina. Their bodies were corporeal and they were solid enough to rend him to pieces.

Malachi's shrieks of agony seemed to go on for a long time. He was finally silenced when a clawed hand swiped his head from his shoulders. It thumped to the ground and lay beside the rest of his mangled body parts.

Slowly returning to normal, the spirits turned to me. I couldn't hear them now, but their gratitude came through loud and clear. The young man who had helped me so often gave me a salute of thanks. I returned it and he slowly faded away until he disappeared entirely. I had a feeling he wouldn't be back this time. Hopefully, they were all finally going to a better place.

Zeus barked in warning, breaking me from my melancholic mood. I sensed a hostile creature approaching and a cold finger seemed to touch the back of my neck. I knew who it was even before my mother stepped out from the trees and into the open.

She crooked a finger, beckoning me to her. My feet automatically obeyed. Katrina might only be a lackey to a master vampire, but she had bitten me more than once and I was forced to do her bidding. I only managed to take a few steps before pain snapped me out of her spell. Zeus leaned against my leg and whined apologetically for nipping my calf.

"Why do you continue to resist me, Alexis?" Katrina called and began walking towards me. Now that I wasn't looking at her, it was easier to ignore her mesmerizing influence. "You know how much I want us to be a family again."

The moon wasn't scheduled to rise for another hour yet, but my wolf surged inside me. This hadn't happened before. It frightened me that my alter ego was so aware of what was happening to me. The wolf was eager to come forward and to take control. She sensed the vampire and knew that she was our mortal enemy. Her plan was to rend my mother apart. If I allowed that to happen, I would die along with Katrina. No servant could survive if they killed their creator. While I wasn't a fully-fledged vampire yet, I didn't want to risk it.

I knew that if I met my mother's eyes, she'd ensnare me in her clutches again. If she fed from me one more time, the vampirism that she'd infected me with would take over. Then the taint would spread to every part of my body. I'd become a soulless creature that craved blood instead of flesh.

"Come to me, my darling," she crooned and a traitorous part of me wanted to obey her.

Spying shiny metal among the bloody ruins of the warlock's clothing, I bent to snatch up my gun. I searched his pockets and found my cell phone and his car keys. Avoiding looking in the vampire's direction, I sprinted to the car. Zeus leaped inside when I opened the door and I slid in after him.

Shrieking in rage that I was defying her, Katrina streaked across the yard with shocking speed as I started the car. I engaged the lock an instant before she hit my door. The car rocked at the impact. She pulled the door handle hard enough to snap it off as I put my foot down and took off.

Refusing to let go, she held on as the car fishtailed, willing me to look at her. In sheer desperation, I powered the window down. Pressing my gun against the cold, unmoving chest of the creature that had birthed me, I fired four rapid shots.

Blown backwards, Katrina hit the road and tumbled for several yards. Barely hurt, she sprang to her feet and stared after me with a malevolence that I could feel. Instead of chasing me, she melted into the trees.

Speeding as fast as I dared along the bumpy road, I tried to lock on to Reece's thoughts and succeeded. Eventually emerging onto the main road, I saw the lights of Bradbury in the distance. The spell that Malachi had cast was gone and I could now follow our link easily.

I felt a swell of panic from Reece and split my concentration. In a highly dangerous move, I watched through his eyes and mine for a few seconds. It was long enough to see that the others were speeding through the woods and that they weren't alone.

The SUV and my father's blue rental car were being chased by several vampires. My mother hadn't come to West Virginia alone. This time, she'd brought her entire nest with her.

Chapter Thirty-Three

My hands were white on the steering wheel when I zoomed through town. It was far too late to worry about stealth now. A figure appeared in front of me and I swerved just in time to avoid the elderly pedestrian. I glanced into the rearview mirror to see him shaking his fist. He shouted something derogatory about my driving skills.

Despite the danger we were in, Zeus was enjoying the ride immensely. Grinning from ear to ear, he had to brace himself against the door to stop from sliding on the seat when I took a corner too fast. I prayed that I wouldn't have to come to a sudden stop. If I did, he'd probably go sailing through the windscreen.

Apart from that single pedestrian, I didn't see another soul as I sped towards the outskirts of town. Even without the bond to guide me, I knew where my friends were heading. Vampires couldn't step onto hallowed ground, which meant the squad had to be racing for the abandoned church.

Taking one of the rutted dirt roads, I retraced the route we'd used and closed in on the church. I sensed the undead before I saw them. They were an irritating itch in the back of my head. The sensation wasn't dissimilar to how I felt when zombies were near.

Reece's relief that I was safe and unharmed increased when I drew close enough for him to feel me. He sent me a picture of what he was seeing. Mark, my father and Beatrice were huddled in the center of the dilapidated old church. Reece, Kala and Flynn were stationed on three sides.

They watched through the open doorway and through the broken windows as the church grounds became surrounded. The vamps couldn't get any closer and could only wander around the perimeter. They were attempting to bamboozle their prey into stepping outside. I counted seven vampires and knew there were more that I couldn't see.

Heads turned when I sped towards the church. Two vampires hissed and moved to intercept me. Avoiding their eyes, I tromped down on the gas pedal. "Get on the floor," I said to Zeus and braced myself for impact as he tucked himself beneath the dashboard. It was a tight squeeze, but at least he was wedged in place and wouldn't be sent crashing through the windshield.

The car slammed into the vamps, sending them

both flying over the fence and onto the sanctified ground. Bursting into flames, they shrieked in agony as their flesh was consumed by a beautiful silver fire.

Leaving the car door open, I bolted towards the church just as I felt my mother's insidious thoughts creeping into my mind. She'd taken a shortcut through the woods, knowing that I'd try to save my friends from her nest. The moment my feet touched the sacred ground, her thoughts became muted.

Zeus bounded along at my side as I burst into the church. My father strode forward and caught me in a hug. "I'm glad to see you're alive, kiddo," he said, taking a step back and placing both hands on my shoulders. "But coming here might not have been a smart move."

"I didn't have a choice," I replied as the others gathered around. "Malachi took me to a farmhouse in the woods on the far side of town. Katrina found me there and she's determined to turn me. This is the only place I could think of where I'd be safe from her."

"Did he hurt you?" Reece asked. His thoughts intruded on mine, searching for answers.

"No," I replied. "Malachi used a spell to knock me out, then took me to an isolated farmhouse. It was another place where they used to perform their rituals. I was out for the whole day and only woke up at twilight. I found the talisman and destroyed it, which set the spirits free. They tore the warlock apart, then faded away. I'm pretty sure they've moved on to wherever they're supposed to go after they die."

"We were worried about you!" Kala scolded me. "The coven figured out that their wards had been tripped by a spell and fled back to town. Mark tried to call you, but you didn't answer your phone. Reece couldn't sense you through your bond."

I flicked a glance at him to see that his expression had turned grim. "Where is the rest of the coven now?" I asked. With Malachi dead, that left five witches and warlocks still unaccounted for. Their power should have been destroyed along with the talisman. Maybe the ghosts had already torn them apart and had completed our mission for us.

"We have no idea," Mark replied. "They turned tail and ran before we could take them down. They used a spell to hide from our sight and other senses." That meant the squad couldn't track them by their smell. "I'm afraid we have a more urgent problem to worry about right now."

I checked my watch to see that we had maybe twenty minutes left before the moon would rise. "What are we going to do?" I asked, trying not to let my despair take over. Even if Reece and I managed to control ourselves again when we changed, Kala and Flynn wouldn't have the same ability. They'd rip the humans to shreds and feast on their meat. Mark, Beatrice and my father would shortly be trapped between bloodsuckers outside and meat eaters inside.

"I don't know," Mark replied softly. "This is the worst possible scenario."

My father stepped over to one of the windows to assess the threat. "How many bullets does it take to kill a vampire?" he asked Mark.

"More than we have with us. You might be able to kill a few of them, but you won't be able to destroy all of them."

"Is that really you, Philip?" Katrina called out with false sweetness as she spied my dad through the window. "I've missed you, darling. Come outside so we can be reunited once more."

Beatrice put her hand on his arm. "Don't listen to her," she warned him. "Every word that comes out of her mouth is a lie. The woman you loved is gone. That thing out there is pure evil."

My father looked stricken for a few moments before hardening his heart against his long dead wife. We shared a look and I read his unspoken promise that he'd rather kill us both than allow us to end up like her.

I looked at Reece and he felt as bleak as I did. *I wish there was some way we could link ourselves to Kala and Flynn,* he thought.

If they'd been werewolves, we might have been able to forge some kind of link with them. As it was, we were practically already a pack. That thought seized me and I turned to face them. They were a different species to me, but didn't I feel kinship with them anyway? Reaching out, I strained to touch their minds and felt a faint, tentative connection.

"Do you feel that?" I asked Reece. He moved to

stand beside me, struggling to pick up what I was feeling. Touching always seemed to boost our bond, so I clasped his hand in mine.

Hope rose inside him when he felt the same connection that I felt to our friends. I sent him a picture of what I wanted to do. "We have to try," he said in response. We'd become bonded by biting each other. I wondered if sharing blood would also forge a stronger connection with the other two shifters.

"Why are you looking at us like that?" Kala asked uneasily.

"What are you two planning?" Flynn was just as wary.

"Do you trust me?" I asked. Kala nodded immediately, but Flynn took longer to reply. He stared into my eyes and I urged him silently to surrender to my will. When he bowed his head submissively, I felt a sense of rightness, as if this was meant to be. "Give me your arm," I commanded and he reached out with his left hand. Reece took Kala's hand and we simultaneously bit down on their wrists.

Swallowing down his blood, I felt Flynn's thoughts whirling around inside my head. It was much fainter than the link I had with Reece, but it was there. I could barely feel Kala and knew that I'd have to mark her as well. Swapping places with Reece, I bit down on the mark that he'd made. Now I had three minds vying for attention, four if I included Zeus.

"I can feel you in my head," Kala said incredulously, touching her forehead with an unsteady hand.

"I can feel them, but I can't feel you," Flynn said to her and they exchanged a long look. Reaching a mutual decision, they bit each other's wrists and we all felt the connection link us together.

"What did you just do?" Mark asked. Even in the face of imminent death, he was still trying to learn as much as he could. My father had pulled his gun and was watching us warily. He could sense the power that was surging between all four of us. Beatrice looked frightened. I wasn't sure if she was more scared of us, or of the vampires.

"We are a pack," I said and Kala laughed in pure joy.

"We are one," Reece said and tears welled in Flynn's eyes. His pupils were beginning to change and the green was now far more vivid. Kala's fingers were growing longer and were turning into vicious claws. The Shifter Squad might have been a team for the past five years, but they'd still felt alone. Now we were linked together, even if it was only temporary.

Any minute now, we'd burst into our animal forms and I didn't want to ruin my clothes. I also didn't want my dad to see me naked. "You'd better move to the far end of the room," I instructed the humans. "You, too," I said to Zeus. With a whine of protest, he followed my father to the only side of the church that didn't have a window in it.

"Do you think you'll be able to control Kala and Flynn?" Mark asked. His tone was hopeful.

"Yes," Reece replied. "We're both alphas and they'll do as we say." He said this as though the answer should have been evident.

We removed our clothing, shoes and weapons, but left our underwear on out of modesty's sake. Excitement mounted and my wolf began to rise inside me as the moon ascended. As if we'd choreographed it, our bodies reacted at exactly the same time.

Far quicker than previously, my hands, feet and face elongated. Claws burst from the ends of my fingers and toes and fangs erupted from my gums. My spine popped, my ribs conformed to a new shape and black fur grew all over my body. I howled in pain and Reece echoed me as he also underwent the same rapid change. It took only seconds for the change to be complete.

Kala screeched in torment as she transformed. It began as a high pitched wail, but ended in a throaty roar. Her fur was the same shade of tawny blonde as her human hair and her eyes gleamed gold. Her fangs and claws were even longer than mine. Sleek and strong, she was a different species from me, but I had to concede that she was beautiful. She grinned fiercely, eager to tear into our enemies. Her long tail twitched, then curled around her leg.

Flynn's transformation was the most startling. His legs merged and lengthened into a long tail, while his head changed into something resembling a cobra. His forked tongue flicked out to taste the air.

From his neck to his waist, he was still humanoid,

but the rest of him was pure constrictor. His shoulders, arms and chest were far more muscular than they were when he was human. His fingers lacked claws, but his fangs more than made up for it. Long and viciously sharp, clear fluid dripped from them and fell to the floor. Steaming when they landed, they began to eat through the wooden boards. His venom was as acidic as it was poisonous.

Light green scales covered his back, sides and tail. They faded to yellow when they reached his chest. The scales on his abdomen were cream. He turned and his hood flared when he spied the humans. Black scales formed an intricate, mesmerizing pattern on the back of his head.

He slithered towards the tasty humans who were handily lined up against the wall. *No, brother,* I thought and he turned back to face me. *They are not food.*

Disappointed, he pointed at the dog. *Can I eat that? It looks tasty.*

I looked at the animal and felt a strange connection to it. My mate shook his head and answered the question for me. *The dog is important to my mate. None of the beings in this building are food.*

The cat stretched, reaching upwards with her impressive claws. *I'm hungry,* she complained. *If we can't eat them, what can we eat?*

Sensing enemies surrounding the building, my human memories welled to the forefront of my mind. *Food will have to wait, sister. First, we must hunt the soulless.*

I sent them a picture of the undead creature who

wanted to turn me into her kind. My mate growled in fury, the cat hissed in rage and the snake clenched his fists. His temper was more even than ours, but when roused to anger, I sensed that he would be formidable. *First, we shall kill the soulless,* he agreed. *Then we can feed.*

With that decision made, we headed for the door.

Chapter Thirty-Four

My mate and I took the lead once we were out in the open. These soulless were different from the ones that we'd previously fought. Instead of being slow and witless, they were fast and cunning. Linked to all three shifters, I felt their eagerness to engage with the enemy. We were made for battle and we weren't going to shy away just because they outnumbered us three to one.

Tilting my head back, I howled at the silver moon that had called us forth from our human bodies. That was the signal to attack. We leaped over the fence and tore into the undead. We instinctively knew not to bite them. Doing so would be deadly.

My mate and I already carried a sickness within us that had been caused by being bitten by one of these things. Our bond was keeping that illness at bay, but we knew that it would take us over sooner or later. If the cat or snake were to ingest the blood of the soulless, they would perish.

My claws rent cold flesh and sent sluggish, dead blood flying. One of the vampires jumped onto my back and sank his fangs into my neck. He thought that would incapacitate me, but he was wrong. Already infected, I couldn't contract the taint again, but fire ignited in my veins as the taint was increased slightly.

Reaching over my shoulder, I tore him free and punched my fist through his chest. Coughing out clots of dark, noisome fluid, his eyes rolled back into his head and his body fell.

I'd slain four of the beings when I sensed something strangely familiar at my back. Whirling around, I beheld another of the soulless. The female was small with long black hair. Her scent was familiar. This was the creature that had infected me.

Before I could snarl in fury and attack, she spoke. It took a moment for me to understand her words. "Come, daughter," she beckoned in a falsely sweet tone. "Let me change you from that bestial form into what you were truly meant to be."

My mate growled in warning when I lumbered forward to stand in front of her. Three of the walking corpses had him surrounded, preventing him from coming to my aid. Standing over the small creature that believed she had a kinship with me, I stared into her dark eyes.

"Give me your hand, darling," she crooned and I obeyed. Her flesh was cold and lifeless, yet it was animated with an evil magic. I felt the same magic within myself and loathed the sensation. I knew that if she were to pierce my flesh with her teeth, that she would own me. Her mouth lowered towards my wrist and her fangs descended.

A loud noise rang out and she stumbled back as a hole appeared in her forehead. I glanced at the building to see a tall human peering through the broken window holding a gun. He took aim again and another of the soulless made a sound of pain. His weapon was all but useless, but it had been enough to break me from the vampire's spell.

Turning to confront her, I grabbed her by the throat. The wound in her forehead was already healing. Lifting the creature off the ground, I snarled into her face and she screamed in fear and fury. Her hands clawed at me, tearing furrows in my arm. They bled freely for a few seconds before closing.

I squeezed down hard and her screams shut off. She was silenced, but choking her wouldn't kill her. How could it when she was already dead? I'd learned one method of killing zombies that I was pretty sure would work on her as well. I put my hand on the top of her head with the intention of pulling her head from her shoulders.

"Stop!" a voice roared. Another vampire stalked from where he'd been hiding among the trees. Ancient and wicked, he wore a dark coat that covered him from his chin to his toes. Arrogance poured from his every pore. So did power. It oozed from him and froze me in place.

All of the remaining undead were linked to him. Their bond was similar to how our small pack was joined. I wasn't sure how it was possible, but the vampire was also linked to me. I sensed that the connection was due to the female who was dangling from my hands. He could control me through the psychic leash she held around my neck.

"Katrina," he admonished, "you did not mention that your daughter is a werewolf."

With my hand still crushing her throat, she could only gasp her response. "I thought that I could turn her, master. I nearly succeeded."

"It is forbidden to attempt to turn those abominations into our kind," he said coldly and she cringed. "It would not have worked even if you'd tried. Shifters always die when our blood is mixed with theirs. I am afraid I will have to punish you severely for this, my love." He turned his dark eyes to me and bared his teeth in a smile. "Let the death of your kin serve as your reprimand."

My mate sent me a frantic thought as he battled his foes. *Why do you not tear their heads from their shoulders?*

I cannot move, I replied. *He is controlling me.* The master vampire took a silver knife from a sheath at his waist. He handled it carefully even while wearing gloves. The metal was almost as deadly to them as it was to us. He wouldn't be harmed as long as he didn't cut himself.

Trapped by his will, I was held immobile as he closed to within touching distance. The female moaned in anguish as he drew his hand back to stab me in the heart.

Another shot came from the church. The bullet passed by me so closely that I felt it brush my shoulder. The shot was true and the creature's head snapped back as the bullet went through his eye.

I sensed my pack mates approaching an instant before they struck. The cougar's claws raked the creature's arm, severing it from his body. The snake hissed, spraying his toxic venom in the vampire's face to blind him. Clawing at his eyes with his remaining hand, bubbling screams came from his melting face.

Slithering forward, the snake wrapped his tail around the vampire's middle and began to squeeze. Mewling in agony, the ancient living corpse writhed, but couldn't dig his nails into the thick scales that protected the reptile's body. Dead, clotted blood burst from his mouth when the snake constricted, tearing his body in two. The cat wasn't satisfied with that. Her claws swiped out, severing his head from his body.

The surviving vampires shrieked as the link that had bound them to their master was broken. The female in my hand wriggled free from my suddenly lax grasp. I staggered at the baffling sense of loss that I felt at his death. Freed from their servitude, the minions went mad and fled in all directions.

My mate appeared beside me and nuzzled my neck where I'd been bitten by one of the foul creatures. *Are you well?*

I am well, I responded. *Let us destroy these creatures utterly.* The ancient vampire had called me an abomination, but that description was more closely suited to his kind. No soulless had a right to exist. It was our duty to wipe them out.

Splitting up, we went in search of prey.

Chasing after the female who was still linked to me, I detoured to swipe the head from the shoulders of one of the other creatures. She was staring up at the sky, screaming at the top of her lungs. I sensed that she'd been linked to her master for so long that she could no longer function without him.

It had been a mistake to stop and finish her off. I looked for the other female and found her to be gone. There were still several of the vampires in the vicinity and I couldn't leave them all to my brethren. By the time we hunted down the filthy nest of undead, only one had escaped. We followed her scent towards a town and lost it near the first set of houses. She'd stolen a vehicle to make her escape. Even we couldn't track her now.

She is gone, my mate said. He flicked an annoyed glance at the feline when she rubbed against my arm.

It was unnatural for us to be a pack, but our instincts to do battle were absent. Her tongue rasped the fur of my face as she licked me affectionately. Her stare when she looked at my mate was bordering on insolent. *Is something the matter?* she asked him with a purr.

My mate now smells like a cat, he complained.

Strong arms came around me and pulled me back against a hard, cold body. *Now she smells like a snake,* our scaly brother said. My mate growled, but he wasn't truly angry. Like me, he finally felt complete. Our family now consisted of four rather than just two. We might be different, but we were united in our affection for each other.

Can we eat now? The cat rubbed her empty belly, which was growling loudly enough for us all to hear it.

There was plenty of food within the town limits, but my mate reminded us that the humans and their pets were taboo. *The woods will have more suitable food,* he said. *Follow me.* I was his equal and could have refused to follow his command, but I surrendered to his logic. We followed him back towards the cemetery where we'd battled the vampires. There hadn't been any humans in the area for many years. We'd be in no danger of being interrupted during the next three nights.

A car approached and the headlights momentarily caught us in its glare. My mate's silver fur almost seemed to glow in the light. Tires screeched as the driver slammed to a halt. The car reversed wildly, turned and headed back from whence it had come. The cat grinned in amusement at the thought of the poor, confused meal inside the metal confines. Our kind was rare enough to be mere legend. His story wouldn't be believed by anyone. We would remain safe as long as no one else saw us.

When we were deep in the woods, the feline and the snake split up. They preferred to hunt alone rather than in a group. The woods were extensive, yet we could still feel them in our minds. We would know if they were in danger, just as they would know if we encountered any enemies.

Before dawn came, we gathered together to sleep in a jumble of limbs. My head rested on the reptile's chest. My mate was at my back with his arms around me. The feline was stretched across our legs, purring loudly in contentment. I snuggled against my mate as the snake lazily stroked a hand down my back. There was nothing sexual in our contact. We were luxuriating in being close rather than locked up in our prisons all alone for once.

On the third and final night of our change, my mate and I chased a small herd of deer deep into the woods. Leaping gracefully through the air, my mate landed on one of the larger does and brought her down. He howled in triumph and I joined his song. Just as our howls petered out, we heard an answering cry coming from a great distance away.

Going still, my mate's ears flicked towards the sound. I picked up the connection he felt with the other shifter through our bond. Another werewolf was somewhere in this area and he now knew that he wasn't alone.

He reached out with his thoughts, making brief

contact with my mate. He recoiled from the stranger's mind immediately, sending me what he'd sensed. I didn't share a connection with the werewolf at all, but I'd sensed what my mate had felt. He didn't know how or when, but he'd met the other shifter before. They'd recognized each other's minds from that one fleeting moment of contact.

We exchanged an uneasy glance as another howl sounded from across the vast expanse of woods. It was lonely, poignant and hinted of madness. My mate sensed that there was something wrong with the other wolf. He was suffering from a sickness of the mind. He didn't have our capacity to retain reason when he changed. He was unpredictable, extremely dangerous and curious about who we were. If we remained in his territory, he would undoubtedly seek us out.

Chapter Thirty-Five

"Aw," a gleeful voice said, waking me from a deep slumber. "That's so sweet."

I opened my eyes to see a very naked Kala standing over me. It took me another second to realize that I was lying on the ground and that Reece's arms were wrapped around me from behind.

"Leave the two lovebirds alone," Flynn said, but I heard the amusement in his voice. He was as naked as the rest of us and didn't seem to be at all bothered by it.

My momentary confusion was wiped away when Reece released me and sat up. My memory of all that had transpired over the past few nights returned and so did his. "We need to check on Mark, Major Levine and Beatrice," he said. He had too much fear and respect for my dad to call him by his first name.

I could still faintly feel Kala and Flynn in the back of my mind as I scrambled to my feet. Our link was fading, but I wasn't sure if it would ever completely dissipate. At least we couldn't read each other's thoughts. That would have been far too intrusive and uncomfortable for all of us.

"Can someone explain to me how we're all still alive?" Kala asked as we began making our way through the dense woods. "Why didn't we tear each other apart?" Shifters from different species usually fought as soon as they came into contact when we were in our animal forms. Neither she, nor Flynn remembered the events that had transpired three nights ago.

"Lexi and I bit both of you to forge a temporary link between us," Reece explained. He'd taken the lead and I followed a few steps behind him. He wasn't at all self-conscious about being naked. Apparently, I was the only one with a sense of modesty.

Picking up on that thought, he glanced back over his shoulder and smirked. My hands automatically moved to cover myself, but I let them drop to my sides. He'd already seen me unclothed several times. It was a bit late to worry about trying to hide now.

"I don't remember anything," Flynn complained. "How can you two manage to retain your memories?"

"It has something to do with our bond," I said and winced when I stood on a sharp stick. The wound healed after a couple of steps. "Our minds are linked when we change and we're able to keep some of our humanity. It seems to help us remember everything."

"So, what exactly did we do after we turned?" Kala queried. "We didn't hurt anyone, did we?"

"We didn't kill any humans," Reece replied. "We eradicated an entire nest of vampires, though. Mark, Beatrice and Lexi's dad were safe in the church when we took off after the vamps."

"We didn't quite take down the entire nest," I said unhappily. "We killed the master and most of his minions, but Katrina got away."

Reece sent me a sympathetic look and Kala reached out to touch my arm. "We'll find her, Lexi," she promised. I hoped so, because both Reece and I were still in danger of becoming vampires.

We'd destroyed the master vampire, which Beatrice had said would give us a chance to stop the taint. Turning into a werewolf had helped to slow it, but it hadn't halted it completely. I could feel the infection spreading through me. Unless we now hunted down my mom, the vampirism would slowly become stronger until our souls were in peril again. Reece was facing the same death sentence. He was as invested in finding her as I was.

With her master dead, Katrina was now free to make a new nest of her own. Somehow, I didn't think she'd waste much time gathering minions. The sooner we found and destroyed her, the better. Otherwise, we'd be facing another mob of blood suckers instead of just one.

Our noses led us to a road and we followed it back to civilization. Reaching the outskirts of Bradbury, we hunkered down near the town line. I examined the area, trying to sense the wards. "I can't see or feel any magic," I said to the others. There was no telltale shimmer in the air.

"Wait here," Reece ordered, then leaped over the fence. My tense shoulders relaxed when he wasn't zapped by a spell. He crossed the yard to a clothesline and pulled a pair of sweatpants off the line. They were too short and much too tight, but they were better than nothing. The rest of us joined him. We chose clothing that didn't fit very well, but at least covered our nakedness.

"Keep your eyes peeled for the rest of the coven," Reece ordered. "They might still be somewhere in town."

Wearing shorts that came down to my knees and a t-shirt that was almost as long, I was just glad to be wearing anything at all. Shoes and underwear would have been welcome, but we were out of luck there.

Sticking to the back streets, we made our way to the center of town. It made sense for us to try to pinpoint where the coven were hiding while we were here.

Kate's Kafé was still closed. We rounded the corner and ducked into the alley behind the building. "I can feel traces of magic," I said. Destroying the talisman had negated Malachi's ability to cast spells, but maybe his siblings had regained their ability to do magic.

Who knew what other spell books and items of power they'd collected over the decades?

"I wish there was some way we could scout out the apartment without actually going inside," Reece said quietly. He was reluctant to enter the building without knowing if the witches were lying in wait for us.

As if sensing our need, I felt a pack of dogs approaching. They rounded the corner, following my scent. It was the same pack that had come to my assistance when Talitha had snared me in her clutches. Overjoyed to see me again, they gathered around us. Quietly snarling at Kala, they ignored Flynn completely. Reece was worthy of respect, but they didn't fawn over him like they were over me. I quietened them before they could start barking happily.

Kala's nose wrinkled in distaste at being surrounded by canines of all sizes. Zeus was the only one missing from the pack. I could feel him at the outer edges of my senses. I figured he was at Dawson's Retreat with the rest of our party.

A strange look came over Flynn and he glanced from the dogs to me. "Could you send one of the dogs inside to scout out the building?"

It was a great idea and I wished I'd thought of it first. "I can try," I replied. Figuring that a smaller dog would draw less notice, I picked a Chihuahua out of the mob. I touched her mind and found it to be a whirling tangle of excitement.

I need you to go inside the building and look around, I said to her. Giving a high pitched yap of agreement, she followed me over to the door. The lock hadn't been fixed yet, so I didn't need to break it open again.

I opened the door just wide enough for her to enter, then concentrated on trying to see through her eyes. The connection between us was weak, but it worked. I saw a cloudy image of the hallway and guided her to the end then to the left.

She climbed the stairs to the second floor and entered the long hallway. She glanced inside each room and saw little of interest until she came to the end of the corridor. Her nose told her that five different people were inside. One of them was Talitha. The Chihuahua recognized her scent from when she'd helped rescue me from the witch.

That was enough confirmation for me. I called her back and opened my eyes. "They're in there all right. They're holed up in the living room. I think they've cast a spell on the room, but I'm not sure what it does."

Ghosts began to materialize as I gave my report until the alley was full of spirits. The young woman I'd seen staring at the photo of the coven in Dawson's Retreat stepped forward. She gave me a beseeching look and pointed up at the second floor of the café.

"Is their spell keeping you out?" I asked her. She nodded in response.

"Do they know if the spell will keep us out?" Flynn asked.

The spirit shook her head. "Does that mean it won't keep us out?" I asked for clarification and she nodded. I smiled and I wondered if it was as nasty as it felt. "Who wants to come with me to kick down the coven's door?"

Kala's smile was just as cruel as mine felt. "You couldn't stop me if you tried."

Reece and Flynn felt the same way. None of us wanted to miss out on our chance to finish off the coven. We'd left our weapons at the church, but we were far from defenseless. If we moved quickly enough, we could barge inside and tear them apart before they even knew what had hit them.

"Let's go," Reece said, taking point again.

He was the first through the door and I was next. The dogs wanted to follow us inside, but I ordered them to stay in the alley to keep watch. The Chihuahua scurried outside as we entered. She was happy that she'd been able to assist me.

Moving as quietly as we could, we crept up the stairs and along the hallway. Reece motioned us to a halt when we were nearly at the door. He wanted to listen in on the witches' conversation.

Talitha was speaking and she was nearly incoherent with rage. "Are we really going to continue hiding from *ghosts*?"

"You saw them," Eunice said in a frightened tone. "They've turned vengeful! They'll rip us to shreds the instant they break through our wards!"

"She's right," one of the warlocks agreed. It wasn't

Jeremiah, so that only left Jonathan. "With the talisman destroyed, we barely have enough power to maintain a shield around this room. We wouldn't stand a chance of holding off the wraiths. They'd overwhelm us in seconds."

Reece turned to me and we shared the same thought. While we wanted to take the witches down, the ghosts had more of a claim on their lives than we did. "It'll be risky," he whispered far too quietly for the witches to be able to hear us.

"We just need to distract them long enough for them to drop their wards," I replied.

Flynn shook his head and muttered beneath his breath when he realized what we were planning.

"What are we waiting for?" Kala said impatiently. "I don't care if it's us or the ghosts who kick their butts. Let's just get it done." She'd figured out our plan as well.

"What if we use more than one distraction?" I mused out loud.

Reading what was on my mind, Reece nodded. "Do it," he said and I called on the pack.

Padding as quietly as they could, the dogs entered the building and climbed the stairs. Whining softly in anticipation, they lined up on both sides of the door, leaving the way clear for Reece.

Ready? he said into my mind and I sent him a mental nod. *Now!* Taking a step forward, he kicked the door. It burst open, revealing the surviving members of the dark coven standing in a huddle.

Talitha's face darkened with rage when she saw me standing behind Reece. "You! You're the one who destroyed our talisman!" Venom nearly dripped from her words.

Banding together, the coven dropped the shield that they'd raised to keep the ghosts out. They zapped Reece and me with a paralysis spell. I could practically see them wilt as they used up their power.

Unable to move or speak, I sent a mental command to the pack. *Attack!*

Chapter Thirty-Six

With snarls and yips of glee, the dogs surged into the room, intent on maiming the coven. Talitha reacted first. Clapping her hands together, the shockwave that she sent out this time was barely strong enough to stir their fur.

Ophelia screamed shrilly and kicked out at a Doberman as he ran at her. He bared his fangs, then sank his teeth into her leg. Our plan had worked. The witches were distracted enough that they didn't even notice the ghosts when they began to appear. In seconds, the room was full of insubstantial spirits.

Jeremiah saw them first and gasped in alarm. His already pale face whitened even more. His siblings became aware of the danger and they moved into a tight circle facing outwards. Surrounded by a pack of dogs and the spirits of the people they'd sent to their deaths, they tried one final spell.

Talitha began to chant and the others joined in. They couldn't maintain the spell that they'd cast against us. It wavered, then dissipated, leaving us free to move again. Kala and Flynn crowded into the doorway with us as I called the dogs back. Things were about to get very nasty and I didn't want them to be harmed.

With backward glances, the pack obeyed my silent command and we stepped aside to allow them to leave. "Good job," I said and bent to pet the Doberman. "Keep watch outside and bark if anyone approaches." He woofed in response and headed for the stairs. He wasn't as attuned to me as Zeus was, but he understood my request.

"What's happening in there?" Kala asked as we crowded around the door again. They couldn't see the ghosts who were staring hungrily at the circle of witches.

When the spirits began to change, I wished I lacked the ability to see them. "The ghosts are turning vengeful," I said. Reece wrapped his hand around mine as he nudged my mind with his, asking for permission to see through my eyes.

Granting his wish, I allowed him to take over a small portion of my brain. Together, we watched the sudden transformation of the lovely young woman into a withered, skeletal hag. Opening her mouth impossibly wide, she hissed and raised her claws. Her clothing had become a wispy, insubstantial black shroud. It billowed around her as she attacked.

Chanting frantically, the coven faltered when the wraith dived into their midst. Eunice shrieked in pain. I could only imagine her agony as the ghost solidified as she exited the witch's body. Blood sprayed the walls as she was torn in half.

"Holy crap," Kala said in awe as the body fell.

Jonathan broke and tried to run. He made it two steps before a trio of wraiths caught him. Two held him by the arms, trying to pull him in opposite directions. The third one wrapped its hands around his head, muffling his screams. He rose several feet into the air, then his arms and head were torn from his body.

"Been there, done that," Flynn noted when what was left of Jonathan thumped to the floor. The psychic known as Greed had been in almost the exact same condition after he, Kala and Reece had finished with her.

Ophelia and Jeremiah lost all semblance of control. They began blasting the spirits with random spells that had little effect. With eerie, hollow laughter, the wraiths struck. Backing away, horror stricken, Talitha watched as her brother and sister were turned into chunks of flesh and splintered bone.

When they were dead, blood and brains were splattered everywhere. Chunks of meat lay on every surface and the walls ran with sticky fluids. It was difficult to tell that the misshapen lumps had ever been human at all. An eyeball sat on the sodden carpet, staring up at us accusingly.

Desperate to escape the same fate that had befallen her siblings, Talitha ran for the window. She leapt through it and glass shattered. Falling headfirst, she screeched in triumph.

We rushed over to the window in time to see her halt just before her head was about to smash into the sidewalk. A wraith had caught her by the ankle and her scream of triumph turned into a wail of despair.

It dragged her kicking and screaming higher and higher as more spirits gathered around. No one stuck their heads out of their windows to investigate the noise. Maybe the spells that controlled the townsfolk were still in effect.

I had a feeling I knew where they were taking her and I leaped out the window in pursuit. Talitha had earned a prolonged and painful death and I wanted to be there to witness it.

The others were right behind me as I raced towards the park where the dark coven had performed their last sacrifice. We pushed our way through the trees to the edge of the clearing. Just as I'd expected, the wraiths were holding Talitha suspended over the inverted pentagram.

"You can't do this to me!" she shrieked in fury.

Hollow chuckles and crazed shrieks came from the spirits. In their vengeful guises, they were capable of sound, if not actual speech. They proved her wrong a second later when they swarmed over her.

This time, I reached out to Reece and took his

hand as blood and body parts began to rain down from the sky. They splattered the pentagram, changing it from black to red. Her screeching finally came to an end and what was left of her was dropped to the barren ground.

With their vengeance finally satisfied, the ghosts lost their frightening forms and returned to normal. In unison, they began to fade. The lovely young woman smiled at me and lifted her hand in a wave. Reece and I returned her wave until we could no longer see her.

Talitha and Malachi's son materialized beside me. I knelt so he could put his arms around me. Cold sank into my bones, but I stayed where I was. He put his hand on my cheek and gave me the sweetest smile that I'd ever seen. Becoming insubstantial, he faded, taking the chill with him. Then he was gone and we were the only monsters left in the clearing.

"Remind me never to piss off a ghost," Flynn said as he surveyed the chunks of flesh.

"I think we're done here," Reece decided. "We should head back to Dawson's Retreat. Mark is probably worried about us by now."

We jogged through the streets openly now that there was no longer any reason for stealth. I made sure we passed by the café again. The pack was still standing guard. I dismissed them, making sure to pet each of them in thanks.

I picked up that they'd taken to roaming together at night when they could break free from their yards.

During the day, they returned to their normal lives as domestic pets. They were the dog equivalent of vigilantes, searching for evil to put down.

Being beneath my control had awakened long buried instincts in them. I hoped they would eventually fade. It would only freak their owners out if they saw their pets roaming the streets at night. Since it was past dawn, they'd been on their way home anyway.

We trotted to the edge of town, then put on a burst of speed once we were out of sight of the buildings. Zeus met us when we were halfway back to the B&B. He barked joyfully when he reached me. I hunkered down to pet him and received a swipe of his tongue across my cheek.

He sent me a few pictures of how frantic he'd been when we'd gone hunting the soulless. He'd sensed that they were unnatural and had shamefully hidden inside the church. It hadn't surprised him that we four had transformed into half-human, half-animals. He already knew about our dual natures. I sent him a reassuring thought that we'd handled the vampires and that I was glad he was safe.

"If you two have finished your happy reunion," Reece said with false patience, "maybe we can continue?"

Reece wasn't only jealous of other men showing me any kind of attention. He was apparently also annoyed with me having a pet dog. I scowled at him and recommenced my run, but at a pace that Zeus could keep up with. He didn't want to stay outside and keep watch, but I promised him I'd come back with food. That was enough to perk him up again.

Chapter Thirty-Seven

We found the backdoor unlocked and filed inside. Mark and Beatrice were sitting in the parlor. Our boss saw us first and surged to his feet. "Thank God you're all okay," he said in heartfelt relief.

He engulfed us all in a brief hug, starting with Kala and ending with me. "Where's my Dad?" I asked and frowned when he tensed up.

"I think he's in the shower," he said vaguely.

I couldn't hear water running, but Beatrice spoke, distracting me. "I have the ingredients I need to cast the spell to find your mother." She indicated a small bag sitting on the floor beside her. Tired and disheveled, her eyes were a little wild. She stood behind Mark, almost using him as a shield. She was back to being petrified. This time she was frightened of all of us rather than just me. Being trapped in a small building while we changed into our deadly alter egos couldn't have been a fun experience.

"Where do you want to cast it?" Mark asked. He'd already had firsthand experience at facing a werewolf. He didn't seem to be affected by seeing all four of us in our other states. "Did you want to use the church again?"

She shook her head. "This spell will require a place of power. I assume the coven has somewhere in Bradbury where they cast their spells?"

I shared a doubtful glance with Kala. "You could use the pentagram where they sacrificed a bunch of people," she said. "But wouldn't that be dangerous?"

Beatrice waved her concern away. "The site itself isn't evil. Only the deeds that were performed there were. Besides, I'll have to dispel their wards. The best place to do that will be from where they first cast them."

"Get changed and meet us at the SUV in five minutes," Mark instructed. Fishing our room keys out of his pocket, he handed them around. He'd kindly retrieved the equipment that we'd left at the church, figuring we'd head here after we'd transformed back into our human forms.

We raced upstairs and I heard my father pacing in his room two down from mine. He must have heard us arrive, but he made no move to join us. Feeling unsettled, I quickly changed into cargo pants and a t-shirt.

Mark had placed my gear in a pile on the bed. My

cell phone was sitting on top. It was fully charged, courtesy of our boss no doubt. I picked up my gun, checked that it was loaded and put it in my pocket. I'd lost some of my ammo when Malachi had taken me prisoner. Fortunately, I'd brought spares along in my suitcase.

Fully equipped once more, I tugged on my boots, then stepped out into the hallway and locked my door. Reece joined me and we jogged back downstairs. While I was glad to be armed, it was even more of a relief to be wearing underwear again.

I took a couple of minutes to feed Zeus, then asked him to stay behind and guard the house in our absence. It was daytime, so Katrina would be holed up in a dark lair somewhere, but I didn't like my father being left alone. Zeus woofed his agreement and gobbled down his food. His table manners were almost as bad as Kala's.

Mark was in the driver's seat of the SUV and Beatrice sat beside him. There wasn't enough room for all four of us in the back. Reece solved the problem by climbing in first and pulling me onto his lap. Kala grumbled about having to be in the middle, but Flynn gave her a light shove and she slid in beside us.

Reece's lap wasn't particularly comfortable, but I couldn't pretend that I didn't enjoy having his arm around me and his chest against my back. If we'd been alone, he wouldn't have been able to fight his reaction to my nearness. Since we weren't alone, he willed his desire away. I was struggling against the almost overwhelming urge to turn around and kiss him.

"Lexi," he warned me and broke me from my daydream of running my hands down his chest to his tight abs.

Kala cut me a look. "Try to ignore the eye candy," she suggested.

"How can I when I'm sitting on his lap?" I asked in a low whisper.

"Think about something else," Flynn offered.

"Such as?" I was open to suggestions.

"Think about how Talitha looked the last time you saw her," he replied with a smirk. "Speaking of which." He directed a question at Mark as we drove away from the B&B. "Are you going to call the Cleanup Crew in to deal with the coven? We found them hiding in the apartment above the café. They didn't last long once we broke through their ward and the ghosts got to them."

Mark would have called in the Crew to dispose of the vampire's that we'd slain. We were keeping them busy during this mission. Only contact with hallowed ground, fire or direct sunlight could burn them down to ash. Staking and beheading always left a body behind.

"I take it the spirits turned vengeful again?" Mark asked and received four nods. He debated about it, then shook his head. "The police won't be able to identify the attackers as from being beyond the grave.

Once the wards are lifted and the coven's spells are removed, the police will find their remains and the bodies they buried. Too many people have died for us to try to sweep this under the carpet. Either they'll discover enough evidence to assume the coven was responsible, or it will remain a mystery."

It was a long speech and he seemed a little nervous. He kept his eyes firmly on the road as he drove the short distance to Bradbury. I couldn't shake the feeling that he was avoiding eye contact with me.

Following Reece's directions, he drove to the park that wasn't far from Talitha's café. The park was warded to keep human intruders away, but it was still too early for most people to be up anyway. Reece opened the door when we pulled to a stop and pushed me out with almost unseemly haste. A light sweat beaded his forehead. I realized he was holding onto his control by a thread. I wasn't sure whether to be flattered that my nearness affected him so strongly, or to be depressed that he only wanted me because of our bond.

Beatrice had to murmur a counter-spell before she or Mark could enter the park. We followed a narrow path through the trees to the pentagram. The smell of fresh blood overlaid the older scent of death. Talitha's bits and pieces still lay where they'd fallen.

"Oh, dear," the witch said in a small voice as she took in the scene. Grimacing at the goat skull, she delicately shoved it aside with her foot and hunkered down to examine the pentagram. "It seems to be intact," she said more to herself than to us.

"What do you need us to do?" Mark asked.

"Just keep your distance and try not to break my concentration," she replied.

Taking his cell phone out of his pocket, he snapped off a few photos of the bloodied pentagram and of the body parts that were strewn all over it. When he was done, he wandered over to the trapdoor. Flynn ambled over to help him and pulled the door open. He made a face at the disgusting odor that wafted out. Mark shook his head in pity and took photos of the bodies.

Morbid curiosity had me moving closer before Flynn could close the door. Unwilling to be left out, Kala joined me. We walked side by side over to the pit. Together, we looked into the dark opening.

It was much worse than the pit at the farmhouse where I'd been held captive. At least those skeletons had been fleshless and dry with age. My vision doubled and Reece looked through me at the sight of dozens of rotting corpses piled up on top of each other.

Four of the bodies were fresh. We could see the remains of last year's sacrifices lying beneath them. The space was too small to be able to contain all of the dead that the coven had killed over the past two hundred years. There had to be other mass graves in the park.

That thought unlocked something in my brain and I could suddenly sense the corpses beneath us. I could feel more scattered around the area. The entire park was riddled with secret death pits.

Kala backed away from the door and stood with her hands wrapped around her upper arms. She looked as spooked as I felt and I moved to stand beside her. She sent me a grateful smile and linked her arm through mine. Reece came to stand on my other side. He was close enough for our arms to brush when I shifted my weight. He'd withdrawn his vision from mine and I was alone in my head again.

Flynn closed the trapdoor then he and Mark joined us. We watched Beatrice as she prepared to cast her spell. She took a small ceramic bowl out of the bag and placed it on the ground. One at a time, she withdrew small parcels from the bag and emptied their contents into the bowl as she chanted her spell. It sounded like mumbo jumbo to me, but I felt power building. Flynn rubbed his arms, sensing it as well.

Taking a deep breath, Beatrice stepped into the middle of the pentagram. She was careful not to tread on the lines or on the globs of flesh. Crouching down, she placed the bowl in the dead center of the diagram and withdrew a final item from the bag. A glint of gold flickered before it disappeared into the bowl. Her chanting grew louder and power gathered until I could see it shimmering around her.

A puff of black smoke issued from the bowl as she finished her spell. A breeze carried it away before I could catch more than a faint whiff. The odor was hard to describe. It was earthy and herb-like, with a hint of metal.

Swaying on her haunches, Beatrice steadied herself with one hand on the ground and picked up the bowl with the other. "It's done," she said and Mark stepped forward to help her to her feet. "Now I just have to dispel the coven's wards and any other spells that they've laid over this town. She didn't look overjoyed at the thought of expending more energy, but she was determined to cleanse the town of the dark coven's influence. "Take this," she said and held the bowl out to me.

I crossed to the pentagram, being careful not to step on the lines. I took the bowl and glanced inside. A gold necklace was the only item left. The other ingredients had been used up during her spell.

"Don't touch it!" she said sharply when I made a move to pick it up. "You can only use the necklace when you're ready to hunt your mother. The spell will only work for a short time. If you fail to locate her within that time, the necklace will become useless."

"What sort of timeframe are we looking at?" Mark asked.

"Roughly twenty-four hours," she replied and motioned for him to step out of the pentagram again. "Putting the necklace on will begin the spell. It will be able to tell Alexis when she is getting close to her mother. It will grow cold when she is facing in the wrong direction and it will grow warmer the closer she gets."

I almost winced every time she described the target

as my parent. Katrina Levine had died a long time ago. The creature wearing her face and body was a monster and I wished I didn't have to be associated with her at all. It would be a relief to end her travesty of a life.

"It won't take me long to dispel the wards," Beatrice said. She lifted her hands and turned in a circle as she chanted another spell. This one didn't require any ingredients and was based on pure power. I felt it emanate from her when she released it. I wasn't even aware of the myriad spells that had been laid over the town until they broke apart and began to dissipate.

Sagging in exhaustion, Beatrice allowed Mark to take her arm. She very deliberately scraped the pentagram with her foot, breaking the diagram. The final spark of evil that had been hanging over Bradbury faded.

"Let's head back to Dawson's Retreat," Mark said. He and Reece supported Beatrice, who was barely able to stand alone. Casting two major spells had worn her out and she needed to rest.

"You're sitting on my lap this time," Kala said to me. "I don't think I can sit through another ten minutes of sexual tension." She said it with a grin, but I was pretty sure she wasn't joking.

"I thought I wasn't your type," I smirked.

"You aren't," she said dryly. "I like men, not skinny little girls."

"Little?" I said as I plonked down on her lap and

cradled the bowl in both hands. "I'm two inches taller than you," I reminded her.

"Yeah, but you weigh half what I do."

"I do not!" Outraged by her exaggeration, I was about to defend my weight when Mark huffed out a sigh as he helped Beatrice inside.

"Cut it out," he ordered us curtly.

"Sorry, Mom," Kala said contritely. I had to put a hand over my mouth to muffle my snicker.

With his usual withering stare, Mark shut the door then rounded the SUV to the driver's side. The guys entered from the other side of the SUV. Flynn was stuck in the middle this time.

"You have a bony backside," Kala whispered too quietly for the humans to hear her.

"I disagree," Reece said just as quietly. "Lexi's backside is the perfect size."

Both Kala and Flynn rolled their eyes in unison while red climbed from my chin to my hairline. That was the first time anyone had ever described any part of my anatomy as perfect.

Chapter Thirty-Eight

Zeus felt us coming long before we parked in the lot behind the B&B. He emerged from the trees when I climbed off Kala's lap and left the SUV. I knelt beside him and endured a lick that started at my jaw and ended at my hairline.

"Gross," Kala complained.

Zeus' tongue lolled happily when I thumped his side a few times. "We'll be leaving here soon," I told him. "You won't have to hide for much longer."

"Can he really understand you?" Flynn asked when the Rottweiler woofed and melted back into the trees.

"He can pick up the general gist of what I'm thinking." Dogs didn't think the same way we did and it was hard to communicate with him. I'd sent him the sense that we'd be going home. That was a concept he could understand.

I took a side trip to the restroom to wash before heading to the parlor. My father was waiting inside. Nerves hit me just before I entered and I hesitated at the door. The last time he'd seen me, I'd been a hulking monster. I almost wished I could read his mind so I'd know how he felt about me now.

Grasping my courage with mental hands, I entered the room. My father sat beside Beatrice on one of the couches. She was half asleep and I wondered why she hadn't gone straight to bed.

Unable to delay any longer, I looked into my father's eyes. For a few long moments, we stared at each other wordlessly. My heart hammered as I waited for his reaction. There was wariness in his eyes that I'd never seen before.

I lifted a hand to push my hair back behind my ear and he almost went for the gun that was hidden in the small of his back. It was only a reflex and he controlled the impulse immediately, but the damage was done. My heart broke when I realized nothing would ever be the same between us again.

"I'm sorry I didn't kill Mom," I said in a dull tone. "At least then you'd only have one monster left in the family to be afraid of."

Sensing my overwhelming grief, Reece reached for me. I knew that if I allowed him to comfort me, that I'd break. I had too much pride to let everyone see me fall apart. I brushed past him and headed for the stairs. Locking myself in my room, I put the bowl with the necklace on the dresser and stripped off.

Slow tears tracked down my face as I took a shower. I wished I could wash away my loneliness and heartache as easily as I washed away the grime. Dressed in fresh clothing, I sat on the bed and stared at the wall. I heard my father packing in the room two doors down from mine.

Leaving his room, his footsteps hesitated outside my door, but he didn't knock. "I'll always love you, Alexis," he said softly, knowing I could hear him. "It's just going to take time for me to come to terms with your new…identity after seeing what you've become."

More tears welled as he walked away. A sob escaped from my tight control. Reece was at the door even before my father's footsteps faded. "Open the door, or I'll break it down," he said in a low voice.

Almost unable to see through my tears, I left the bed, unlocked the door, then was engulfed in his arms. He closed the door then leaned back against it and pulled me in close. His cheek rested on my head as I held onto his shirt tightly and sobbed out my heartache.

"You aren't alone, Lexi," he said. "You'll never be alone again. Mark, Kala, Flynn and I are your family as well now. We'll never leave you." *I'll never leave you,* he said silently and I believed him.

I sensed his own loneliness and despair and he dropped his shields for me to see the cause of his pain. My breath caught when I saw his earliest memories. He should have been too young to remember it, but he knew he'd once been part of a true werewolf pack. He hadn't been turned into a shifter like Kala and Flynn had been. He'd been born one.

Something had happened to his parents and he'd been left on his own. His memories were muddled, but his grief was clear. He didn't know how long he'd been alone before Mark had found him and had taken him under his wing. Kala and Flynn had joined them shortly afterwards and they'd become his new family.

Now he had me. Even though our bond had been forced on us, he was happy. He was no longer a lone wolf. I was his mate and he was content.

Wrapping my arms around his waist, I allowed myself to sink into his embrace. What we had wasn't perfect, but he had accepted our bond and he was willing to make the best of it. I had a choice to make and it was the most important decision of my young life. I could accept our bond and attempt to become his true mate, or I could reject the olive branch that he was extending and ostracize myself from our pack.

In the end, it wasn't a difficult choice at all. I went onto my tippy toes and kissed him. His hands came up to frame my face and he returned the kiss with a passion that was far more gentle than usual. Eventually, we pulled away, marveling in our mutual surrender to the inevitable. We jumped when a knock came at the door.

"If you two can bear to tear yourselves away from each other, Mark needs us in the parlor," Kala said and walked away before we could respond. I didn't have to see her face to know she was smirking.

I spent a few moments in the bathroom to wash my face and to tidy up before I joined the others downstairs. Mark's expression was serious when I took the spare seat across from him. Beatrice had gone to bed while I'd been falling apart. She was upstairs, sleeping deeply and snoring lightly.

"I've just received word that the remains of a body were found on the far side of the woods," Mark said.

"Do you know what was responsible for the death?" Flynn asked.

"My source believes it was a werewolf," he replied and a foreboding silence descended.

I turned to Reece and he looked back at me in stunned horror. Any shifters who killed a human were considered to be rogue and were automatically sentenced to death. As far as I knew, we were the only two werewolves in West Virginia.

"No we aren't," Reece said in response to my thought. "We sensed another werewolf in the woods, remember?"

I recalled it now and I also remembered that the shifter had been somehow familiar. Reece had met this rogue sometime in his distant and hazy past.

"We have to figure out who they are and find them as soon as possible," Mark said.

"That's kind of our job, isn't it?" I queried. I was unsure why he was so grim about it.

Kala said what they were all thinking. "We have to find out who did it before Reece or you get the blame."

"Oh." I hadn't thought of the possibility that either Reece or I might be blamed for the murder. We might be the bad guys when we turned, but when we were human, we worked for the good guys.

I wasn't sure how many people in the PIA knew who and what we were, but at least a few of them did. The TAK Squad weren't the only hunters who worked for the organization. If we couldn't find the creature responsible, Mark's superiors might indeed blame us and blow the whistle on our secret. If that happened, we might very well end up facing our colleagues.

Every single one of them were expert hunters and they'd be hell bent on eradicating our squad. While they might be good, we were better. None of them would stand a chance against us. We'd be forced to defend ourselves and we'd leave a swathe of bodies in our wake. It would be a no win situation that we needed to avoid at all costs.

We have to find this guy and put him down, Reece thought to me bleakly. In tune with his mind, I felt how much that thought hurt him. He'd been alone for so long and now he'd finally found someone from his past. There would be no happy reunion for the pair. The other shifter had gone rogue and there was only one possible outcome for him; death.

Made in the USA
Monee, IL
16 June 2022